Jupiter Justice
by Donald J. Hunt

Jupiter Justice

by Donald J. Hunt

Christine ~
Thanks for helping
me reach for the stars!
Enjoy! Don

DJH oct. 2015

Cover Design by **www.BespokeBookCovers.com**

Edited by James Denny Townsend.

ISBN-13: 978-1516972548

- FIRST EDITION -

This book is dedicated to my wife, Deb,
and our two children, Nathaniel and Marissa.

Without my wife's patience and support this book
would not exist.
Thank-you, *mon ami*!

ACKNOWLEDGMENTS

Special thanks to: Dr. Theodore Hall for his insights, simulations, and programs. I highly encourage any authors or interested others to visit his webpages on artificial gravity:

http://www.artificial-gravity.com

My fantastic early readers for their tremendous insights and feedback, especially: Phyllis Hunt, Sue Colella, and Phil Steadman.

I would like to do a special call out to the **Inklings & Speculations Writing Group** in Geneva, IL, especially Peter Borger, Lauren Cidell, Chris Gerrib, Toni Johnson, and Wren Roberts. We poke fun at our work with humor and candor, and this book would not be nearly as good without their insights.

I would also like to thank Dr. Stephen Tonks for his help translating English to Japanese; Dr. Mark Hammergren of the Adler Planetarium in Chicago, IL for his patience with my many questions; and Steve Tortorici for insights regarding the terminology, mechanics and maintenance of large-scale piping.

Lastly, I'd like to thank my editor, James Denny Townsend, for his expertise and for the polish that any book worth its salt deserves before being shared with the universe.

A NOTE TO YOU, THE READER

Special thanks to you, Reader, for picking up this book. *You* are why we writers spend so many hours weaving tales and creating worlds to explore. I hope you enjoy this book as much as I have enjoyed writing it.

I strive to make the tone of each book match the story, so a hard-science fiction story will read differently from epic fantasy, etc. Keep an eye out for other books as they become available:

www.donaldjhunt.com

I would love to hear from you. Let me know what you liked; if you see an error, let me know that, too. Every effort has been made to present you with an engaging story while keeping the science realistic. I also tried to follow the "guidelines of grammar" as much as possible, although I did break them intentionally on occasion for effect. In this age of electronic books, I will do my best to make periodic corrections.

Write to me at:

theworldsofdonhunt@gmail.com

"Ah, I know that look on your face, Captain Schroeder. You think we are paranoid, but we are paranoid by necessity."

Jupiter 2269.

A suspicious shuttle explosion. Two deaths.
Rico Schroeder must unravel the mystery before a terrorist plot plunges the colonized solar system into war with the deadliest weapons ever created by humanity.

- ONE -

Taz seemed distracted, which was not normal for him at all. Test pilots were a strange breed—focused like a laser, full of bravado, and half crazy. Whatever else they might be, they almost never came across as scared, regardless of what they might feel inside.

"Hey, Taz, good luck with the test flight today," Rico said.

"Thanks, *broja*." "I just wish you were here watching my back, Rico, like down in French Guiana, you know?"

The way he said it gave Rico a chill, even over the OptiComm. Taz had been a friend a long time—since basic training, when they were both in the Corps. A few years after basic, after his cousin had been murdered, Taz had called Rico when an officer had been murdered down in French Guiana.

The case had been rough, and they had both almost been killed.

Taz hesitated and then said, "There's–" and then faltered into silence.

"What's up, Taz?"

"Nothing, Rico. Nada. Just nerves I suppose."

Rico gave a light chuckle. "You? I've seen less stable asteroids."

Tiago Vaz—Taz to his friends—gave him a wry smile. "Yeah. Just watch your back, okay?"

"Always." The screen pixilated and the young pilot's face disappeared for a moment. Rico frowned and double-checked his ship's instrument panel. Some higher magnetic fields from Jupiter today, but all the other sensors read five-by-five. His friend's face reassembled on the screen and he asked, "What aren't you telling me, Taz? What's going on?"

"I wish I could tell you more, *broja*. Confidentiality agreement, you know?"

Rico's screen flashed red. A request came through from Tiago to go off-log and encrypt their transmission. Highly irregular, and typically against team policy between competing ships. Rico hit the Accept icon.

"I could get yanked from the test today for going dark, Rico, but a lot of weird stuff is going on. Juarez was asking a lot of questions a few weeks ago and now she's dead."

Rico's penchant for doggedly pursuing details kicked in. "Weird how?"

"Like Sistema Solar's new business partner last year, for one. It just doesn't add up. Sistema had plenty of credits. Why add in another company and lose half the prize money? Plus, when they came in, they were pushy, you know?"

"What new company? Pushy how? I'm not following you, bud."

"Look, I've got to get out of encrypted mode before someone notices. If…" again he paused. "If anything happens, Rico, check into it. For me, *broja*. But be careful."

Three hours later, Tiago Vaz was dead. The *Domínguez,* the experimental ship for team Sistema Solar, had exploded. Taz never stood a chance.

#

"Did you hear about the *Domínguez*?" Jane asked over the Optical Communication array, after she'd welcomed him back.

"Yeah." Rico heard the tension in his own voice. He swallowed it down. "I knew him. Just spoke to him today. We went way back."

"Oh, Rico, I'm sorry."

"Yeah. Me, too."

Silence took over for a heartbeat or two. When you live and travel in fragile cans that, if ruptured, will leave you dying in the dark void of space, anytime a pilot dies it gives you pause. Fortunately, few accidents occurred on ships or stations. Redundant safety protocols helped prevent any but the most cataclysmic events, but if you wanted to live, you never relied on protocols. There was no such thing as "foolproof" in space.

But Rico suspected that mechanical failure had nothing to do with Taz's death. He felt a hollow chasm in his chest, and all the losses of his life tried to escape from the box he had locked them in. Murder had touched his life too many times. The ghosts from his past threatened to well up and drag him under.

Mostly to distract himself from the dark alley he'd wandered into, Rico pushed the dead aside and asked, How's the *Amazing Grace* coming?"

"Well, she's beautiful, but the latest sims are definitely not." Jane hesitated, and Rico's radar for trouble went off. *What did she mean by that?* He started to ask, but she said, "Uesugi's waiting for you in the lab. We'll meet you there, and she'll fill you in. She's called a meeting as soon as you're station-side."

"Okay, thanks. Rico out."

Rico had put on his team jacket—required to be worn at all times while in potential public venues by their team sponsor contracts—and entered the enclosed screening room while talking with Jane, leaving behind the chill and the smells of lubricants and coolants that permeated the hangar bay. He stepped up to the retinal scanner, and a red laser beam flitted across his eye.

"Welcome back to Axion Station, Rico," the bodiless computer voice of the station said. The station CPU was a Candra IV-R. "All nano-technological organisms have been verified. Rico, your nan-bots report that they have removed all of the plaque from your teeth and your arteries."

"Thanks, Candra," he said with a half smile. "My doctor and my dentist will both be thrilled. Security update?"

"All systems operating within normal parameters. You have a haircut scheduled for today."

Rico hit the smartwall and then the mirror icon. He gave himself an exaggerated, suave smile and chuckled. He examined his face in detail. He needed a shave, that was for sure. He had considered nanobot iris coloring, but a girl he'd dated once had gushed over his "chocolate brown, soulful eyes," and, after an endorsement like that, he'd decided to leave well enough alone. His thick, dark-brown-almost-black hair was just past the tops of his ears and brushing the top of his collar. A few bangs kept falling down—a constant nuisance—but they weren't in his eyes. The haircut could wait.

"Candra, reschedule please. I think I can hold off

another week."

"As you wish, Rico."

The hatch door opened with a hiss of equalizing air pressure, and he entered the main hallway of the donut-shaped station. He stopped and breathed deeply, enjoying the filtered air. His ship, the *Outlier,* needed some new filters. At the moment it had the pungent tang of locker room. Compared to the air on his ship, the station smelled like springtime in Puerto Rico.

As he walked down the hall, Rico marveled once again at the real wood panels alternating with stone in this sector of the station. The expense involved in harvesting and shipping the wood to Axion must have been huge, even from the relatively nearby Wong Arboretum.

Rico pushed open the door to the lab and saw Dr. Kita Uesugi, retired Captain of the United States Air and Space Corps, as well as several other team members, among them Jane Osgood, head of communications, and the test pilot, Zavier Sorrenguard.

"Hello, Useugi-sama," Rico said, using the Japanese honorific. After her retirement, Kita had been invited to teach the next generation of space pilots and researchers for the island nation and so had returned to the land of her ancestors for a few years. Rico had visited her a few times in Tokyo and had been impressed with the deference they paid her. As a result, he'd adopted the honorific as his own to show his respect and affection for her.

She *tsked* at him. "Not so formal. Greetings, Rico-san. Welcome home." Kita smiled. Her black, shoulder-length hair framed deep brown eyes. She brushed it back, and returned her gaze to the computer display in her hand.

"Hey, Hot Shot," Zavier said. "How was the Europa run?" Zavier stood a little under two meters tall, blond, and towered over Uesugi at only a meter-and-a-half. The broad-shouldered man appeared more as an asteroid miner than Axion's star pilot. His bronze skin divulged the fact that he stayed in the tanning booth longer than needed to simply create vitamin D.

"Same old. Got the replacement parts we needed." He'd wanted to put in some hours at the stick and, after the antimatter shipment got stolen, Uesugi had put Rico in charge of supply runs.

"D'you hear about the *Domínguez*?" the pilot asked. To Rico, he practically mimicked the old men from his grandmother's church, eager to gossip and spread bad news.

Rico didn't sigh, but he wanted to. He did not want to rehash this topic all day. "Yeah, Zavier," he said. He directed his next question to Jane. "Any clue what happened?"

Jane shook her head, her medium brown curls swaying and dark brown eyes somber. "They're going over traffic vids and reworking their numbers now. They claim their calculations were spot-on, their sims clean, and a remote controlled test went down without any problems. They thought they had the prize sewn up. They've been over the numbers dozens of times now, but nothing yet."

Uesugi said, "I spoke with their team leader, Joseph Juarez, to express my condolences. His niece,

Lucille, died last month in a decompression accident." She paused and her eyes were hard flints of brown granite. "They believe Adala had a hand in the explosion onboard the *Domínguez*."

Rico whistled. He knew of Adala, of course. After the destruction of the Iranian city of Karaj in 2071, the Sinai Accords ended millennia of fighting. The governments finally found a way to work through their differences without leveling another city, but fringe elements such as Adala clung to the older beliefs. Adala meant "justice" in Arabic. Their *raison d'être* was the overthrow of governments corrupted by religious tolerance and the re-establishment of orthodox sharia law—as interpreted by their own imams, of course. They saw space trade and colonization as a particular threat to the cohesion of Muslim beliefs. Back in 2132, they rammed a supply ship through both cylinders of Hilm al-Salaam Colony—or something similar to that—he could not remember the exact name. They killed almost everyone except for half a dozen people in a hydroponics lab. It had been on the news and blogs for months.

"Any clue why they're pointing the finger at Adala? Why would they care about a space race?"

Jane shook her head. "No. Nothing yet. Um, There's a service on Prime Station tomorrow for the pilot."

"Anyone going?" Rico asked. Jane deferred to Uesugi with a glance.

"I've asked people to stay on station," Uesugi said, "until we solve our own simulation difficulty, so we do not have a similar accident. However, Jane tells me you knew the pilot."

"Yeah," Rico said. "I knew him."

"I expect you will want to attend the service?"

Rico nodded. "I'd appreciate it, Cap." He didn't want to go into his connection to Taz, at least not in a public setting. His past was his own damn business.

She nodded in return. "Of course, Rico-san."

"I heard the *Domínguez* lit up the sky near Himalia like a new star," Zavier said. "Dem's da' breaks, as they say." Zavier let out a short laugh.

Rico had only been back fifteen minutes, but already he'd had enough of Zavier. "Shut up, Zavier. A pilot died out there. A Jupe. One of us."

Zavier gave an arrogant smirk that made Rico fume even more. "Not one of us, Rico. One of *them*. One of the other teams out there fighting for the AMMATT Prize, in case you forgot. Pardon me for not crying because those sun-baked Sammies suffered a set back that might help us win."

Rico snorted in disgust and turned away. Although he was not from South America, derogatory terms like that one got into his spacesuit. He wanted to pop him one, but he'd learned to keep his cool a long time ago.

Zavier talked to his back, feeling defensive, no doubt. "Hey, man. We're talking about 117 *trillion* credits, and if you think–"

"Enough, gentlemen." Kita interrupted quietly. "I cannot concentrate with all your babbling; we have our own problems."

She walked away from them, and over to the sim table. They passed an old, unlabeled photo with several people in lab coats hung on the wall. Rico was amazed at all the people with bald heads. *I'm glad they found a cure for that problem,* he thought to himself.

Jane spoke softly to him as they followed Uesugi. "People are pretty tense. With the explosion of the *Domínguez,* and the arrival of more antimatter, teams are pushing harder than ever to launch. A New Delhi coder claimed on one of the forums that they'll be ready for a test run within a week. The post got pulled, but I saw it before it did." She stopped talking as Uesugi began the sim and began speaking.

"In the simulations we have run, when we combine the matter and antimatter the magnetic field cannot contain the reaction. Candra, please bring up simulation 43-b-17."

The computer carried out the command and *The Amazing Grace*—named after the naval admiral and computer-programming pioneer Grace Hopper—appeared instantly on the holo. Her sleek lines practically sang of speed. Shape did not matter out here in space, but aesthetics were still a point of pride for a lot of spacers. She looked tremendous. The simulation ran through various stages. "Maximum plasma speed obtained," the computer said. "Magnetic antimatter containment holding."

Other than Candra, the ubiquitous hum of air being forced through the station was the only sound. Grim faces gathered around the table. Rico already felt as if he was at a funeral. Zavier's pale face glowed in the simulator's light.

Jane cast her eyes at Uesugi, who gave a nod without moving her eyes from the screen. "Initiating anti-particle teleportation," she said.

"Antimatter-matter combustion successful." In this case, combustion seemed one the greatest understatements in the history of humanity.

"Magnetic combustion chamber holding at effective one-hundred percent. Gamma shielding one-hundred percent." the computer said.

"Opening nozzle. Engaging thrust." The ship shot dramatically ahead.

Jane read the numbers scrolling across the bottom. "Point one gigameters per hour. Point five gigs. One Gig. One point five. Two."

The simulated ship exploded in a spectacular ball of orange flames. Rico watched the simulation with a queasy feeling, knowing it would be Zavier or someone else he knew in the pilot's seat.

Federico "Rico" Schroeder knew the risks. He'd broken a leg flying hang gliders off the mountains near his grandmother's home in Isabela, Puerto Rico. Rico had not been a test pilot in the ACS, but he hung out with a lot of them. When there was a new engine to try, Rico flew it at first opportunity. He knew that if you wanted big gains, you had to take risks.

Uesugi turned to Zavier while the sparks from the simulation flickered out. "The rules specify a human-piloted ship. We would much prefer to break the one gig mark and have our pilot live through the experience." She shifted her gaze around the room. "Okay. As you know, a new shipment of antimatter has recently arrived from beyond the heliosphere on the robot ship," Kita Uesugi continued. The heliosphere was the outer edge of our solar system, and the place where robot ships could collect comparatively large amounts of antimatter for the first time in human history. With just a fingernail's worth—and a working drive—the solar system could open up in brand new ways. If they could get their antimatter drive working, the Jovian Planetary Zone would be less than four *days* away from Earth, instead of taking up to two years. Regular trade with the Jupiter orbital colonies would finally be possible, but only if they could avoid creating a miniature sun when they hit the thrusters. The changes within the solar system would be as dramatic as when the combustion engine became the dominant form of transportation back on earth.

"We must resolve this before Prime Station releases the antimatter to the teams. Everyone. Regardless of your role, go over everything again. We'll meet tomorrow evening at nineteen hundred hours."

* * *

Flying had always been Rico's passion—anything and everything and, of course, the faster, the better. His grandmother always worried about him. "Federico, I don't like you jetting around the solar system," she'd said one cool summer night while they sat on the porch listening to the sounds of the evening. Strange how noisy planetside was. He'd teased her and said, "They don't use jets in space, abuela." She'd tsked and snapped at him with her dishtowel. Rico always chuckled when he thought of his grandma's reactions to the speeds involved in space travel. When Rico had told his old-school grandmother that he had flown at a little over 160,000 kilometers per hour before her eyes got wide and she just stared at him.

He loved flying atmospheric and space ships, and reading about them, and was an obsessive trivia buff when it came to aerospace history. It had been his escape as a kid, after his parents had died. They had only been the first in a long string of deaths that had led him to where he was today. First his parents, then his grandmother, and then his uncle. Others, too. Too painful to think about, so he had formed a hard shell around those memories, and trained his mind to no longer go there.

Joining the United States Air and Space Corps ROTC program had been a fairly easy decision. Fly and get money for college. After a hitch in the Reserves, you were done and out. That had been his plan, anyway. Then his cousin, Jackie, had been murdered during his senior year. She had been murdered on Mars while at college there while he had, literally, been a world away. Even if he'd been there, what could he have done? Nothing.

Rico and Jackie had both been betrayed by someone they trusted. Then she was dead, just like so many others in his life. When he'd gone through his psych profiling, as part of his vetting for the military police, the psychiatrist had warned him that with the extensive losses in his life, forming intimate relationships would require special attention and effort, moreso even than other military personnel.

That was a lot of psycho-babble for, "Dude, you have had a crappy life, and it has messed you up."

It was not quite as bad as all that. Close. But not quite. Fortunately, he'd also had some good influences along the way, to help him get back on track.

In spite of no investigative training, Rico had taken leave and gone to Mars. He'd found his cousin's killer, and held the man's life in his hands. Rico could have killed him easily. He'd not merely been tempted to kill him—he'd *wanted* to kill him.

He'd blotted the name from the ledger of his mind. Banished. Outcast. Scrubbed from existence. Since that day, he'd refused to allow himself to even think the man's name. He was only *the killer*.

Jackie's killer had taunted him, laughed at him, and her death had just been the last of a long string of betrayals that Rico had not even been aware of until that last encounter. In retrospect, his naiveté had been understandable. The killer's mocking revelations had made Rico's face hot with embarrassment and anger and had made the betrayals all the more profound.

After Jackie's funeral, Rico went back home to Branson Rings. He'd been coasting through the Air & Space Corps up until then, at least as much as anyone can coast through the military. Rico surprised his instructors. He applied himself to his studies with the vengeance he had withheld from the killer. He went from a mediocre student to virtually straight A's. Rico had found his calling and, until The Unfortunate Incident, he never looked back and never changed his trajectory.

He studied forensics, criminal psychology, and even xenology. Although earth's expatriates strongly objected to being considered aliens, definite differences had emerged in the psychology and physiology of colonies in earth's orbit, around Venus, on Mars, in the Belt, and now around Jupiter. Rico had always been fascinated by how quickly distinct cultures had emerged. Much the way children will cast aside the traditions and mores of their first generation immigrant parents, the bold pioneers of space forged new societies on whatever rock or habitat they clung to in their efforts to survive.

After he graduated from Hallsworth University, he'd done four years as a greenhorn officer, and then eight more in the Office of Criminal Investigation. He'd been happy serving in ASC, and his career had been promising—at least until French Guiana. He didn't want to think about that part much, but his mind went there anyway—a dog licking a wound.

Rico's assignment in French Guiana had changed his life—not all for the better, but one bright spot had been meeting Inés Villaverde. Taz had introduced them. That thought made him smile, because they had been running from thugs with machetes at the time. The three of them eluded their pursuers and then drank Jeune Gueule beers nonchalantly at an oceanside café while eating a Vietnamese dish called Pho.

He flashed back to Cayenne's Central Market where the café sat, reaching out into the Atlantic Ocean. He remembered the way the sun shone on Inés' black hair that day.

Inés Villaverde. She gave one hell of a good backrub. He remembered the graceful curves of her body, wonderfully in shape, but not all muscle and bones.

Rico blew out a sigh. That had been a falling star—fast and fleeting—with a fiery crash at the end.

He tsked to himself. Man, he wished things had gone differently.

French Guiana was also how he'd met,Major Kita Uesugi of the United States Air and Space Corps. She'd been stationed there at the time and they'd crossed paths during his investigation. He'd saved hundreds, maybe thousands, but thirteen people had still died. Thirteen. He knew all their names to this day.

Major Uesugi had stood by him, and her testimony had helped considerably at his trial. He'd been exonerated at the court martial proceedings, but the whole ordeal left a bitter taste in his mouth. It had been a shark feeding frenzy, and he had been chum in the water. Rico had resigned his commission after that.

Rico had made a difference, maybe, for a while, but it had not ended well.

After he left the Corps, he got a job as a "star jockey." Really, he was nothing more than a glorified truck driver, picking up and delivering Helium 3. Still, it was cheaper than therapy and more fun, if you didn't mind spending weeks at a time alone. Rico had always been comfortable with his own company. He enjoyed people's company, but he appreciated quiet time as well.

Two years ago, he had just arrived back at Chou Station for another shipment when he received a message from Kita Uesugi. They were getting ready to test a breakthrough matter-antimatter engine, and she wanted him to handle security for the team. With the high stakes riding on the contest, the team worried about espionage or sabotage.

Flying for a while had been fun, but it was definitely not challenging with all the automation these days. And, truth be told, you can only watch so many vids, play so many games, and read so many books on the long flight from Jupiter to Earth or even Mars or the Belt. Rico wanted to get back to something more challenging. He gave notice with Chou InterGalactic, and he had been working with Axion ever since.

Rico drank a cup of JavaJazz and stared at the data on his board again before he launched for the funeral service over on Prime Station. Everyone had gone over them before, and even Candra had redone the computations with the same results. No one had found a critical error thus far. So Rico sipped his fourth cup of Jazz. He figured the teleportation of antiparticles into the combustion chamber must be the problem. Teleporting *regular* particles posed a substantial challenge and had only recently become reliable. Even so, only particles could be teleported. Not even something as simple as a pebble had been successfully teleported. Their team was the first to attempt teleporting antiparticles, at least as far as they knew. If the teleport coordinates "landed" slightly off, this could cause the explosion when anti-molecules contacted real matter outside the combustion chamber. Or maybe the magnetic field for the combustion chamber deteriorated in a rapid cascade failure. But the computer had failed to detect any such problem.

Candra interrupted his thoughts. "Rico. You asked me to inform you when it was 0-six hundred hours. It is now 6 AM."

"Thanks, Candra. Hey, Candra, while we're gone, pull up the simulations from this past April. Compare all the programming code and the mathematical equations and flag all differences between each sim and the most recent one."

"Yes, sir."

"*Gracias, Amiga.*"

"*De nada, Señor.*"

- TWO -

Rico's trip over to Prime Station took a little longer than an hour, and the time to reflect brought up memories of his own first home in space, Branson Station. Branson Station was larger than his current home, Axion Station, and even larger than Prime Station. Branson also had the best views in the solar system of both the earth and the moon, as far as Rico was concerned, since it was fairly close to both.

Most stations start out with one small ring to house the construction workers. They are small in circumference, to save costs and get things going. That small size, however, means that they have a dizzying rotation speed. They need it to create a near-earth gravity. From that small ring, a central axis is built, and then additional, larger rings are added. The larger size means a slower—and far more comfortable—rotation speed.

Branson had been no exception. Her first ring had been only 100 meters in diameter. Even if you were sleepwalking, you could make it around that old metal donut in less than ten minutes. That wheel cruised along at close to four revolutions per minute. Plus, on the smaller rings, the gravitational pull is greater on one's feet than on one's head. It can be pretty disconcerting. Even many experienced spacers could lose their lunch under those conditions.

The workers had been a tough, raucous band— hard working, hard drinking, and hard fighting. They'd been proud of their ability to ride the ring, and they'd wanted it commemorated. When the station was done, they'd suggested that the first ring be kept as a tourist attraction, quasi-amusement park ride, and historic monument. The CEO had loved the idea. Visitors and locals could all test their mettle on the First Ring.

When Rico's cousin, Jackie had come up from Earth to Branson Station, before she'd been killed. He'd taken her into that smallest ring when playing tour guide for her. They'd both been about sixteen. Jackie'd described it as, "sorta like when yer on a roller coaster, at just the right spot in a loop, where your body is mashed into the seat, but your head feels lighter—only not quite as extreme as that. Close, though!" She'd laughed. She'd also told him that adjusting too suddenly gave her vertigo.

Walking straight, in line with the ring's rotation, wasn't too bad, but if you tried to turn to talk to someone, or walk at an angle, then you felt like someone was pushing you upright. "I feel like I'm a gyroscope," she'd said over drinks while they watched the planet below them from the Earthgazer Lounge. "Or, remember when we were all at the ocean? When the waves were behind us, they weren't much of a problem. But as soon as you tried to go sideways to get the beachball, the water took you out!" He did remember and they both laughed. Rico poked her arm. "Yeah, but I'm not sure that's a fair comparison—that wave was over my head!"

"Excuses, excuses! Anyway, that's how it feels in the small ring." She frowned in thought, not satisfied with her illustration. She sat there a moment, trying to grab an elusive thought. "No! No, I got it!" She grabbed his arm. "Remember when we were at that amusement park, where we were on the spinning wheel?"

Rico nodded. "*Sí*, and we thought Lucia was going to be sick?"

"Yes, but before that, we tried lifting our arms and legs away from the wall, but the spin would push our arms and legs back down? *That's* how it feels for me, if I move wrong. Not as strong, you know? But that pushing sensation.

"For the most part, the larger rings aren't like that now that I've been up here awhile. The worst is bending over and feeling as if I'm losing my balance because of that spinward thing. That still gets me. Ugh!"

Rico chuckled. He'd never had that problem.

"The wall fountains and stripes help, though." Throughout all seven rings that were eventually built onto Branson Station, architects recessed flat, enclosed water fountains into the walls. The addition added a more organic, less sterile feel to the station. However, they also had another equally important benefit. Instead of the water falling straight down, as it would on earth, the droplets curved in the opposite direction of the station's spin as they fell. Earthers said the curving water reminded them of pouring water out a sprinkling can in a high wind, or pouring soda out a car window. Most stations that accepted "space virgins" also had prefab walls with periodic indented curves painted in relief for the same reason. The water and the curved stripes reminded visitors that items—and people—fell in that direction and to watch their step. Jackie had adjusted in three or four days but other poor souls could take weeks to adjust.

Prime Station workers on the other hand, had cut up and repurposed their first ring. She was months from Earth and supplies. Everything that could be reused was.

Prime Station had five rings now: Command ring, two agricultural rings, a dedicated research ring, and Farside Ring. The tourists preferred the larger and newer, Farside Ring, which was more than a thousand times bigger than Command Ring. It took a full hour to completely circle around to the same spot and boasted earth-normal gravity. It contained three hotels, dozens of bars, and condo units. There was even a recreation sphere at the center of Farside. Rico had been there, of course, but he preferred the less flashy Command Ring.

The Command ring had replaced that initial small torus habitat. Command still served as the main docking ring for supply ships and provided temporary berths for their crews, as needed. It also housed the station traffic control personnel, security, as well as various research and administrative offices.

For the most part, Command Ring on Prime Station, orbiting Jupiter, retained the same utilitarian décor as when it was first built, with steel, plas, and plastic comprising the walls, and a functional, plain grip-floor. At over 1,600 meters in diameter, Command Ring had a reasonable gravity of .85 of Earth's, and a leisurely one revolution per minute. At a brisk walk, it would take about 45 minutes to walk all the way around the ring. Techs and researchers from the other stations came here to socialize and to trade goods.

At the moment, Rico sat in Command Ring's only bar, The Spartan, watching the moon Callisto on the viewscreen. The bar smelled of mold and rancid fruit juice from too many spilled drinks. The real-time viewing screens had been installed years after the ring had been completed; neon lights, a huge fish tank along the inner wall, and color-shifting chairs had also been added in an attempt to brighten up the place. The tank burbled happily. If nothing else, the amazingly close view of Callisto, with Jupiter looming beyond, still struck awe in even the oldest space hands. Even at this distance, the planet, with its swirling mass of storms, took over so much of the view that it always gave Rico the impression they were being sucked in.

Rico raised his glass in silent salute to his friend and sipped at an Old Fashioned, enjoying the sweet-bitter taste. Today, they would be honoring Taz. A pilot, a spacer and a "Jupe"—one of their own. He wondered how many of them had a personal connection to the man, as he had. Doubtless some of his teammates would be here.

The service was disappointingly short, however. Tiago's fellow team members listed the pilot's accomplishments, with just a few anecdotes that gave a brief glimpse of the man's life and personality. Seems as if a guy should have more of an epitaph than a twenty-minute synopsis of his life and a commemorative chocolate bar. Tiago Vaz had been a huge fan of Brazilian chocolate, so his friends had created chocolate bars wrapped in a collage of his favorite things and accomplishments in bold colors. A nice touch, but it still left Rico feeling shortchanged and glum.

"Hell of a way to wrap up a life," Rico muttered to himself.

Rico observed the moon and stars beyond the window and let out a deep breath. He gestured and a middle-aged man with salt and pepper hair came over and refilled his drink.

The doors to the bar whisked open and four security guards stepped in, preceded by a short, hawk-eyed man. The guards carried state-of-the art Lambs: LLAMs, the Less Lethal Auto-adjusting-to-Mass Riot Gun.

"Ladies and Gentlemen," Hawk-eye said in a no-nonsense tone. "There is an emergency situation, and Prime Station is under lockdown until further notice."

A din of protests rose from the assembled crowd.

"What about the antimatter shipment?" a man called out.

Hawk-eye glowered at the man as if he might pounce and devour him whole then and there. After a slight pause, not heavy-handed, but long enough to make the point, he replied in the politest tone, "Sir, it took more than twelve years for the robot ship to come from beyond the heliosphere to arrive at our humble station. Another few hours will not make a difference." He held up a hand, forestalling any objections. "I know you are concerned about the AMMATT Prize. All the teams are under the same constraint. That will have to suffice." The man turned his steely gaze on Rico. "Federico Schroeder, would you come with me, please?"

Rico peered at the man skeptically, but shrugged and finished off his drink. He followed Hawk-eye out the door, and he felt the eyes of the mob following him. Two guards came with them, and two more remained behind just inside the doors.

The man spoke crisply and with bold confidence. "Walk with me, please. My name is Rueben Holt, Assistant Chief Security Officer. I just got promoted, you might say, to temporary head of security, and we need your help.

"What kind of help? And what happened to Bahru Wagle?"

"Ah. You know the Chief of Security?"

"Yes. We met at a workshop on security for Jupiter stations."

"Well, my boss has been missing for several hours; we cannot raise him by comm, and we cannot track him using his locator beacon. We're quite concerned. Especially given what's happened." He walked on for two beats before continuing. "I understand you have some experience with investigations, Captain Schroeder?"

Rico nodded. "A little. Um, it's just mister now. I'm retired."

"Well, you, sir, are the best we have. There's been a murder. My boss has disappeared, and I have little experience in this area. We have received orders directly from Earth—from the United States government—recalling you to active duty for the duration of this investigation. Dr. Uesugi has been informed of the situation and has agreed to cooperate." He handed Rico his AI pad and showed him the order.

Rico grunted. Typical.

Holt, a short, sparse man, walked at a fast clip. He

was probably five years older than Rico. He had a gaunt face, drawn tight and bony.

"The victim's berth is on the opposite side of Command Ring, within the Sector 270 hangar bays." Every sector of Command Ring was identified by the degrees of a circle. Station Control, by tradition, always sat at zero degrees (or 360 degrees), which had added more opportunities to make administration the butt of jokes. Command Ring had two primary hangar bays, located on opposite sides of the habitat, one set centered around 90 degrees, and the other at 270 degrees. "A few things you should know before we get there. The victim, Hujjat Malik, worked for Dubai Intergalactic. As such, they want one of their own people in on the investigation."

Rico stopped walking and stared at the man. "That's highly irregular. What if someone from Dubai is involved?"

Holt walked a few more steps before realizing that Rico had stopped walking. "You've been out here awhile now, Captain. You know how it works. Money makes most of the rules, and Dubai has a considerable amount of that. You'll have to do the best you can. The person they want on board seems decent enough, though. His file presents him in a good light. He's a doctor of sorts."

Rico set his mouth in a flat line. He was not at all happy about being drafted into this mess without a say, much less having the investigation compromised from the get-go. However, he also knew Holt was right. Rico couldn't do anything about the situation, except refuse the post, and he wouldn't do that—not if it meant letting a killer get away.

"Fine. But I want it on record that I'm protesting this 'representative's' involvement, and I object to being strong-armed into taking him."

Holt inclined his head. "Duly noted."

Rico started to ask what, "doctor of sorts" meant when they arrived outside a door with two more guards, also armed with LLAMs.

"I realize you have experience with this, but you still might want to brace yourself."

The door whisked open, retracting into the wall to save space. The body laying on the bed caught his attention immediately because of the gruesome hole that erupted from his stomach. Folds of skin peeled back like a macabre flower in bloom. Rico caught the heavy-sweet tang of iron and copper from the blood that covered the bed and pooled on the floor. It was a grisly scene.

As Rico examined the room from the doorway, another person walked up, but other than giving the man a quick glance, Rico remained focused on the tight temporary quarters. The deceased clutched a physical book in his hands. Printed books were rare these days. Rico could not make out the title from the hall. Based on the wrinkles on his face and the extra weight around his mid-section, the man on the bed was between the age of 40 and 50. Middle Eastern, dark hair and dark complexion. Married, by the ring on his finger. Two daughters from the framed picture on his nightstand. Possibly nieces or family friends, but a person does not usually bring a photo for an overnight—especially a stand-alone frame—unless it is someone important to them.

"Did you serve, Mr. Holt?"

"I was an E5, sir. Staff Sergeant," Reuben Holt replied. Rico had figured as much. He had the bearing and efficient manner of someone ex-military.

The new arrival wore a heavy green suit with a satiny sheen to it, a high square collar with rounded lapels, no tie, a button shirt, and pearl buttons. He had a neatly trimmed mustache and beard and dark skin. He had the looks of a movie star. His brown eyes watched Rico but gave nothing away.

"Right," Rico said.

Holt cleared his throat uncomfortably, and gestured to the newcomer. "This is Dr. Raheem Kuzbari, and this is Captain Federico Schroeder. Dr. Kuzbari is the Dubai Intergalactic Chemicals representative. He rode over from Dubai station with a retired couple, and the victim, Hujjat Malik. The victim was one of their team members." The two guards who had followed them took up positions at both ends of the hallway.

Rico gave him a polite nod. "Call me Rico." They shook hands.

Dr. Raheem Kuzbari stood tall—close to two meters in height—but not as tall as a spacer. The crisp, well-tailored lines of a formal emerald-green Nehru-style suit showed style and meticulousness. The current style of a wider opening from the chest to the throat showed a silken white shirt with pearl buttons. He had strong, but not overstated cheekbones, adorned with a close-cropped beard. His complexion was light, but darker than Rico's own. He gave Rico the impression more of a Middle Eastern model or shuttlebuster than a real doctor.

"Any investigative experience?" Rico asked him.

"I have a medical degree, and I have done autopsies, Kuzbari replied. "Mr. Holt told Dubai Intergalactic Chemicals of the situation and, since I was already here, they assigned me to assist. Do you want me to preserve the scene?" Kuzbari held up a 3D cam.

Rico cast a glance over at him and nodded. "Sure, that would be helpful." Kuzbari's preparedness surprised him, but Rico kept his face neutral. Efficient. Maybe he'd be useful to have on the investigation, but he disliked having the Dubai doctor pushed onto his investigation—it compromised anything the man touched.

Holt tipped his head, eyebrows knit together. "Dr. Kuzbari is being modest. He's an expert in nano-medical programming. He's published papers on the topic."

"Really?" Rico replied noncommittally. "Were you and Dr. Malik friends?"

Kuzbari shook his head. "No. I just met him on the trip over. Dubai Intergalactic is a large station, and I just came out from Earth two months ago."

Rico gestured into the room. "What can you tell me about the victim?"

Kuzbari answered. "Not too much. Physicist and engineer. He told me that he and the pilot from the Sistema Solar team who died, Tiago Vaz, shared a passion for the Royal Game of Ur. An ancient board game, similar to Parcheesi. They would play it by computer over optical signal. I believe you call it the OptiComm."

"What brought you over for the funeral?"

Kuzbari, distracted by the body in the room, said,

"The shuttle." Then, realizing how that sounded, he gave an apologetic smile and added, "I did not come for the funeral. I merely hitched a ride. I am giving a lecture in a few days on medical advances."

They examined the corpse again. Rico said, "It almost looks like he got hit from behind with some sort of archaic bullet. See the way the wound is much larger in the back and peels open? How big is that exit wound? 20 or 30 centimeters? Any ideas what caused it?"

Kuzbari hesitated. "Without closer examination, it would be hard to say. A rat could possibly do that; it's improbable but we are close to the docks. He turned to Holt. Any rats in this area?

Holt shook his head. "Unlikely. They're around; where there are ships, there are rats, but they tend to stay in the conduits, work tunnels, and near food storage.

Probably some sort of weapon." The doctor pulled out an electronic device and flipped it on. It made a warbling noise until he ran his fingers over the glide screen.

"What's that?" Rico asked.

"Bioelectric scanner. Detects electrical activity as subtle as that put out by a human body. It can help determine time of death."

Rico grunted. "That reminds me of a shrapnel wound. I just never saw one from a guy just laying in bed."

Rico and Kuzbari slipped on sterine gloves and booties and broke the seals activating the heat pack. The covers instantly shrink-wrapped around their hands and feet forming a thin, durable shield. Rico walked in and did a quick perusal all the way around. He preferred to take in the room before he examined the body. His instructor had told him, "Skim the surroundings first. Check the body, but don't let it distract you. He's dead. He's not going anywhere. Inspect the room. Look for threats. Watch for evidence."

An AI pad sat undisturbed in the corner. The victim's unicard, a combination of ID and bank/credit card, sat on a dresser. Three books lay on the bed. Up close, Rico could make out the book in the man's hands: *Antimatter Collection Beyond the Bow Shock.*

To the man's left, toward the wall, a book with Arabic letters on the cover lay on top of blood-soaked blankets. Pointing it out, Kuzbari said, "*Qur'an*. Not an overly conservative Muslim, however."

Rico gave him a quizzical expression. "You can tell that from the *Qur'an*?"

"No, the wedding ring. Although more accepted in recent years, for many they are still *haram*. That is to say, sinful."

"Enough that someone might kill over it?"

Kuzbari hesitated. "Possibly."

Rico wondered if something as minor as a wedding ring, at least from his perspective, anyway, was enough to get a terrorist group such as Adala involved. It seemed dubious, but maybe someone went rogue, or they were trying to issue a warning to others, or both. Maybe someone stepped off the ring from crazy-fanatic to just plain crazy.

Rico considered Kuzbari's second theory about a weapon. It seemed almost as if a giant spear had thrust up through the bottom of the bed. Impossible, but that's how it appeared. Drawers occupied the space under the bed, and they appeared undisturbed. The man's eyes stared at the ceiling, wide circles of horror, as if he knew that he lay dying. His hands and face, drained of blood, had a gray pallor.

Kuzbari said, "Based on the wound location, he took awhile to die. Stomach wounds can be particularly painful and slow to kill. This certainly seems personal."

Rico said, "I agree. It sure appears gruesome enough to be personal, or perhaps to send a message. I saw a guy last for days with a stomach wound once. We were pinned down. Anyway, it wasn't pretty."

The doctor gestured toward the hallway and asked, "Did he activate the emergency call system by wallscreen or voice?"

Reuben Holt shook his head from the doorway.

Rico shook his head in turn. "From all appearances, he just laid here, even after his stomach erupted. Why wouldn't he have called for help? This is definitely one screwy case." He spoke directly to Holt. "I'll do what I can, but I can't make any promises."

"I'm done," Kuzbari said. "With your permission?" The man held his hand over the victim's eyes, which stared at the ceiling.

Rico hesitated and then nodded.

Kuzbari closed the dead man's eyes and said something Rico did not understand, presumably a prayer in Arabic. When he finished, with Rico's help, they spread out some sort of plastic sheet. They picked up the body of Hujjat Malik and lowered it onto the plastic. The doctor unfolded a frame and placed it around the body. Next, he sprayed a chemical on the plastic, and it transformed into a hard, opaque shell to preserve any evidence.

Holt, Schroeder and Kuzbari stood in the hall while the medical team moved the body to the med lab. Two guards remained in the hallway while others searched for the missing head of security.

"So," Rico said, "Tiago Vaz, a pilot from Sistema Solar Recursos Ilimitados, dies in the first test flight any team has been able to pull off. While at his funeral, an acquaintance of his from Dubai Intergalactic, Dr. Hujjat Malik, gets killed."

"That hardly seems a coincidence," Kuzbari said.

"Agreed. Reuben, can you have all Tiago's and Hujjat's communications pulled and sent to my AI pad? Let's see if we can find some connection besides some ancient Parcheesi game."

"Yes, sir." He pulled up his own pad and typed in a few lines. "I've got someone working the protocols. We'll have it in a few minutes."

Reuben held up a finger and touched his earpiece. "Holt here. Go." He frowned, listening. "Well, tell them they can't." Another pause. "No, I—Bah— Space me. All right. I'll be right there." He gestured at Rico and Kuzbari to follow. "Come on. One of our guests has called a vote to force us to let them all go."

"Before the investigation is complete?" Kuzbari asked.

"They can't do that," Rico said. "We haven't even interviewed anyone yet."

"Yes, they can," Holt said.

"I better get down to the lab, then, and see what I can find out from the body, stat," Kuzbari said. He peeled out of his sterine gloves and booties, and tossed them into a reclamation chute. He snapped the sleeves of his shirt and jacket back into place.

"Computer, provide Dr. Kuzbari with the route to the medical lab." A red line with a matching arrow appeared on a nearby smartwall and pulsed its way down the corridor, leading the way to the lab. Kuzbari nodded and hurried off, his heavy bag in tow.

Holt marched crisply through the halls, staring straight ahead and deadly serious. Rico kept pace with him while the man talked. "Someone's using the Jupiter Articles of Mutual Cooperation to throw his weight around. He's called a vote."

"A vote? On what?"

"The constraint clause. At any time, any one of the member organizations can call a vote challenging any policy issue that restricts the activity of any other member, even if it does not constrain themselves or their interests. They only need a one-third vote to overturn any constraint."

"Right. I remember reading about that when I relocated out here. Struck me as pretty nuts. That's almost anarchy." Rico said.

"Pretty much so," Holt agreed. "It is about as *laissez-faire* as you can get. Anarchy with the illusion of governance. Passing a regulation takes 85 percent. Overturning one is as easy as floating in zero-g. It is intended to give corporations the maximum freedom possible; none of the corporations or the governments wanted any interference out here. Raw materials are not the only reason groups set up operations so far from earth. You think it's difficult getting a resolution passed at the United Nations?" Holt gave a grim laugh. "Try Jupiter."

They walked on in silence for only a meter or two before Holt continued, "There's another complication. I knew I was running low on air when I tried stopping all traffic out of the station, anyway. Closing the rings down starts costing a fortune pretty quickly. A few hours aren't much, given the distances between here and the belt or Earth. Keep it up for much longer, however, and we're talking millions of credits lost each day. With my supervisor missing, I'm in charge, so I had to make the call. Was it the right call? I don't know. Regardless, even without the group of citizens and employees clamoring in the bar, if I try to lock down the station for long, my ass will be tossed out an airlock."

They hurried along, exchanging trivial talk for the rest of the fifteen-minute walk back to the bar. Holt stopped talking as they entered the bar to a harangue of shouts and protests. Rico followed behind him.

"All right, all right!" the hawk-eyed man shouted. "That's enough!" The crowd quieted and he said, "Who called the vote?"

"I did." A stocky dark-haired man with light skin and blue eyes said. He had an accent Rico could not quite place. South American. Portuguese, maybe, but not quite.

"You are?"

"Ted Martel. The Articles are quite clear, Mr. Holt. We can call a vote on any situation that inhibits our actions."

"I'm sorry, Mr. Martel. Who do you represent?"

"I'm from French Guiana. I represent Sistema Solar Recursos."

At the mention of French Guiana, Rico's nerves sent a wakeup alarm through his body. Taz dies and suddenly there's this guy Martel who is from French Guiana, but also claiming to be part of Sistema Solar Recursos. Unusual to have a French Guianan working for a Brazilian company. The two nationalities did not get along all that well.

That was both odd and interesting,. French Guiana sat on the northeast coast of South America, north of Brazil. After a string of economic crises, Asia—primarily India, Japan, and China—and the Middle East's Dubai emerged as the leader, and led the way in the development of robots, nan-bots, nanomedicine and space development. South America emerged just behind those nations as a hub of space activity, largely because of the French Guiana Space Centre. Since the tiny nation was part of both the European Union and the Unión de Naciones Suramericanas (UNASUR), it stood uniquely positioned to facilitate trade between the powers. They marketed themselves as "The Center of Space," and the wealth flowed to those in power, while those living in the ghettos surrounding the port scrabbled to survive and hoped for the chance to get into space for a better life.

Reuben worked his mouth as if biting back words or trying not to spit. "Fine." He addressed the crowd of researchers, pilots, and others confined to The Spartan. "A man has been murdered. A scientist. If you leave now, we will lose vital information that may help us catch the killer, and you will be letting the murderer escape."

"Well, I don't know anything about it," a man of

enormous girth said.

"We've got a prize to win!" someone yelled out.

"And shipments of H3 to get moving," a man with a Mandarin Chinese accent said. Rico spotted him, but did not recognize him.

"Call the vote!" a woman toward the back shouted. A chorus of "Call the vote!" rang out and then a tense silence again fell over the room.

Martel gave a sad smile. Rico didn't believe it for a minute. "We grieve for our compatriot, inspector. However, we are very close to winning the Prize, and Tiago would want us to press on. It is the best tribute we could give him." He raised his voice to reach the entire room, while still keeping his eyes locked on Holt's. "All those in favor of ending our confinement and releasing the antimatter to the teams, say Aye."

"Aye!" erupted from the crowd.

"I believe that satisfies the vote, inspector."

Holt turned to the two men guarding the sliding doors and said, "Let 'em go." The crowd surged through the doors and in moments had dispersed through the narrow corridors to ready their ships.

"I'll delay them as long as I can," Holt told him.

"All right," Rico said. "Put in a priority request to all the companies for whatever recordings they have on Tiago's flight. I know everyone was watching. Maybe we'll see something."

"Where will you start?" the station officer asked.

"Always start with the victim's known associates," Rico said. "I think I'll go see what our Sistema Solar representative, Mr. Martel, can tell us while Dr. Kuzbari is doing the autopsy."

- THREE -

Rico caught up with Ted Martel who was giving orders to a man outside his ship, a mid-sized interzone vessel capable of traveling the distance between Earth and Jupiter.

"Pedro, *vamos*. Open the cargo doors. I want us ready to launch as soon as the antimatter arrives."

As Rico approached, Martel glowered. "What're you doing here? Where's your little Arab friend?"

Rico ignored the hostility. "I'm investigating Hujjat Malik's death."

Martel's face flushed red with rage. "Ah. And what about my teammate Tiago's death, eh? Who is investigating that? Pah!" He threw up an arm in disgust.

"You think someone sabotaged the *Domínguez*?" Rico asked.

"Ask your friend," Martel said, still glaring. "You got a lot of guts coming here." He stepped toward Rico with his fist clenched. Rico's first impression of the man as stocky was not quite right. Rico did have a few inches on the guy, and Martel's broad shoulders and bulky arms were evident under the cold-resistant flight jacket, but he was not heavyset or awkward in the least. His sinewy grace gave the impression of a predator about to pounce. The other man, Pedro, had disappeared inside the ship.

"Who? You mean Dr. Kuzbari? Do you have something you want to say, Mr. Martel?" He shifted his feet and his balance, ready in case Martel came at him, but kept his hands by his side and his face blank.

"I don't want any trouble. I'm not threatening anybody," Martel sneered, turning his face aside.

Rico said, "Mr. Martel, if you have any information that can help us catch Tiago's killer, I want to do that. He was a friend of mine."

Martel softened his tone, but not by much. "Catch him and do what? There is no justice out here except Jupiter justice, eh?. You are American, right? Just as with your Old West frontier, we fight our own battles out here."

"Do you have information about Tiago's death?" Rico pressed.

Martel stepped closer and jabbed a finger in Rico's face. "You've got a lot of *cojones* asking me that." He clenched his jaw and leaned in close. "We know what your friend and his team did." Rico did not give ground. He kept his breathing even and his body relaxed, waiting for Martel to make his move.

Instead, Martel stepped back. "Keep that piece of flotsam off my dock, and you stay off it, too. I didn't kill Higgit. But if we figured out what Dubai Intergalactic has been up to, maybe somebody else did, too. *Adios, adieux.*" He spat on the dock and stalked into his ship.

#

Kuzbari watched through the scope as the nan-bots he'd injected into the hard carapace made their way over to the body. Although he'd worked with nan-bots for years, he'd never ceased to be fascinated by them. It amazed him that they could fly through the air, actually move through a person's lungs examining for signs of cancer or some other problem and then, just as easily, enter through a blood vessel wall and swim through a person's bloodstream. They truly were miraculous inventions.

Kuzbari leaned forward as the group of nan-bots sent their observations of Malik's body to his terminal in real-time. Something was wrong. As soon as their scans hit the cavity, a different cloud of nan-bots rose up like a swarm of angry hornets. They charged Kuzbari's nan-bots, and the video feeds all winked out. Panicked, he switched channels to the group he'd sent toward the head and had them pivot back. A score of nan-bots raced toward his team. Ignoring the aggressors, the doctor zoomed in on the background, where a group of them had emerged from the body. Hundreds if not thousands of them were settling against the hard shell of the autopsy carapace.

They were trying to cut their way through.

Kuzbari stumbled backward off his stool. "Oh no, oh no, oh no," he muttered as he scrambled for his black cloth bag, his normally calm reserve shattered. His nan-bots must have triggered a defense response: eliminate anyone probing the body. His head jerked up. Was that his imagination? Had he heard the shell cracking? Sweat broke out on his forehead as he pawed through his bag. "Come on, come on!"

He pulled out a rod that looked like a miniature satellite dish, his own invention. *Finally!* He pulled the trigger, sending an intense rapid-flux magnetic field at the carapace. He couldn't see the microscopic robots, of course, so he went over every millimeter of the shell. Then, just to be safe he ran the field over his own body. He sat down on the floor, setting the degausser down next to him with trembling hands.

#

Rico lounged in a simple but comfortable chair in his assigned room, sipped coffee he'd made with his own portable brewer, and considered Ted Martel from French Guiana. The man seemed convinced that Dubai Intergalactic, or someone on the team, intentionally blew up the *Domínguez*, but why? What did he know? The question nagged at him.

When Rico had gone planet-side for the first time at the age of twelve he had ridden down the world's first successful space elevator, anchored in the city of Saint-Élie in French Guiana. Although he had been scared and alone, the view had been spectacular. The elevator, however, had hitched along slowly, its seats with cracked upholstery lining graffiti-marked walls. The port city also had a seedy, dangerous edge. Missing persons and murders dominated the local news blogs. Ted Martel would fit right in there, Rico thought. Still, the guy seemed adamant in his accusations.

"Candra, pull up all videos from Axion station of the last *Domínguez* flight, please." The file popped up on the smartwall, courtesy of the station computer, and Rico began scrutinizing it. He played it through once to its grim conclusion. "Magnify times 10. Play video. Note any anomalies."

"None noted," the station computer reported.

"Pull any feeds supplied from the other stations and data from proximity telescopes. Include infrared to ultraviolet."

The computer said, "Three energy pulses detected in the infrared range, sir, two-point-three seconds before the explosion."

Energy pulses? *Ni Pa*, Rico thought, slipping into a phrase his late father used, which meant, "no way."

"Candra, overlay all available data on star and satellite positions. Add in all images and data from other stations, satellites, etc. Extrapolate energy source point of origin, size and shape."

He waited impatiently for the results. As they came up on the screen and he began sifting through them, Rico's wrist-comm chirruped. Dr. Raheem Kuzbari's name was on the screen.

"Accept video. Kuzbari. Whaddya got?" He peered closely at the wrist-comm. It was hard to tell on the small screen, but the doctor's face seemed drawn and tense.

"No DNA, other than the victim's. Listen, Rico, we need to talk." He leaned in toward the cam to emphasize his point. "In person. Can you meet me in the medical lab? Right away?"

Puzzled, Rico agreed. Judging from Kuzbari's demeanor something was off with the autopsy, and he didn't want to talk about it over a comm. Rico headed down there right away, his service bag over his shoulder.

As he walked along the gently curving floor of the rotating space ring, he considered what to do next. Apparently someone had fired on Tiago's ship. As much as Martel was an ass he had been right, at least about the ship being sabotaged. Martel seemed to think that Tiago had been killed by someone on the

Dubai team.

That definitely put Rico in a bind. Damn system politics. He needed to talk to people from Dubai Intergalactic Chemicals, starting with the CEO. He also needed to ask some pointed questions and see if he could stir up the pot; he didn't need this robotics doctor getting in his way, maybe running interference and tripping him up.

That also meant that someone on Martel's team, if not Martel himself, could have easily killed Hujjat Malik out of revenge. Revenge is a dish best served out in the cold depths of space.

From there, his thoughts shifted to a different trajectory, and he pondered what could possibly be wrong with his own team's engine design? They'd made incredible progress lately, and when Rico had left for the supply run, Uesugi had been getting ready to apply for a test flight. Good thing they didn't, or Zavier might have ended up like Taz.

Rico had been honored and thrilled when Uesugi had asked him to be part of the team, but none of that would mean anything if they couldn't identify the problem! Maybe he should check the ratio of antimatter again, but he put that in a holding pattern for now.

When Rico walked into the lab, Kuzbari's face was absolutely grim. Surprisingly, the dead body still lay under the plastic shell.

"That bad?" Rico asked.

"Worse," Kuzbari said. He tapped some buttons on a computer pad and said, "Dr. Raheem Kuzbari." He put his thumb on the touchpad and then held his eye up to the camera. He tapped another couple of buttons and an image appeared on the screen. "Look at this," he said.

Rico saw pictures that created the impression of zero-g mining machines, with large protruding teeth, except that they had turbines or propellers set at various angles. What kinds of bots were these, and what did this have to do with...? He shifted his gaze from the screen to the corpse to Kuzbari, and realized the connection. Hundreds of miniature robots floated in the body of Hujjat Malik. They were military grade with armored plating and large mandible piercers that made him think of mutant beetles.

Rico gave out a low whistle. "I take it you found the murder weapon?"

Raheem nodded.

Nan-weapons had been banned since the North Korean Technocrat Coup, when a woman named Kwan, working with a band of programmers, and less than two thousand nan-bots, had eliminated every member of the Supreme People's Assembly, the Politburo, the Presidium, and Central Electoral Committee—and, of course, the Supreme Leader, Kim Hwan-ji. It was one of the most thorough and bloodless coups in history. Each of the politicians died simultaneously of a massive heart attack and stroke. Apparently, Kwan had not wanted to risk having any survivors. The leaders of Earth, Mars, and the habitats—even the criminal elements—had all been alarmed by the relative ease of the assassinations and their own vulnerability, and had acted swiftly to ban nano-weaponry.

"Shouldn't the AI have detected any non-registered nan-bots when we entered the station?"

Rico asked.

The doctor shrugged. "There are ways around that. I can tell you these were Earth-made, from an ASEAN company, probably China or Korea, based on the prefix code, but the station's database library does not carry specific manufacturers. I can request more details from Earth, but that will take at least two or three hours on the bounce-back. Add in any red tape and figure two to five days."

Rico said, "We'll need the results faster than that. Send the report and the manufacturing codes over to my pad, and I'll see what I can do through my channels."

"Of course."

Rico sat in silence for a few moments, weighing the situation. If Kuzbari knew that much about nanbots, he undoubtedly could have killed Malik, but what would be his motive? Some sort of religious conflict or inner-ship turmoil? Or, maybe something more personal? He had pointed out the ring on Malik's finger. An affair, maybe?

Rico told Kuzbari about Martel's accusations. "Stay alert," he told the slender man.

"I had not considered it from their perspective," Kuzbari said. "With Sistema Solar out of commission for the time being, that probably makes Dubai Intergalactic the frontrunner in the race for the AMMATT Prize. We filed a petition for an antimatter test flight last week. We've been approved for two days from now. We've tried to keep it a secret, but you never know who may have found out."

That raised some interesting possibilities. Dubai Intergalactic could have killed Tiago Vaz to give themselves more time to win the prize. Sistema Solar could have killed Malik out of revenge, or as a counter-delay. Or another team altogether could have taken out one or both of them. He made a mental note to ask Holt if any other teams had filed test flight requests.

"There's something more you should know regarding the nan-bots inside Malik," Kuzbari said, grimacing. He let out a long sigh. "I don't want this coming out through other channels, and you deserve to know up front. If you check the lab records, you'll see that I destroyed the memory cores of the nan-bots, potentially eliminating valuable evidence."

"Well, I don't ... wait, you did *what*?" Rico's eyes went wide, and he sat up as if the room had started to depressurize.

Kuzbari gave him a wry smile. "Yes. The lab records will show that I sent a magnetic field through them. In my defense, they had reactivated and had chosen me as their next target. You almost had another body on your hands. I decided if it came down to them or me I did not want to be eviscerated."

"Son of a space monkey," Rico said. He stared at Kuzbari in shock. He could not believe that there were nanite assassins less than two meters away, and that they had almost gotten the doctor. But was it the truth, or a well-crafted lie?

"Not the phrase I would choose, but I agree with the sentiment." Kuzbari slouched in his chair, worn out from his recent ordeal. His olive skin shone with sweat.

"Ah, old joke. A monkey was the first animal— mammal—sent into space."

Kuzbari closed his eyes and shook his head.

After a moment, he said, "The circumstances are rather damning, Rico. Since Dubai could be involved, perhaps I should remove myself. Do you want me to step aside?"

Rico scrutinized the man, trying to size him up. He pursed his lips and made a judgment call. "Holt put you on the team. We have a job to do. If something changes, I'll let you know. Do you want to solve these murders?"

"I do, indeed."

"Then until I decide otherwise, you're on the case."

"What about Martel's objections?" Kuzbari asked. "He has a valid point, you know. Most Earthers and ex-Terrans of Arabic descent have connections to Adala. It's in our genetic makeup. Collaborators and wannabe terrorists all."

Rico ignored the dry humor. "Forget him. He can gripe all he wants. Let him take it up with Holt."

Kuzbari nodded a thank you and said, "We have another issue. We cannot let word of how Hujjat was killed get out to the general public. If they lose trust in nanite technology all sorts of health issues will resurge that had been controlled for decades. If people panic and start dumping nanobots, we'll have to dig out treatments from last century for obesity, diabetes, high blood pressure, and high cholesterol—and those are just the obvious ones that come to mind. Of more immediate concern for us on the station, many people could be killed if news of assassin bots gets out and causes a massive panic."

Rico retrieved a container of coffee from his

service bag while he considered Kuzbari's words. He never went anywhere without his own portable brewer and vacuum flask. The flask came with a cup attached to top and bottom, and Rico filled them both. He recalled hearing about the lines of panicked people trying to get off of Mars when the prisoners took control of first the prison, then an entire dome. Dozens of people were killed trying to get out on a ship.

"Agreed," Rico said, "but if this is already out there, then we need to run this up the chain of command. We've got to get them in the loop."

Kuzbari took a sip of the coffee and grimaced. Rico laughed and the doctor smirked sheepishly, then laughed as well. They were both grateful for the release. "Sorry, but this is awful! Egh!"

"What are you talking about? That's Grade-A coffee. Besides you get used to it. Six hundred million klicks from earth means the coffee gets a little old by the time the next shipment comes in. A good cup of Java is my main motivation for a working antimatter drive, you know."

"Ahh." He took another sip and winced a little less. He gestured with the cup and raised an eyebrow. "Yes, I can, ah, see your point."

"I've got news as well. Check this out," Rico said. He linked the results from the recent computer analysis between his pad and a nearby smartwall. He started to talk and then paused. "Are you sure those creepy mini-carnivores are dead?"

"Yes. After the initial shot with the degausser, I did another, *very* meticulous one. They're neutralized."

"Right. Okay then. Check this out." He went through what he'd found from overlaying all the system data he could get hold of. A few minutes later he wrapped up. "The first pulse was low power, wide radius—just the type of laser fire used for determining speed, range, and trajectory of a target. The second was also low power but tighter—the kind of beam used to locate the engine. The last pulse," he tapped the pad in front of him, "breached containment."

"Are you sure? You realize what you are saying? That a stealthed ship blew up the *Domínguez*?"

"Yes," Rico said emphatically. "Based on the angles of the various vids and imagery, the computer estimates it as a relatively small craft, not much larger than my shuttle."

"Since laser weapons and stealth technology are both banned from commercial and research vessels—" Kuzbari said, and left the conclusion hanging.

"Exactly. This is a military ship or an illegal. Someone with a great deal of cash killed Tiago Vaz. Martel clearly thinks it was someone working for Dubai Intergalactic."

"Which provides motive."

Rico nodded. "Revenge for Tiago's death would be a strong motive. Illegal stealth vehicles and killer nan-bots, though? That's a whole different kind of operation."

Rico's brain cells were firing fast. There was a very remote chance that whoever killed Tiago or Malik did so on their own, but it was not likely with those kinds of resources. Micro-manufacturing cost a fortune. Whoever did these murders had a lot of credits behind them. Could these deaths be fallout from two corporations duking it out? Or maybe Adala and some South American faction they had not identified as yet? Was Adala sending a message to non-devout Muslims? If so, was this just the first of more deaths to follow? Were the two deaths unrelated, and the timing just a coincidence? Was some corporation trying to derail the development of a working antimatter engine? There were always rumors. One of his squad had claimed that teleportation had been invented back in the '90s, but that a bunch of power people had purchased the tech and buried it. No doubt, when the antimatter engine actually worked, the manufacturers and shippers of H3 stood to lose a fortune.

Rico broke out of his reverie and rubbed at his temples, feeling a headache coming on. "The computer is examining all the vids and running the pattern of stars against any missing ones that should be there to extrapolate shape, heat signatures, and possible makes and models of the stealthed ship. We'll see if we can get some more information. Meanwhile, isn't there some rule for Muslims about burying the dead within three days or something?"

Kuzbari gave him a thin smile. "Not exactly. Within 24 hours. Even though the days are longer here at Jupiter, the rule has held. Those close to him will have arrived by shuttle recently. Once I finish the autopsy, they will do the ritual cleansing, shroud the body, and then the community will gather for the funeral prayer."

"Do you need to attend?"

"Ah, no, I am not welcome there, Rico. Not for

religious ceremonies." Seeing his puzzled expression, the doctor drew in a deep breath and let it out. "I am not a Muslim. It causes some friction occasionally, but not a great deal at the moment. Religious tolerance ebbs and flows. This year we are tolerated. There are a handful of us kufar—non-believers— working on Dubai Intergalactic."

"Sorry," Rico said, "Didn't mean to pry."

"We are in the midst of an investigation," Kuzbari said. "It is your job and mine to pry. To that end, we must ask questions of the people on Dubai Intergalactic. While it is unpleasant to think they could have sabotaged the *Domínguez*, it bears exploring. How can I be of assistance?"

Rico grunted. Now what? If he set Kuzbari loose, then anyone involved would be tipped that they were investigating the explosion as well as the murder. On the other hand, that information would undoubtedly get out soon anyway. Nothing stayed secret on a space station. Plus, Kuzbari might get access to some inner rings that Rico, as an outsider, would never penetrate.

"All right, Raheem," Rico said. "I'll go through official channels. You see what you can find out through any crew members you're on good terms with."

The doctor raised an eyebrow at the use of his first name, but nodded his assent.

- FOUR -

Rico left Raheem in the autopsy room, grabbed a snack at a food stall in the medical and science suites after his stomach growled for the third time, and headed back to his room to make some calls in private. Rico's temporary berth was half way between Raheem's room, which happened to be in between Hujjat Malik's and an elderly couple's room. The latter, a Mr. and Mrs. Nejem, had been on Dubai Intergalactic visiting their son, and were headed back home to Mars. Holt had interviewed them and sent him a summary. They appeared to be clean. Kuzbari's room being right next to Malik's made sense, especially since they came over on the same shuttle from the same station. However, the coincidence, explainable or not, still made the nerves between his shoulder blades tingle.

The undercurrent of suspicion made the tingling turn to tense muscles in his shoulders and neck. He needed a good backrub, which again made him think of Inés Villaverde. He hadn't thought of her in months, if not a few years. Why was she cropping up now? He pushed thoughts of her aside as best he could.

Rico wondered where Kuzbari came from. The man spoke in formal and precise English. His formality came across as British boarding school, but he had no trace of the Queen's accented English. His accent also lacked the lolling trill often present from Smith City on Mars. Earth? Harvard, maybe?

A quick computer search revealed that Kuzbari currently worked as a researcher for Microdigitomics in Boston. The company also had offices in a dozen other cities. Kuzbari's bio did not mention much personal background. He went to school at University at Albany, then Yale, and then Harvard. No surprise there. Lots of academic papers. Three awards. Multi-million credit grant. No mention of pre-college or family, not that Rico had expected that on a work site.

After another ten minutes of queries to Candra, he came to the conclusion that Dr. Raheem Kuzbari had no social media presence at all. He apparently had no CyberToll account, no PsiSync account, no 4D account. Nothing.

"Who are you, Raheem Kuzbari? What's your game?"

He sent Uesugi a secure message. "Please send a message to ASC. I need a background check on Dr. Raheem Kuzbari, currently employed by Microdigitomics. Thanks."

Next, he commed Holt, ran Kuzbari's thought by him about some team taking out the *Domínguez* to stall for time, and then asked which teams had filed petitions for use of antimatter in tests. Holt stared back at him with a flat expression before replying, "Captain Schroeder. You know I cannot give you that information."

Rico let his irritation show. "Not even for a murder investigation that *you* put me on?"

"No, sir. I'm afraid not. My orders are quite clear regarding the contest."

Annoyed, Rico punched the off button, not bothering to say goodbye. He understood the benefits of an AMMATT drive, as well as the tourist income the contest brought in, but the powers that be were wound just a little too tight when it came to this contest. Did they expect he would tell his team members what he found out? Well, perhaps not, but it most likely would color his future actions if he did know, but how much faster or harder could they work than they were already? Those thoughts led him back to some other ideas he had. He checked his comm. Almost 1 PM.

"Candra, call Uesugi."

The smartwall—computer interfaces located throughout most rooms and hallways—lit up and Uesugi appeared. He recognized her office in the background.

"Ah, Rico-san. I just sent off the request to ASC. Is there something else I can do for you?"

He filled her in on what had happened and then said, "I've sent you the numbers from the nan-bots. I need to know the origin and the purchaser." He paused. "I don't have much time, Kita. The antimatter will be released any time. Once that happens, everyone scatters back to their own stations."

"One moment, Rico-san." She focused on her console for a few moments and then returned her attention to him. "I have sent the request. What else?" All business.

"On a different topic. Our simulations from four months ago – they had a green light, yes?"

Kita gave him a quizzical expression. "They did."

"So what's different?"

Kita Uesugi's gaze drifted off to the right as she considered the question. "Not much, really. We changed the flow modulator for greater efficiency. And we applied Hanson's Theorem to the magnetic field to create a more stable resonance. But we went back and double-checked both of those sets of calculations, together and independently. Candra also verified our numbers. We're missing something."

Rico's lips twitched up into an impish smile. "Maybe. But not necessarily what you think. Have you re-run the last simulation, before the modifications?"

"No. I considered that, but there seemed no point, since we had time to find our error while the extra-solar bots secured more antimatter." Kita touched her ear, reflecting. "What are you thinking, Rico-san?"

"Can you bring up the last sim and share it on my screen?"

"Certainly, but–"

"Trust me. I'm playing a hunch."

Uesugi pulled up the old sim, prior to the modifications, and had the computer run it. At 2.1 gigs, the ship on the screen erupted into a silent fireball.

Uesugi's mouth turned into a grim line. "I do not understand, Rico-san. These simulations worked perfectly before. Has someone altered our calculations?"

"Not exactly," he said. "We've been hacked."

After Uesugi got over her shocked outrage, Rico told her his plan. He explained what he wanted the crew back at Axion to do, and they were about to disconnect the call when a soft chime sounded from her end.

"One moment," Uesugi said. Rico waited while

she read something out of his line of sight. Still staring at the data, she said, "According to the codes you sent me, and the company manifests, the nan-bots were purchased by a Lara Kohler for a Brazilian company called Vargas. The investigators are searching for any connections to Sistema Solar. Nothing yet." She raised her head and pierced him with the commanding gaze that often took people by surprise, but that Rico knew well. "Be careful, Captain. When I receive more information, I will pass it along."

"Yes, ma'am. Thank you, Kita. Rico, out."

#

"Did you find out anything?" Rico asked as they ordered a late lunch/early dinner at the Command Ring cafeteria. Raheem had suggested they go back to the Spartan, but it might be the only meal they got today, and Rico wanted some fresh shrimp with linguine. Raheem ordered *al harees*, with a side of falafel.

They sat and Raheem took a sip of coffee. He grimaced and raised an eyebrow. "This is not much better than yours."

"Hey!" Rico said. "I'm wounded."

While they were eating, they compared progress. "I could not find anything of substance. After I finished the autopsy, I made a few personal comms to Dubai Intergalactic. Even when I called people I know decently well, however, the researchers and team members would not make eye contact with me. Because I am kufar, as I said before, this is not altogether unusual … to a degree. However, it seemed even more than usual and, given the possible connection with Tiago Vaz's death, I found this behavior disturbing. One of the crew with whom I am friendly told me, 'Raheem, we have done nothing that would have warranted the murder of Hujjat, and we did not sabotage the *Domínguez*. You should know that. Are you trying to cause trouble for all the other kufar and yourself? Stop asking such questions and leave it at that.'" Raheem shrugged.

"Do you think someone on your team killed Tiago or Hujjat?" Rico asked.

"Hujjat, I doubt. His expertise benefited the team. Tiago?" He held his hands wide. "I cannot say."

"If they consider you some kind of heretic, how'd you get invited to the party in the first place?"

"I am good at what I do. That, and my family has some degree of influence."

Raheem's less than informative answers felt evasive. "And what exactly do you do?"

"As Reuben Holt told you, I am one of the best medical nano-programmers in the Middle East," he said levelly.

"Ah. Where do you work?"

"Microdigitomics. I'm on a leave of absence to work on the Dubai team."

"How does nanotechnology fit in with creating an antimatter drive?"

The doctor smiled at him, and while the grin did not seem exactly predatory, it did seem to Rico to be rather feral. Perhaps his overactive imagination was just playing tricks on him.

"I cannot answer that one, Captain Schroeder.

Trade secrets and all."

Rico chuckled. "What about your family? What do they do?"

Raheem sipped more coffee and set the cup down before replying. "My mother is in artificial intelligence. My father is in the markets. My thirteen siblings have a variety of jobs. I have no pets, no wives, and no significant others. I have no alibi for the murder of Hujjat Malik, or for Tiago Vaz for that matter. I was watching the latter test the Sistema Solar antimatter drive, but any witnesses on board Dubai Intergalactic must, understandably, be suspect. Is there anything else you want to know?"

The investigator chuckled. The man knew how to cut to the axis of the matter. "So, you had enough pull to get onboard, but you got stuck harvesting shiitake mushrooms with me?"

Raheem spread his hands wide and grinned, as if to say, "You said it, not me."

Rico gave a robust laugh, and people at a nearby table cast a glance his way. He did not ask about Raheem's ability to program nan-bots to kill. He had no doubt the man could do it, given his expertise.

"I've contacted both Dubai and Sistema Solar," Rico said. "Nothing interesting in his comms with Hujjat – no debt, no illicit behaviors, a few girlfriends. What was more interesting is that neither Dubai Intergalactic nor Sistema Solar wanted to give me the comm messages."

"Really?"

"Yes, I had to have Holt threaten to hold up their antimatter delivery." He did not share with Raheem that Holt had been totally bluffing. Given the stringent rules, he could not have withheld the shipment from a given team. "He assures me this is all of the communiqués."

"Hmm. Maybe Hujjat discovered something that got him killed. Did you check his docs as well?" Raheem asked.

"Yes, nothing on his pad or the Dubai station computer. After Holt got me access, I checked his files and Tiago's remotely but found nothing obvious. One odd thing did stand out, though."

Raheem sat forward. "Yes? Do tell."

"It wasn't so much what was in the communications. It was the number of them. Far more than seemed called for just to play a game. But I read through them and had Candra do an analysis, and they seem innocuous. Apparently, Tiago and Hujjat had struck up a genuine if unlikely friendship, and they just naturally covered a lot of topics."

"Why unlikely?"

"Tiago was a maverick. He did his own thing. Broke a lot of rules. Gave away Brazilian chocolate and Cuban cigars everywhere he went. Partied hard, gambled big, loved the ladies, pushed the limits as a pilot. He was brusque, macho, opinionated-——Larger than life, you know? No offense, but a friendship based on playing Parcheesi—

"Ur."

"Pardon me?"

"Ur. The Royal Game of Ur." He waved it aside. "Nevermind. Minor detail. I didn't mean to sidetrack you."

"Right. Well, playing Ur with an astrophysicist seems out of character to me, but one thing I've learned in life, people can always surprise you."

Raheem nodded in agreement. "What else can you tell me about Tiago Vaz?"

Rico decided to leave out the part about Taz saving his life and, after the investigation was over, going hiking and fishing together with Inés. While Rico was on leave, for that brief time, the three of them had formed a tight friendship.

"Taz encouraged everyone; made a lot of people laugh; broke through barriers. He had a great many friends, but he pissed off people, too. I just don't see them having the resources or the access to kill him off through sabotaging his ship."

Raheem smiled sadly. "Sounds like an interesting man. I take it you considered him a friend?"

Rico nodded. "I did. We'd meet here on Command Ring to play cards once in awhile. Someone on his team may have wanted revenge for his death."

"So, you think someone from Sistema Solar killed Hujjat? "

"Maybe. That's where the evidence seems to be pointing. Martel sure thinks so."

"Revenge is a compelling motive," Raheem said. He tapped his chin with a knuckle, his expression troubled, clearly thinking about the *Domínguez*. "Martel also seems to be a fan of Jupiter Justice."

Rico grunted. "You said you've only been out here a few months, right?"

"Two months, almost three."

"Martel's right to a degree. You have to protect yourself and your own out here: frontier justice. That much is true. But the spacers' code still applies."

Raheem knew the spacers' code, as did anyone who travelled by ship or did not live under a rock back on Earth. Simply put, it was always give aid. Always. It was the one inviolate rule that cut across all races and beliefs and helped people survive the challenges of space. Only criminal sociopaths and fanatics disregarded the spacers' code. "He's got it all wrong if he thinks that, because we're way out here on the edge of inhabited space, that that justifies vigilantism. There may not be a lot of laws out here, but you still have to work within the law, such as it is."

Raheem gave him a skeptical stare. "Even when the law can be overturned by a simple vote of the Jupes? Even though the corporations are effectively totalitarian regimes out here in the dark edge of space?"

"Well, there is that, isn't there? Each company is its own little kingdom; I'll grant you that. And there are plenty of desperate people that want these jobs, so they waive a lot of rights. It's questionable, legally and ethically, but it happens. I get that, but we can't go around killing anyone we want. It's too easy to cross that line."

Rico was remembering another time and place, the feel of the blaster in his hand. His finger tightening on the trigger and wanting, so damn badly, to pull that spacin' trigger. He remembered his cousin Jackie's dead body, and *The Killer's* mocking smirk when he'd shoved him against the wall. Yes, Rico knew all about the throbbing, hot desire for vengeance. That day had been the darkest one of his life. He'd hated himself for not taking that bastard's life ... and he'd hated himself for wanting to take his life in the first place.

"When we give in to that gut-level desire for revenge, it changes us. We become nothing more than a pack of wolves circling each other, waiting for an opening to tear each other apart. We're out here—a community of colonies circling a planet—in the most hostile environment humanity occupies; we should pull together, instead of reverting to barbarism, but we don't. Instead, we call it Jupiter Justice, as if that makes it all right, and we call it a day."

Rico took a deep breath and let it out. "Sorry. Didn't mean to go off on a rant."

Raheem waved it off with a dismissive hand. "I may disagree on the merits of taking justice into one's own hands, but I asked, didn't I? Either way, revenge requires an offending action. Your analysis shows someone did, indeed, kill Tiago. Martel has essentially accused Dubai Intergalactic."

He stopped, letting the statement—and the connection between the two murders—hang in the air between them.

"Have you decided yet?" Raheem asked.

"Decided?"

"Yes. If I'm guilty or not. I obviously have the skills. I had opportunity. Perhaps I had a motive. You have not asked to see the communications between Malik and myself, although presumably you requested that formally from Dubai Intergalactic."

Rico leaned back in his chair, frowning. "You're right. I did, along with all his other messages." There had been no messages from or to Malik. "But, I already told you. If I want you off the case, I'll let you know. Hey, Raheem, if you want to step off the case,

I understand. It can't be easy for you, either. There's no shame in it."

Rico examined the tall, thin man before him. He searched his face, seeking answers as thoughts fired rapidly through his brain. Did he know more than he conveyed? Was he involved? If so, what was his angle? No point in asking for an alibi, not when his berth was right next door; even then, he suspected the murder weapon could be programmed years in advance. That being the case, why not just release the bots and have them kill Malik three months from now? There were certainly religious fanatics in any belief system who could justify lying to and killing heretics not of their faith. Was Dubai Intergalactic connected to Adala? Raheem's apparent stance in favor of vigilantism disconcerted Rico. He'd encountered that mindset in ASC often enough; however, in the military, soldiers were trained to button-up that anger and follow orders instead, to varying degrees of success, true, but that was the intent. Was Raheem really on the outs with the rest of the Dubai team? He liked the guy, wanted to trust him, but he'd been burned before. He'd keep him close, keep an eye on him, and keep his guard up. He knew he was taking a chance, but he didn't have much choice, did he?

"No, Rico. I may be jaded at times, but I do believe in justice and truth. I will follow the comet, even if it leads to my own team members."

Could he follow the trail, even if it led to murderers on the Dubai team? Rico hated the not knowing. This was the worst part of the investigation—having enough answers that the picture was emerging but still not clear. He was close, he could feel it. But some crucial puzzle pieces were still missing. And, as when waking up from a dream, the answers could slip away into mist before they coalesced in his mind.

"Listen, I have to ask. Does Dubai Intergalactic have stealth-capable ships?"

"Not to my knowledge," Raheem said. Without hesitation, he added, "However, we could definitely afford them."

"Unfortunately, any company that can afford a station around Jupiter could probably afford them." Rico blew out a heavy breath. "C'mon," he said. "We're not getting anywhere sitting here. Let's go rattle Ted Martel's cage and see what crawls out."

Rico tossed back the rest of his coffee. Raheem left most of his on the table, and Rico suppressed a grin.

- FIVE -

"What do you mean, he's not here? Where did he go?" Rico asked. He stared at Martel's ship as if he could will the man to be onboard and come out for questioning.

The dockworker shrugged. "*No se'*," he said. "His station berth, I think."

"You're Pedro, right?" Rico asked.

"*Sí*," the short, squat man said. He gave the appearance of having grown up under Jupiter's heavier gravity, if that were realistic. He had dark skin, but with a more golden tone than Raheem's, with thick, short-cropped hair that reminded Rico of the bristle brush his grandmother used for her horses.

Raheem stepped forward holding his unicard so that Pedro could see it. "It would be helpful if we could take a quick peek at his quarters," Raheem said.

Pedro licked his thick lips. "El capitán no like," he said. Raheem pulled the card back, and Rico saw it was set on the bank transaction screen. Raheem pushed a few buttons. The amount of cash he transferred would easily be six months salary for Pedro.

"Hopefully, this will offset any inconvenience."

"*Señor Martel es el capitan de la nave espacial*," Pedro said in a whisper.

"*Luego nos debe apresurarse antes capitán Martel devuelve*," Rico said, and then translated in case Raheem did not speak Spanish. "He says that Martel is the captain of the space shuttle. I told him we'd better hurry, then, before Captain Martel returns."

With furtive glances around the docking bay, Pedro pulled out his own unicard. Raheem touched his card to Pedro's and completed the transfer. The stout dockworker hurried up the ramp, gesturing them to follow.

"Cinco minutos—five minutes," Pedro said and hurried back outside.

They searched quickly but thoroughly. At the end of five minutes, Rico straightened up in disgust. Nothing. Not a bloody thing. Raheem shrugged.

"Well, sugar and cream," Rico said. "I thought for sure–"

Loud clarions ripped through the air. For half a second, Rico thought they'd set off an alarm, but then realized it was the alarm that only sounded for imminent catastrophic threats to the station, such as collision, atmosphere breach, or solar flare. It meant get to a shielded internal chamber immediately or die. That sound made even a lifelong spacers' blood freeze.

Rico and Raheem, on the other hand, smiled at one another.

"Sounds as if your plan is working," the native of Dubai said.

Rico's wrist-comm chirruped. "Rico here."

Jane appeared on the small screen. "Hey! We found the nan-bots hard fixed to our system just as you predicted. We ran the jinn-wyrm and it did its job." The alarm continued to blare outside the ship.

"That was fast," Rico said.

The jinn-wyrm was an invasive computer

program designed to act independently and under exact conditions. No one knew whether the "jinn" referred to the Chinese dialect or the Arabic word meaning, "hidden"—and the basis of the word "djinn."

Zavier stuck his head into view. "Actually, I wrote it. It was easy. I just modified a ... uh ... program I'd already written. Only took me ten minutes."

Jane rolled her eyes upward and then frowned at the big oaf. "Yes, he's an ass, but apparently good with JWs. The part that took the longest was finding the planted bots."

Rico's plan had been simple. Use the spy nan-bots against whoever had put them there by sending a virus back up the pipeline, so to speak. Whoever had been stealing data received a wyrm that then fired off its thrusters, dramatically pushing it away from Jupiter and Callisto. Rico had specified that the wyrm should include safety precautions requiring that no obstacles, such as ships, probes, satellites, space debris, etc. be in the way when the station's thrusters were triggered. No harm, but it waved a nice big flag that would establish where the corporate spy was sending information.

Jane leaned in close to the view screen. "But, the jinn-wyrm didn't infect Sistema Solar, as you expected." She paused a moment, enjoying the suspense. "It hit Centurion Station instead!"

Rico gaped, incredulous. "What? One of the European teams?!"

"You got it. Centurion's planetside thrusters are firing full bore and pushing them out of Callisto's orbit even as we speak! Of course, with that much mass, they're still moving slow enough not to be a flight hazard. Our jinn-wyrm definitely nailed 'em. They have no idea what's going on." A mischievous grin played across Jane's face. "Their comm officer sounded a little panicked."

Zavier jumped in again. "A little? He's raising holy hell!" He barked out a laugh, and for once it didn't annoy Rico. He actually found himself grinning.

"Great job! That'll keep them busy. Keep me posted. Rico out." He sat back, bemused. He'd been right that nan-bots had, indeed, been planted on Axion Station. They must have lain dormant until triggered by the sims, at which time, they faked a cascade failure. His second guess, that the bots were transmitting data out, had also been correct. Though Jane's revelation that the bugs had *not* been planted by the South Americans, as he'd thought, definitely surprised him.

"Presumably, Centurion has been doing the same with other teams, including Sistema Solar and Dubai Intergalactic," Raheem said.

Rico ran a hand through his hair and sighed. "That still does not mean that Dubai did not mistakenly think Sistema Solar planted the nan-bots. The question is, who else knew, or who else could benefit by killing Tiago?"

"The Centurions would have as much to gain as any other team by keeping Solar from claiming the prize," Raheem said. "Even if the South Americans believed that Dubai Intergalactic destroyed the *Domínguez*, why kill Hujjat? Revenge, of course. I see that, but why not go to the authorities?" Raheem asked, nonplussed.

"Lack of evidence? Maybe without solid proof they decided to take out a little Jupiter Justice of their own? Maybe they wanted to take revenge themselves. That view's fairly prevalent out here. Martel seems to fit that mold, but I don't know. It doesn't make a lot of sense to me. They had to know that two deaths so close together time-wise would be linked and bring up questions. Why risk raising suspicions?"

When the alarm ceased blaring, Raheem said, "I suggest using the station to locate Martel."

Rico nodded, and they left Martel's ship. Pedro was nowhere to be seen. They went out into the corridor, found the 90 hangar bay office and charged in. "Excuse us," Rico said to the controller on duty, who practically fell over as he stood up in surprise. Rico touched a smartwall panel and it luminesced. "Rico to Holt," he said.

"I'm a little busy with a runaway station, at the moment, Schroeder. What is it?" The man gave the impression that he had just eaten a mouse.

"Don't worry about the Centurion. She won't go anywhere else unexpected. Pull up Ted Martel's location for me, would you?" Rico could not resist a slight grin.

"How do you … never mind. One sec." The "on hold" screen automatically switched to a live shot of one of Jupiter's "Red IV," the cyclone that formed a few decades ago. The datascreen informed Rico that the wind speed was 588 km/h. The view of the great oval practically hypnotized him with all its churning energy.

Holt was back before a minute had passed. "Apparently, he just left Distribution at sector 315, irate that he could not get his antimatter. Do you want security to pick him up? He should be passing right by here.

Rico hesitated a moment and then shook his head. "No. We've got it. We don't have anything solid on the guy. At this point we just want to talk to him."

"If you head toward Station Control, you should intercept him around sector forty-five, unless he's figured out you're after him and ducks into side corridors." A map appeared on the wall beside them, and arrows lit up on the wall. "I'd say he's going to his quarters or the hangar bay."

"If he heads off somewhere else, keep us posted. Rico out."

They walked along the outermost of three main corridors—what stationers called the outer tread. Rico did not even think about the slight "upward" curve of the floor as they walked along. As you walked along, the floor and walls appeared to go up and disappear into the ceiling. It was simply a natural phenomenon for Rico, one that he didn't think about.

Until, that is, they found Martel. They saw Martel right where Holt predicted. After he came through the 'lock, Rico called out, "Mr. Martel. We'd need to ask you a few more questions."

"Sure, why not?" the man replied, but Rico saw him reach into his pocket a little too quickly, and something did not feel right.

Martel pulled a compact can out of a side pocket, and Rico's nerves thrummed, instantly on alert. Unfortunately, Martel was on the "lift side," and anything he threw at them would roll "downhill," right at Rico and Raheem, making them sitting ducks.

"Down!" Rico yelled. He went to push Raheem, but he had already dived backward. Rico fell to the floor, closed his eyes and covered his ears, praying that Martel wasn't a suicide bomber. The blast rocked Rico's head, and even with his face buried in his arms, the flash of light still blinded him. He felt as if he'd opened a station shade into unfiltered sunlight. He could not see or hear, but he knew a flash grenade when it concussed him. He'd experienced enough of them in training and in the field.

What might come next made him lurch to his feet. He stumbled, the ringing in his ears and his distressed inner ear canal throwing off his balance. He bounced off a wall with his shoulder, groped for Raheem, grabbed his suit, and hauled him anti-spinward with brute force. They made it maybe two meters when the second wave hit. Officially called a CZX49, the combination flash grenade and tear gas had nicknames such as Bangers & Mash, Doppel-banger, and the One-Two, short for one-two punch. The first part was the brilliant flash and boom that disrupted eyesight, hearing and balance. The second part, designed to go off seconds later, churned out a cloud of tear gas.

Even though he'd known the gas was coming, shut his eyes and held his breath, Rico's already abused eyes watered uncontrollably. His sinuses burned, and his nose ran like he'd caught the plague. He gagged, but didn't puke, thank God. He hated puking. Designed specifically for fighting and crowd control in space, the second combustion also had fire suppressants in the chemical compound, and the propellant lasted only a few seconds, long enough to incapacitate those nearby, but not long enough to overtax a habitat's filtration systems. Lucky them.

Rico found the doors to the "inner tube" and hit the panel. The two doors slid open and he pulled Raheem—gagging, coughing and spitting—inside. A cloud of vapor followed them in, and an office worker took in a lungful. As tears filled the clerical worker's eyes, he started coughing, retched, and then vomited all over the nice carpet of someone's reception area.

- SIX -

Ten minutes later, Raheem sat on a couch with a cold rag on his eyes, his head resting against the off-white silkren walls. Rico blinked at the wall panel in front of him, tears still running down his own face.

"Yeah, we're fine," he typed, in response to Holt's question. "Med-bots have fixed the nausea and headache. Mostly anyway." He tried to ignore the pulsing in his head, and his stinging sinuses. "Just can't hear yet. Ears ringing like an elementary school orchestra tuning up. The nans are working on equalizing the inner-ear fluids. Anything on Martel?"

Rico could see the chagrin on Holt's face as the man spoke, and the computer transcribed his words. "Nothing yet. I already have guards at his cabin, but I've got one officer down, and his LLAM is missing. Martel's also not showing up as on station."

Rico nodded. "What about the ship?"

The security officer frowned. "The grenade must have blasted some conduits or something. The door locks in that sector have all malfunctioned. I've got at least 200 people trapped."

"Keep me in the loop," Rico said. and clicked off. Gratefully, he took a cup of water from the med bot. Several concerned office workers hovered nearby. He ignored them and sat down with a thump next to Raheem. The man groaned at being jostled, and gave Rico a sideways glance with bloodshot eyes.

Rico gestured with his head toward the inner door, and immediately regretted it. "Come on," he said, even though he knew Raheem could not hear him. With effort, he stood and pulled the other man up. Raheem spread his hands with a questioning expression.

Rico made a face, unsure how to communicate, and then had an idea. He spoke into his wrist-comm, and gestured at Raheem's. The text message from Rico to Raheem read, "Going to Martel's room for clues." Raheem nodded. "Computer, show us the way to Ted Martel's room."

Rico waited, and when no arrows appeared on the wall and nothing appeared on the screen, he shook his scrambled head and winced. I'm an idiot, he thought. "Computer, text mode. Repeat."

A smart panel lit up on the wall with text on it: "Emergency lockdown in place. Hull breach, sectors 43 through 64. Proceed to inner core."

Rico and Raheem exchanged glances, and the latter raised an eyebrow and tapped his close-cropped beard, shaking his head. Raheem opened a text window of his own. "Hull breach? No."

"Agreed. We would have felt something." Rico reopened the text window to Holt, explained their suspicions, and asked if Holt could authorize him to manually override the 'locks. He watched the screen and tapped the wall while he waited.

Holt gave them the go-ahead but added, "There are twelve airlocks just in that 150-meter stretch." Rico swore and Raheem shrugged. What choice did they have? The two men took off at a run toward Martel's hangar. As they ran, Rico's ears began to clear. Holt, thankfully, had killed the alarms, but the smartwalls rippled with red as the warning lights cascaded by them.

They reached the first airlock, and Rico opened the emergency panel door. A laser scanned his hand as he grasped the handle and turned it half way before it clicked and stopped. He heard the muffled voice of the station computer: "Warning! Hull breach beyond this point. Authorized personnel only." Rico wet his dry lips and peered through the plas window of the 'lock, just to be sure. He'd seen the bodies of people who'd died in vacuum, and he had no desire to meet his end that way. He could see another airlock far ahead with the doors in place. A good sign, but no guarantee.

Rico made eye contact with Raheem, and the other man gave him a thumbs-up. Rico saw him speaking in an exaggerated manner and lip read, "Go for it."

A red light flashed three times inside the panel, followed by a yellow light, and then finally a green one. The handle released and Rico turned it the rest of the way. The sliding doors popped open enough for them to get their hands in between, tug them further apart, and squeeze through.

They were at their third airlock when Holt's face popped up on the smartwall next to them.

"Schroeder. Can you hear yet?" he practically snarled.

"Enough. Why?" Rico caught the irritated tone in Holt's voice. Something had gone wrong.

"Martel bypassed our system somehow, and overrode the hangar-bay protocols. His shuttle, *The Scimitar*, just launched. He's not responding to hails."

"Space me," Rico said. He took a deep breath and stared at the ceiling.

They heard a male voice from somewhere out of visual. "Scans are iffy because of shielding, sir, but I'm reading only one person on board. Full thrusters or close to."

"Weapons, bring cannons online!" Holt said. The laser cannons were primarily intended for asteroid defense, but between terrorists and the rare pirate every station carried some type of munitions. "Sensors, probable trajectory?" Holt asked.

"Canons ready," a female voice said.

"Apparent slingshot around Callisto or perh–" the male voice stopped suddenly.

"Sensors, confirm explosion!" Holt snapped.

"Affirmative, sir. That flash was the shuttle."

"Weapons, did you fire canons?" Holt asked, more puzzled than angry.

"Negative, sir," the woman replied.

"We have debris," the male came back.

Rico leaned in toward his display as if he could peer around the corner to the other screens. "Holt, don't leave us floating out here."

Eyebrows arched, Holt, said, "It would appear that Martel has committed suicide."

Raheem shook his head. "That seems improbable."

"I agree," said Rico. "I recommend Sensors analyze the debris mass."

Holt nodded to someone off screen and, after a lengthy pause, the man's voice said, "Minimal debris. Less than 20 percent of an IZ class, sir."

Raheem rubbed the back of his head. "Well, this is as inconceivable as Martel committing suicide, but I think we found your stealthed ship."

"Wait a minute. What stealthed ship?" Holt demanded.

Rico quickly filled him in on what they'd found out about the destruction of the *Domínguez* and Tiago's death. He finished by saying "I think that *The Scimitar* is still out there and hiding in plain sight."

"Sensors, figure out a way to find that ship," Holt ordered.

"I can't right away, sir," the man covering sensors said. "There's too much interference from the explosion. It'll take awhile to sort out the background noise and render a trajectory, and even then…"

"I know, I know," Holt interrupted, growling. "We can assume that will not be his final trajectory. Right."

Rico cut in. "Holt, I may be able to help, but I need to see where the AI is with my routine. I'll get back to you, STAT." Since the whole area was on lockdown, Rico simply opened a smartwall right where they were. Raheem gave him a quizzical glance, but asked no questions.

"Candra, do you have results for the last work request from Federico Schroeder?"

"Affirmative. The heat signature from the unidentified stealth craft corresponds to a crescendo ship, a short-range shuttle of European design with a .677 probability."

"The Europeans again. Interesting," Raheem said. "However, the results are definitely not conclusive."

Rico agreed. On a hunch, he asked the station's computer to run another analysis. The results revealed that, although the *pattern* of the thrusters matched, some of the heat signatures were weaker than the others. Rico had Candra recalculate without the weak heat signals. With the fake thruster signals removed, the result came back as a probable match to a Qátala-class ship, probability .938.

Rico gave a low whistle. The fact that the ship was Qátala class stood out to both of them. Raheem normally olive complexion turned pallid and his expression grim. In Arabic, Qátala meant "to kill" or "assassin."

The ships were made by Etihad Station. Etihad, roughly pronounced eti-hy-ad, meant "Union" in Arabic, and was the Middle Eastern Union's orbital manufacturing facility around Earth. Etihad had widely been considered a front for, or at least a supporter of, Adala. Drug manufacturers, dealers, and smugglers preferred Etihad ships and habitats for their low cost, high speed, and lack of questions. Adala had used Etihad ships when it destroyed the Salaam habitat colonies. Etihad had condemned the attack and disavowed any connection to the terrorist group at that time. They claimed that Adala stole the ships. While they acknowledged that the thefts might have been an inside job, they held no liability for the actions of Adala.

Perhaps the lady had protested too much.

"Adala again," Raheem said, his face stony.

Rico made an affirmative noise. "And it seems they may have been trying to point a finger at the Euros."

"Those guys give Arabians and Muslims a bad name." His face had gone from stony to downright stormy. It was the most emotion Rico had seen on the guy's face since they'd met earlier that morning. It had already been a long day.

Rico sent a priority update to Holt, and a smartwall up near them with a crystalline alert chime. Reuben's face appeared. "Thanks for the data, Rico, Raheem. That will help us search, but if this is government-level tech, I doubt we'll find him. I've heard you can piss on someone in this camo and not know until they protest."

"Colorful analogy," Raheem said mildly.

Holt glanced at Raheem, opened his mouth to say something, and closed it again, biting his lip to keep from smiling. At least he was not the only one who sometimes had a hard time getting a read on Raheem. Holt finally settled on, "So what's your next step, Captain?"

"We're going to see what we can find in Martel's room. We'll keep you posted. Rico and Raheem out."

#

They found two guards on duty, each carrying LLAMs. As expected, there was little in the cabin, but they did find a computer pad on the desk, password protected, of course. They also found clothes and toiletries, including a hairbrush. Raheem called up a delivery bot and, when it arrived, placed a hair sample in the robot's holding compartment and sent it off to the med lab for DNA analysis.

In the toiletry bag, they noticed a small hose, less than a finger-width in diameter, and a blunt needle. Neither one of them had a guess as to their purpose. They scoured the room, but discovered nothing else of interest. As they were getting ready to leave, Rico scanned the room once more. The spinward wall had some sort of access panel, about the size of a small backpack, and the gray color stood out in contrast to the off-white walls. He examined the edges. He tugged on it, but the panel held. Raheem smiled, amused.

"What?" Rico said. "Any better ideas?"

"Well, yes, actually." Raheem laid down on the floor and squinted up at the bottom. "That's odd. There's a tiny circle down here." He stood up. "I think Officer Holt would prefer you not break any other space stations today, especially his." Still grinning, he said, "Computer, relay to Weapons Mechanics, please."

"Wep-Mech, Kristy Harris." She pronounced it, "Wep-Mac." "What can I do for you gents?"

Raheem used his wrist-comm to show the woman the box on the wall.

"Nope. Not one of ours. I'll send over some can-do's right away. Might be more of those spy-bots we're scanning for." Her laser gaze snapped from Rico to Raheem and back again. "Have you touched it?"

Rico turned sheepish and mumbled.

She shook her head. "You're ASC, right? And the fugitive already used a One-Two, right? You should know better, Sir."

"Yes, ma'am, you're right. Been a while since active duty."

She gave him her best put-upon face, and disconnected without saying goodbye.

"Is my ass still there, Raheem? Because I think she just chewed it off. Not that I didn't deserve it, but ouch."

The Wep-Mech team showed up within fifteen minutes, three men and two women. They scanned the box and Martel's other gear, and declared all of it free of explosives, poisons, corrosives, and biological agents.

A squat woman with Asian features set in a round face framed by blue-black hair greeted them. "Sorry it took us a bit. The hatches are all on lockdown. We're going section by section and getting the people out, so we're all scrambling." She asked them if they wanted the team to try cutting off the box. They had no idea how it was attached, but a LaserX could cut through anything.

As they were discussing options, the other woman, a young tech with close-cropped, red hair, said, "Sirs, this toothbrush has a pump hidden in it." She opened the handle and showed them the miniature pump. She reassembled it, took off the toothbrush head, and pushed the button. The pump kicked on with an audible hiss.

"Interesting," Raheem said. "Hand me that needle from Martel's kit."

They all watched as the man crawled under the fake access box. He raised the needle and, although Rico could not see what he was doing, he heard a quick intake of air and a soft pop. The panel came off the wall, and Raheem caught it as it came loose. "Vacuum sealed to the wall. I realized it once you found the pump. I pushed the needle in the hole underneath and it popped right off. Nice work, tech," he said to the young redhead. She nodded, trying to maintain a professional demeanor, but the corners of her mouth edged up into a smile.

Taped inside the panel, they found a highly illegal, old-fashioned pistol--—the kind that fired gunpowder gunpowder-based bullets. Pistols were illegal on most stations except as collector's pieces due to the risk of depressurization. Unlikely since the stations and ships could withstand minor impacts from space debris, but guns were still rare up in in space.

The Wep-Mech team excused themselves and left to help with the search for the bugs.

The pictures showed Ted Martel's face, but the name on one ID read, "Tobias Munson," with an address in London, England. A second ID listed him as, "Tariq Al-Mardini," with an address in Janus Dome, Smith City, Mars."

"This guy, Martel, 'TM,' really gets around," Rico said. It surprised Rico that the guy used the same initials each time, and he said as much.

"Probably everyone craves some small bit of continuity, some sense of identity," Rhaeem said. "I would expect that is even more the case when you change identities often." He pulled a ceramic-appearing tube with a matching cap out of the kit. "Check this out."

Rico scrutinized it, and shook his head. "What is it?"

"A special container for smuggling nan-bots." Rico raised his eyebrows, and Raheem gave him a thin smile. "I saw one at a conference once. In L.A., actually. Quite remarkable. Simple, yet effective. The composite is very similar to the human tooth."

He let that last remark go by without commenting.

"There's no chance those things are going to become active is there?" Rico asked.

"No, they should be dormant in this container."

The wall screen blipped for Raheem, and a tech came on to tell them the DNA belonged to Tobias Munson, assigned to Centurion Team.

"Munson? What about Martel?"

The tech double-checked his screen. "No, it definitely says Munson. One second." He typed some more. "No genetic ID for Martel. Looks as if it never made it into the system, or it was deleted."

"Convenient. Does the name Tariq Al-Mardini show up in your system?" Rico asked.

"One sec … Yes, it's red-flagged as an alias for Talib Mokri, a terrorist with Adala. Mokri killed 43 people on Mars."

Rico said, "Well, we can add aliases of Ted Martel and Tobias Munson to that list of known aliases."

Rico went through the pieces that were starting to fall into place. They had thought Sistema Solar planted the spy nan-bots on Axion Station and maybe the others, but Centurion Station's thrusters had fired instead. "TM," whoever he really was, had ties with South America, French Guiana, Europe, Mars, Adala, and potentially Etihad.

What kind of game was he playing? If his motive was purely money, why pose as Ted Martel on the Sistema Solar Team? More nan-bots could have stolen data from Solar, just as with the other stations. Why do it in person? Why risk the exposure? One more question on top of a mountain of others.

- SEVEN -

Raheem got off the comm and said, "This fellow, Martel, or whomever, seems as if he's playing several games at once," echoing Rico's own thoughts. "If he's connected to Adala, and he's got assassination bots, the implications are devastating."

Now that was an unpleasant thought. Adala with nan-bot assassins. Son of a space monkey.

Rico said, "Computer, engage OptiComm, Rico Schroeder to Sistema Solar, Commander Inés Villaverde, Private Comm." Rico sat at the small desk, and Raheem sat on the bed. Rico opened a second wall screen and sent it across the wall to Raheem, so that he could see better, but with the latter video feed muted.

While they waited for Inés to find a private spot to take the call, Raheem asked, "Are you going to fill me in, or do I have to wait in suspense?"

"Someone I dated." Rico said, a grim expression on his face.

"I take it the relationship did not end well?" Raheem asked, his own features nonchalant.

"You might say that."

After a few minutes of tense silence, a woman with dark brown hair and chocolate eyes peered at them through the wall screen. "Rico? Well, look what washed up on the beach. Captain Federico Schroeder. *Qué pasa*?" Not outright cold, but not warm either.

"Hey, Inés. How are you?"

The woman gave a heavy sigh. "Life is grand,

Chico." Her old nickname for him. So, maybe not so bad. "What do you want? I'm on duty."

"What can you tell me about Ted Martel?" Rico asked, getting to the point.

"I figured this was no social call. Too bad." She pointed at the screen. "You still owe me a nice dinner, Chico. Don't think I've forgotten about that."

Uh oh. He had forgotten about that, given how things had ended between them. He figured she'd never want to lay eyes on him again after he'd shot her cousin and locked him up.

"Martel's an ass. Arrogant, bossy. A bully. Why?"

Rico ignored the question. "Inés, I've got a delicate question…"

Inés snorted. "Baby, you and me, we are waaaay past delicate. Ask."

Rico felt his face heat up; Raheem was probably biting his tongue to keep from laughing.

"I know this is not your style, but could Martel be feeding someone on your team stolen info?"

"What are you talking about, Rico? What kind of info?"

"Engine designs. Antimatter protocols. You name it. Anything."

The Latina opened her mouth. Closed it. Then she sat back from the screen, her expression unreadable. "Santa Mãe. This is bad."

Rico gave a slight nod. "So it's possible, then. Would he have access to a stealth ship?"

Inés started to laugh at the absurd question, but immediately stopped herself. "Not that I know of, but he got thrust on us from another company named Vargas that partnered up with Sistema—brought their own station modules, with hangar bays and ships. Caused a big ripple, you know?" She turned her head to the side, thinking, and Rico admired the profile of her face. "It was a big boost." She turned back to the camera. "They brought in a ton of money and a lot of technical expertise."

Rico heard Raheem's subtle intake of breath and saw a message pop up on his own screen a second later. He was reminding him that Vargas also supplied the nan-bots that killed Malik.

"Federico Lorenzo Schroeder, you better tell me what the hell is going on, or so help me, I will come over there and kick your ass."

Rico gave her a genuine smile. "Two more. Does he seem to know a lot about nan-bots?"

"Nan-bots? What?"

"You know, those tiny little robots?"

"Very funny, Chico. I don't know. He could, yes. He does some of the programming here. The languages are different. What–"

Rico held up a hand to stop her. "Does he ever go over to Centurion Station?"

"All the time. He's got a woman over there. Her name is … What was that? Something … Arla? Klara? Laura? No, Lara, that's it. I don't recall her last name."

Lara, something? Rico joined a couple of dots. Probably the same one who bought the nan-bots. So, old Teddy has an accomplice. He searched his memory.

"Lara Kohler?"

"Yes"

"Excellent. Listen, Innie," he said, using his old

nickname for her and leaning in close. "I need a favor."

She shook her head and her mouth quirked up, in a half-smile. "What, another one? I don' know why I help you other than that irresistible charm of yours. You are so much trouble, Chico, and you still have not told me anything yet."

"I know. I am, aren't I?" He gave her his most winning smile. "See what you can find in the ship's communications between Martel and anyone on the research team, but be careful. Martel's already used a Doppel-banger on Prime, and he had a pistol here. A gunpowder pistol, not an s-g."

Inés' eyes widened. "But that's crazy! Why wouldn't he just use a smart-gun?"

"Good question."

She said she'd get back to him as soon as she could, and the screen went blank.

He had a hunch that TM had left a bunch of evidence framing Sistema Solar for corporate espionage. From the way the Sistema folk were acting, some of it might even be true. Rico resisted the temptation to pace. Instead, he called Holt.

Following another intuition, Rico asked about the video feeds, and Holt confirmed that all the stations supplied vids of the *Domínguez's* destruction except for Centurion and Sistema. Why wouldn't Sistema Solar turn over video evidence that would help catch the saboteur and Tiago's killer? They should have been the first ones on the line. They were up to something, but if not the nano-spy game, then what?

Rico filled Holt in on what they'd found in Martel's room.

"I'll put out an Arrest on Sight on Martel, but it's hard to say where he's headed."

"We've got an idea on that regard. He's got a girlfriend named Lara. Over on Centurion Station. Last name Kohler."

"One sec … Lara Kohler." He typed a few keys. "Specialist in geothermal research. I'll send out a patrol for her. I can only do a Detain for Questioning on her, not an AoS, you understand?"

Rico gave a nod. Not enough evidence in her case. Not yet, anyway. Rico asked Holt to have some of his team run a decrypt on the two pads they'd found. Holt said he'd take care of it, and they signed off.

"C'mon, let's get the hell out of this room. I need some more coffee."

Raheem grimaced and followed him into the corridor. "Only if we hit the cafeteria," he said. "I could use some more food."

Rico suspected that was merely an excuse to avoid his own fine brew, but he let it slide and checked his wrist-comm: 6:03 PM.

An "Incoming Message" framed in red for "urgent" popped up on the table top while Rico was talking about the finer points and strategies of moving in zero-g, while playing Bashi Ball, his favorite sport. He stopped and tapped the new message icon, and Holt's face appeared. "Rico, I sent the DFQ over to Centurion, and Lara Kohler took off without clearance. She must have been tipped off somehow."

"Lifesigns?"

"Confirmed."

"Are they pursuing?"

"Three Splitters. On screen."

Holt sent them another frame, and they saw the pursuit from the perspective of one of the ships. The lead ship told Kohler to cut her thrusters, but she sped on. Laser fire cut the dark, thin and brief, for all its deadly power. A warning shot. Still no response. The research vessel must be up to maximum speed by now. Rico could imagine the ship's safety alarms blaring, and it vibrating so hard your teeth rattled in your head. She was headed toward the moon Callisto, probably hoping to use it as a shield or to use the gravity well as a slingshot for more speed. Another order to cut thrusters or they would fire on her engines. Rico held his breath.

Laser fire hit the engines. A small chunk of the ship erupted outward as a laser tore into the engine compartment. Two seconds later a much larger explosion ripped out of the sidewall as oxygen and fuel vented into space. Throughout Prime, every smartwall in the area went live, with a strobing red border. When a ship put out a distress call, it preempted all channels, unless an imminent impact with the station itself took priority. A woman's voice said, "Mayday, May … This is …. a Kohler. Expl ……. no con …. Mayd … Mayday."

Computer sensors pulled video feeds and automatically transmitted them to assist with search and rescue. They watched as the ship plummeted toward the planet. She clearly had no controls whatsoever. The vessel went in hard, a missile plummeting right toward Lake Pele, a vast pool of molten lava. Planet hoppers were designed to withstand reentry temperatures hotter than the volcano by a good 400 degrees Celsius, but not a direct, unimpeded impact with the surface of a moon. The shuttle struck the lake and exploded, sending a plume of lava back up into space. Droplets of molten lava broke free of the moon's weak gravity and drifted outward into space to join with Jupiter's rings.

Silence descended on the station control room. Holt's face turned ashen.

- EIGHT -

Hushed murmurs came from the various occupied tables of the cafeteria as the station occupants tried to come to terms with three deaths in less than a week. Rico and Raheem finished their meals in silence, mulling over what they knew, and each reflecting on their own lives and losses.

Raheem broke the silence first. "Do you think the shots caused Kohler's ship to explode?"

Rico shook his head. "No, Martel was probably cleaning up loose ends. That's probably why we only saw one life sign on his ship before he faked the explosion. My guess is that Pedro was stuffed in a closet somewhere."

"Well, that's a pleasant thought." Raheem put his fork down.

"Sorry," Rico said. He sat back and ran both his hands through his dark hair.

"No, no need to apologize. I–"

"OptiComm signal for Federico Schroeder from Inés Villaverde, Private Comm." The computer directed them to an unused privacy booth at the edge of the cafeteria. Once they got settled, Rico hit the accept icon.

"*Hola*, Inés. This is my partner, Dr. Raheem Kuzbari."

"*Hola*, Rico. Dr. Kuzbari." She didn't smile and she practically glowered as she dragged a short, slightly overweight man into the screen area. He had the puffy face of someone who spends too much time sitting in front of a computer and eating instead of hitting the gym. Clearly he had been rousted out of his bed. Inés introduced the guy as Harley Bosch and then said, "Tell him what you told me and the captain. All of it." She shook him by the shirt, and the man winced.

"M-martel was giving me information. About the antimatter designs and tests." The man's eyes darted around and licked his lips. "He told me that Vargas made a deal with Sistema Solar, because the company heard how far along we were. Martel joined Sistema Solar through them."

"How did he give you the information?" Rico asked.

"Right in my mail."

"Do you know anything about Taigo's or Malik's murders?" Rico asked.

He could see Inés' nostrils flare a little at the question.

The little fellow squirmed, giving the impression of a turtle trying to pull his head back into his shell. "Martel said he'd 'take care of those bastards' for Tiago's death. He didn't say how," he said. "I ... I didn't have anything to do with that!"

The chipmunk-faced fellow kept talking. Martel had conveniently left Sistema Solar's station on his own shuttle to watch the test flight over on Centurion with Lara. Yes, Martel was an expert in nan-bots. No, he didn't say anything about using nan-bots to spy on the other teams. When he came onboard he'd asked a lot of questions about defense measures against nan-bots. Sistema Solar had several lines of defense against hard-wired attacks.

Harley started to explain, but Inés cut him off. "Sorry, Captain Schroeder. That's classified," but she'd had a hint of a smile when she said it. "You can rest assured, though, that nan-bot spies wouldn't stand a chance here."

"That explains why Martel was on your station, then. He wasn't giving you information, at least not much. He was stealing it. Because the bots wouldn't work, he came in person."

"Son of a–" Inés cut herself off.

"Did he talk about the Centurion Team?" Raheem asked.

"He talked about Lara, his girlfriend, and how she sent him reports. He said she was one of his sources and," chipmunk swallowed, "he said he was 'pumping her' for information."

"All right. Stay on Sistema Solar Station," Rico said. "I may have more questions for you."

The man nodded several times and wrung his hands together nervously.

Inés gave a command to someone off screen. "Confine him to quarters. No visitors, no comms, no smartwall access." The man whimpered as he walked out of the room, and Rico shook his head.

"Martel and that little weasel may have disqualified us for the race," Inés fumed.

"Maybe," Rico said, not sugar coating the truth.

"I've got something else, too. We searched Martel's quarters and found this." She held up a smart pad. "Harley knew his password somehow. Not sure why Martel left it here on station, but he did. We haven't had time to dive into it yet."

Rico and Raheem exchanged a glance. Another

pad? That was odd. Or perhaps not, with this guy.

"We also found something resembling a cigar holder, but we haven't been able to open it. It's got some sort of electronic seal on it." Rico felt the blood rush out of his face and into his rapidly beating chest. The tube matched the one they found in Martel's room and that Kuzbari said spies and criminals used for transporting nan-bots clandestinely.

Rico and Raheem both shouted out, "Don't open that!"

Inés' eyes widened. "Well, okay then," and she set the vial down with exaggerated care.

"Seal that in a container, STAT. Have your AI check the pad for malicious sleeper programs. If it's clean, shoot me a message. I'll check it over remotely when I can. And, if Martel shows up, comm Holt, priority 1. Thanks, Inés. "

"Wait a minute, Rico. What about this tube?"

"Sorry, Innie, I've got a priority comm coming in from the Station Commander. Have to fly."

She glared at him as he cut the connection.

"You're going to pay for that, you know."

"Don't I know it. It won't be the first time either."

He had spoken tongue in cheek, but the quip made him remember, with a mild pang of guilt, the last time he'd been in a hurry—and cut Inés out of the loop. Taz had almost been killed. That had been back in French Guiana, of course, and now he was dead. With a mental start, he realized that Inés had been friends with Taz even longer than he had. He wondered how she was handling his death. His face grew hot at the realization that he'd been too caught up in his mission to think about her feelings when he'd first contacted her.

That had been the main reason that Inés and he had crashed and burned the first time around. Ever since Jackie's murder, and the betrayal that had been a knife in his own heart, when Rico was working a case, it consumed him. Sleep eluded him. He couldn't focus on anything else. He had to find out the truth. He had to bring closure to the family—and justice to the victim. Until a killer was caught, the case became his obsession. It was just how he was. Inés had many redeeming qualities, but patience with his lopsided approach to his job had not been one of them.

Rico clicked the red-bordered icon and Holt's bony face appeared. "We think we found the Qátala. The ship is headed toward Jupiter, maybe Ganymede. He fired up thrusters while his lover was crashing into Callisto."

"Perhaps hoping for us to be distracted," Raheem said, commenting on Martel's timing. Rico had the same thought. So much for true love. This guy was cold.

"Have you got any Splitters near us?"

"Yes, three bays retro from your shuttle, Rico, but I've got pilots that can–"

"No way, Holt. You gave me this job. I'm going to finish it. Save one of the Splitters for us. Warm up the engines. We're on our way!" They took off at a full run.

- NINE -

They reached the hangar bay in less than five minutes. The crew had the Splitter hot and cleared the bay for takeoff. A man—practically a kid—with white-blond hair and a jumpsuit said, "Commander Holt said to tell you there's two LLAMs in the cockpit storage. You know how to use them?" Rico nodded. The dark-haired man who would be riding shotgun nodded with the hint of a smile of his lips. "Okay then," the younger lad said. "Good luck."

As soon as they strapped in, the alarm and clarion went off, warning the unwary of imminent depressurization. The air whisked out of the bay, recycled back into the station, and the doors opened. Rico set a course and eased them clear of the bay area.

Raheem watched Ganymede on one of the viewer screens. Rico didn't head that way, though. Instead, he used the small thrusters to set them up for a journey toward the asteroid belt. Raheem inclined his head but didn't say anything. They both knew Rico was taking a big gamble. If Martel went another direction, they'd lose him. But the asteroid belt was the most popular place to sell stolen goods—and information—off-planet, especially since more teams were trying to develop antimatter drives there as well. It was also the best place to refuel on the way back to earth, if the belt was not his final destination. Plus, if Martel was working with Adala, and if they had a base of operations in space, then the tens of thousands of asteroids between Jupiter and the earth provided plenty of places to hide.

Rico said a prayer that he was right, and punched the thrusters.

He put the ship on AI, and then pulled out the LLAMs and the other equipment. He had Raheem show him his knowledge of the smart-gun just to be sure he knew what he was doing. The man passed with flying colors.

After that, there was nothing to do but wait and watch. Raheem and Rico scanned the viewers, but these stealth ships actually bent light waves, so even if one were right in front of you, you might not see it. Only computer analysis could semi-reliably find a stealthed ship. A stationary object was virtually impossible to find, but Rico felt pretty sure Martel would be on the move. The Qátala ship had a big lead on them but, if Rico was right, and he was heading for the asteroid belt, then he'd be slipping into Ganymede's gravity well to get a little speed boost.

"Captain Schroeder, we lost him below Ganymede. Repeat, we've lost telemetry on Qátala ship below Ganymede, declination -.23 degrees. Minus two-three."

"Computer, reply: Roger. Last known location negative point two three. Schroeder out."

Ni pa. Rico felt the tension between his shoulder blades climbing into his neck. To Raheem he said, "Martel's riding low if he's trying to accelerate by drafting on Ganymede's speed around the sun. Either he's an inexperienced pilot, which I doubt, or he's up to something."

"Could he be trying to hide from station sensors?"

Raheem asked. "After all, they did lose him."

"Maybe," Rico said, but he wasn't convinced. Something wasn't right. Martel already had a jump on them; if Rico had guessed wrong, they'd already lost valuable time or, even worse, lost him altogether. At this point, ten or fifteen minutes wouldn't make much of a difference. Rico held his course.

They waited in tense silence as the Splitter headed into the void between Jupiter system and the Asteroid Belt, with no sign of Martel before or behind them. The worst part about chasing another ship in space, or space battles in general, was the distances involved. Or, more precisely, the waiting. It would take Martel at least two hours to slingshot around Ganymede, and for Rico and Raheem to hopefully intersect his trajectory. In the past, space military crews often experienced Prolonged Engagement Reaction Syndrome brought on by spikes of adrenalin, followed by long periods of waiting. Fortunately, drugs and nan-bots could handle most of the symptoms these days. Rico's body thrummed with tension.

Twenty minutes later, a voice-only came over the OptiComm. "Captain Schroeder, this is Lt. Avery on Communications at Prime Station. You have a Priority-One-Urgent message coming from Mister Wu, Chou Refinery. Stand by."

Rico's smooth face, lit only by instrument panel lights, frowned at the words. Wu Feng appeared on the screen. His friend's face had the same pronounced cheekbones that Rico remembered, as if they had been carved from stone. Tiny brown mouse-eyes peered timidly out from beneath disproportionately large, heavy eyelids and almost nonexistent eyebrows. "*Ni Hao*, Rico. Eh." The strong chin went up in greeting.

"*Ni Hao*, Feng," Rico said in greeting. "Raheem, this is Wu Feng," he said, providing Feng's surname first, as custom still dictated. He gestured to his side, "This is Raheem."

Wu nodded at Raheem, smiled broadly, and then, in his heavily accented English, he said, "You call me Feng. Rumor on OptiComm say you looking for killer of Muslim scientist." Feng cast his head to either side, alert for any eavesdroppers. "He on way here. Come in planetside. Contro' cleared. Hallway cleared. Workers all held over. In factory or quarters only. All lock down."

"Son of a Martian," Rico muttered. He hit the thrusters to bring the ship around. He'd been wrong, but at least Martel was still in system. He'd taken them an hour the wrong way. He checked the time. 8:25 PM. He resisted the urge to hit the console.

"My cousin find out. Other cousin get me on the OptiComm." Wu sat up quickly. "Someone coming. Got to go. You come in Bay 33. I meet you there." The feed went dark.

For a full minute, Rico and Raheem rode in silence. Officially, Chou InterGalactic was not in the race for the AMMATT Prize, but that didn't mean they wouldn't grab the purse if they could get away with it. Certain management people on Chou Station were not above making an extra few credits if someone, say someone on the run, slipped some creds their way. Although criticized by some of the more modern Chinese, bribery remained a prevalent and time-honored tradition. Plus, Chou stood to lose a lot if antimatter engines became a reality, so his ex-employer could be involved. Rico couldn't rule it out; that was for sure.

Rico filled Raheem in on his connection with Feng Wu. When Rico worked for Chou Intergalactic, Feng worked the gas lines, filling up freighters on their way back to the asteroid belt, Earth, Mars and various space habitats, with Helium 3 fuel. The company frequently ignored recommended safety protocols and, a few years back, a freighter came in too fast. The ship slammed through the back wall of the hangar and trapped Wu and three other workers, while a fire spread around them. Worse, H3 would blow if it hit -267 Celsius, and the regulating pipes were not designed to handle fires. With flames heating his back and the valves burning his hands, despite the space gloves he'd grabbed, Rico diverted the H3 while others put out the fire. It had been a close call. He'd been in the infirmary a week while they peeled away burned flesh, did medicated wraps, and finally skin regrowth. Wu clearly felt as if he owed him, and maybe he did, but Rico'd never felt that way. He'd just done what needed doing.

They deliberated on filling in Holt, to alert the other two Splitters, but they didn't want to tip off Martel. Rico decided to take another gamble. Hopefully this one would pay off better than the last.

As they approached, Rico shook his head, not for the first time, in bemused amazement at the haphazard appearance of the refinery. Chou Station did not have the standard torus-shape prevalent among space habitations. Rather, it gave the impression of a donut that had rolled off to a corner and had subsequently sprouted odd spores, which now stuck out in every direction. The station had several hangar bays, many of them placed erratically around the structure. Rico figured the station was designed that way to allow Chou a feasible out for denying the smuggling activities that were a poorly kept secret. Wu met them at a recessed hangar bay at the end of a narrow alley with no viewing ports and, presumably, no cams either.

As soon as the bay repressurized, Wu stepped through the airlock.

Rico said, "Thanks, Feng. *Xie xie, xie xie.*"

The Chinese man, wire-thin—a stack of wooden blocks loosely wired together—lifted his chin as he'd done earlier, his characteristic assent. "*Bu Ke Qi*, Rico. You welcome. The man you want. He lay low. Stay on ship. Come."

Rico and Raheem followed him, carrying two LLAMs, and not very low key at all, but Feng did not react to the weapons. He led them to the service tunnels. Gravity on Chou was only about half that of Earth's. At this level of g, moving quickly meant they had to run-leap in a gazelle-like motion, without hitting the ceiling or slamming into a wall on the turn. Rico thought hurrying might be a problem for Raheem, but he moved with a martial artist's precision. Raheem lifted off with one stride as they came to a corner and pushed off the wall with the next step, not even slowing. Rico smiled, surprised, as he followed behind the other two men. He wondered if Raheem practiced *kyoku-atsu*, and where he would have learned it.

They arrived outside the hangar bay, and Wu tapped a code into a computer panel—no smartwalls here—and a view of the ship came on screen. Rico had seen this technology before. The ship material bent light waves, hid heat signatures, and dissipated shadows. If they had not known for a certainty the Qátala sat in this particular bay, Rico would've sworn the hangar lay empty.

"Son of a space monkey," he said.

"No doubt it is equipped with ship-to-ship lasers, as well as canons," Raheem said.

"Yup. Those, plus inversion bombs, and probably all kinds of other nastiness," Rico said. "A direct assault would be suicide."

"Are there any breaching weapons near here?" Raheem asked.

"No," Wu said.

"Is he taking on any supplies? Food, water, fuel?"

A shake of the head. No dice.

"Are there any H3 lines near this hangar?"

Wu nodded, his eyes round with alarm at what Raheem might be proposing.

"Um," Raheem started to say, hesitating at Wu's facial expression, "can we blow the line?"

Rico grinned at the two of them. "Not without taking out half the station. Don't worry, Feng. We won't take the place out. Not without a good reason." Wu started to smile and to nod, and then did a double take and stared at Rico.

As they stood in the "back" service corridor trying to figure out what to do, the main corridor 'lock opened and Martel walked into the hangar bay, grinning and talking with Yi Lin, plant manager of

Chou's Jupiter refinery. Rico realized that because he and Raheem were all the way on the far side of the hangar, they'd only have one shot at Martel before he retreated back into the station or onto his ship.

"Feng, I thought you said he was on the ship!" Wu started to say something, but Rico interrupted. "Never mind. Can you jam that door?" Rico whispered urgently, indicating the door Martel and Lin had just come through.

"No," Feng said, shaking his head. He contorted his mouth in odd directions as he thought. "Maybe cousin can."

"Okay, get on it. And stay here! I don't want you getting shot."

"What about me?" Raheem asked. "You don't seem concerned about my getting shot."

Rico grunted. "You signed up for this tour, cowboy. Pony up."

Wu started chattering into his wrist-comm in Chinese. Rico knew Feng could get into a lot of trouble for helping them. The person on the other end did not sound happy. He really hoped Wu could get that door locked down.

"Raheem, you go left," he said. A stack of plas crates partially blocked their entrance to the hangar. Two more stacks lay along the left wall, but with a considerable gap to get there. Kuzbari would be exposed while he ran for them. The stealthed ship lay between them and the main door, and slightly off to the left, which might help provide Raheem some cover. Rico opened the door and ran straight toward the ship, keeping it between him and the large door Martel and Yi had just come through.

He made it to the ship and saw Raheem moving up on the left. Rico resisted the urge to touch the odd material of the stealthed ship, just in case Martel had touch-sensors activated, which he probably did. Rico stepped out from behind the ship and moved toward the two men with long, bounding strides. Luckily for him, the two were watching the corridor more than the supposedly secured bay.

Moving at half-g and then stopping where you want is tricky, but Rico had practice, having grown up playing Bashi Ball on Branson Station, and through more hours of military training exercises than he cared to count. He did a stutter-step braking motion, and Martel whirled his way. Rico tagged him, so the smart-gun bullets would activate only if they hit Martel. If they hit Yi, he might get a slight stinging sensation, but no more, if he was lucky.

"Hold it right there, Martel," Rico said, his LLAM pointed at the man. He hit ShockGel on his ammo selection. The fugitive's smile disappeared. He drew a pistol from his pocket and pointed it at Yi. *A cellular disruptor. Great.*

"You again," he said. "Well done. Before you get any ideas, though, I'm sure you recognize this," he pointed at the pistol. "I had this one specially modified. Once in my hand, unless I deactivate it, it has a dummy switch that will fire the weapon if I lose consciousness." He grinned a self-satisfied grin and then his face went flat again. "Now, if you will excuse me, Mr. Yi and I will be going."

Martel poked Yi in the back with the disruptor, and the unfortunate hostage started moving toward the ship.

Rico pursed his lips, thinking fast but coming up empty. He had no other options. "Fine, okay, Martel. Easy does it. You get on your ship and go, but leave Yi here." He kept the LLAM trained on Martel's chest. He didn't want to give the killer the chance to eliminate him as a threat. He'd rather live through this ordeal, thanks anyway.

Martel started walking toward the ship and chuckled softly. "No, I don't think so. Yi comes with me. I'll release him in an escape pod after I'm safely underway." As he walked toward the ship a ramp descended seemingly from nowhere, revealing a ship's hallway that appeared carved into the air. The stealth material of the ship continued its illusion. *Right*, Rico thought. *If you release him, it will be out a 'lock, and not with any escape pod.*

Yi must have been of the same opinion because, at the foot of the ramp, he balked and began talking rapidly in Chinese, his hands in the air in front of his chest. Martel just glared at him, jaw muscles tight, but otherwise expressionless, and Rico thought for sure that he was going to shoot Chou's plant manager point blank. Instead, he just continued dragging the man backward, pulling on his collar. Rico caught the words "money" and something about a "vacation" and "pleasure habitat."

That was when the manager's personal shield snapped on, obscuring the man in a staticky haze. He stepped backward into Martel, pushing him off balance. With surprising agility, Yi crouched and, after a single step, bounded toward the door like Superman. A fat, Chinese Superman, but still.

Martel's legs went up in the air as he tumbled in

the low g. Martel ignored Chou at first as a non-threat and fired at Rico instead. Even though Martel fired while falling backward, the disruptor beam only missed by centimeters. Behind him, Rico could hear a cargo bin sizzling and bubbling. Burning plas stung his nostrils and eyes. His already irritated eyes and sinuses protested the additional abuse.

Raheem stepped out from behind some cargo bins and fired, but his shot went high and rebounded up the ramp. Raheem had chosen Pounders, a rubber-like ball that expanded outward when it hit, adding to the blunt force, and knocked the target down if not out.

With incredible agility, Martel turned his falling motion into a tuck and flip. He fired off a shot even as he came around. A hole the size of a fist dematerialized in the crate Raheem was hiding behind. The smell of burning metal and plastic increased.

Yi, the plant manager, made it to the doors, but they wouldn't open. Rico quirked half a smile. Well, Wu had gotten the bay locked down, at least.

Martel came to a full standing position and raised his pistol to fire. Rico shot him in the chest with three ShockGels. Martel's body jerked and twisted as thousands of volts short-circuited his brain, and fast-acting neurochemicals finished off the job. He fell, a feather incongruously drifting down to the ramp floor.

Yi overrode whatever block Wu's cousin had managed to put in place, and the doors wooshed open. The plant manager fled the room without looking back.

Rico and Raheem rushed up the ramp to secure Martel. As they ran up, two laser rifles suddenly appeared to greet them. A man and a woman leaned around either side at the top of the ramp.

"Well, now, that's disappointing," Raheem said, raising his hands.

"Yes, I'm sure it is," the woman said. The man beside her gave an evil grin.

"Lara Kohler and Pedro-what's-his-name," Rico said. It was childish, but he enjoyed seeing the smile disappear off the man's face. "Nice job faking your death, Lara. Sorry to mess that up for you."

Lara gave Rico a smug expression. Her high cheekbones, dark burgundy-purple lipstick, mahogany hair and copper highlights accentuated her wild, commanding visage.

With a lift of his chin, he asked, "How did you get off the ship?"

She gave a coy smile, noting his puzzled demeanor. "Why, Rico, haven't you figured that out yet? An old space cop such as yourself? Oh, yes, we know your background. Teddy researches the background of everyone he meets—the local cops, ex-military or ex-law enforcement, politicians, business leaders. Knowledge pays, right?" She gave him a wink.

"Well, now, darling. As to my amazing escape, we rigged the shuttle for remote control. After it left the bay, I dropped out using a space suit and flew my little self right on over to Teddy's ship. He hovered under Centurion Station, and they could not even see it! Ha!"

She lowered her chin, met his eyes seductively. "A few quick thrusts and I was inside." She worked it well, and her wild beauty promised all kinds of dangerous pleasures, but Rico wasn't buying what she was peddling. The price tag was too high, and there was no warranty.

"What about the life sign?" Raheem asked. "Did you stash some hapless soul on board to cover your escape?"

She peered at Raheem, scrutinizing him slowly, from head to toe. "Dr. Raheem Kuzbari. Illustrious scientist. Researcher. Programmer. Man of mystery. Your public profile seems rather Spartan, Dr. Kuzbari. Why is that?" She tilted her head to the side with a thoughtful pout on her face. Raheem declined to answer.

"No, we did not kidnap anyone and stuff them into the captain's chair. What do you think we are? Barbaric? We used a robot Teddy designed to mimic human life signs. Less likely to undermine our ruse."

"What's your play now?" Rico asked, his face impassive.

She pursed her lips in mild disappointment and shrugged. "Pretty simple really. You get off our ship, and then we get off the station."

"Simple? I see. Why should we let you go? Other than the rifles pointed at our heads, I mean. I'll admit that that is a compelling argument. However, one call to Prime, and you'll have Splitters all over you."

"Teddy always has a back-up plan," Lara said cheerily. She peeked down at her apparent lover, who lay drooling unconsciously between them.

"My. He'll be pissed when he wakes up. I should kill you, you know," she said, long black lashes and thick, wide eyeliner making her eyes appear just a little bit crazier, if that were possible. "If I kill you, then you'll be dead, and I'll stay dead. No one will be the wiser regarding my sad demise." She gave a thin smile. "Then we can be dead together. Like Romeo and Juliet, except that you'll really be dead, and I won't be." She gave him a perky little smile.

"So why don't you then?" Rico asked.

Kohler sighed. "I might, but I prefer not to. I'm attracted to you, Rico. I have a weakness for handsome Galahad-types, and I collect favors the way some women collect tattoos. See, if I let you go, and let you save this station, then you'll owe me, Rico Schroeder." She pierced him with her gaze. "Won't you?"

"Save the station?" That did not sound good.

She wagged a finger at him and shook her head. "Mmm, hmmm. Do we have a deal, pretty boy? If I ever need a favor, then…" She paused, and leaned forward ever so slightly, and her eyes pierced him, and she emphasized her next words but still managed to say them in a sultry stage-whisper: "You'll … owe … me."

Pedro shuffled next to her, clearly uncomfortable with this impromptu negotiating. No doubt, he was adding up the balance sheets, and wondering what this might mean for his future prospects. *I'd be worried if I were you, too, Pedro.*

"Sure." What did he have to lose at this point, especially if Chou Station was in danger? "I'll owe you."

She gave him a skeptical sneer and tsked.

"My word. Scout's honor."

She threw her head back and laughed, her curls bouncing gracefully in the low-g. "That's rich. You probably actually were a Scout, weren't you?"

"I was, now what's the threat?"

"Oh, didn't I mention it? Teddy planted a bomb near the main H3 delivery node." She checked her comm. "If you hurry, you just might make it. Sixty-four minutes, thirty-three seconds. Give or take. Besides, you do *not* want to be here when Teddy wakes up. He hates loose ends." She leaned forward, conspiratorially and whispered, "Personally, I think they make life so much more exciting, don't you?" She laughed. Rico looked at his own comm. The bomb was set to go off at 11:11 PM. Give or take.

"Bye boys." She blew Rico a kiss, winked at Raheem, and then waved a hand at them in a go-away motion. "Shoo."

As they walked backwards, Raheem whispered, "She is a tiger, that one."

They kept their hands in the air. As soon as they stepped off the ramp, it lifted upwards, closed with a snick and hiss, and virtually disappeared before their eyes. Only cargo containers and supplies remained visible in the room. The depressurization alarm sounded and pumps started sucking the atmosphere into temporary reclamation tanks. Rico and Raheem ran for the access door.

- TEN -

Out in the hall, Rico tried to comm station control, but all that came up was "No Signal" on a black screen with white letters. The computer screen only produced an error panel. Martel and Kohler had done a good job of bolloxing up the communication system.

They couldn't waste any more time. Rico realized they'd have to take care of it themselves.

"Feng, I need an external door to the main H3 node! Quick!" Wu gave a nod, and waved them after him as he bounded off in a new direction.

"What about Martel?" Raheem asked.

Rico shook his head. "No contest. Save the station first."

Raheem frowned but gave a firm nod.

They ran down non-descript gray corridors, the same as all the other hallways. However, within five minutes, Feng Wu stopped by a florescent green bar on the wall. Orange characters in Mandarin read, "Emergency: Low-Pressure Suits." Feng flipped a latch and a frame clicked into place, perpendicular to the hallway. A one-piece, syntactic-polymer spacesuit stretched out within the frame, open in the back, with gloves, boots and helmet all built in. Feng opened the attached syringe container and injected Rico with isotonic saline meant to decrease the symptoms of decompression sickness, a known risk of such low-pressure emergency suits and the pure oxygen they contained.

Rico set his jaw and tried not to think about the hangover coming his way. Because both carbon dioxide and decompression hammered a person afterword, the emergency syntactic suits were nicknamed C2D2 suits. C2D2 apparently made some reference to an obscure movie from the early days of cinema. It didn't help that Chou tended to do things on the cheap, so these suits were undoubtedly even less protective than usual. At least they had the suits. He just hoped the seals held.

Well, the hangover gave him something to look forward to—if he lived. He'd have to survive the bomb first. He inserted his arms, stepped into the suit, and kept moving forward until snap-ringlets brought the material together in the back. The chemical reaction sealed the seams, and a second reaction filled any potential leaks with vacuum-impervious foam. A tube in the frame connected the suit to the station air supply. It automatically filled the suit and tested for leaks. Inside, poly-amine materials insulated the suit, absorbed blood, waste, and some of his carbon-dioxide. In moments, Rico had an airtight suit with about forty-five minutes of air, depending on activity level and stress. He'd have plenty of both, so he'd be cutting it close.

He punched at the suit's built-in wrist-comm, and set up a countdown on the timer. Forty-six minutes to find and deactivate the bomb. He'd better find it before then, or he'd be running out of air. "Space me," he muttered. *We are so gonna die, but might as well go down swinging*, he thought. He ignored the knots in his stomach.

"Wu, get the pig outside the main retention tank. I

want it ready to go when I find the bomb. Raheem, you'll have to figure out how to reprogram the pig." He quickly outlined his plan.

Back on Earth, for more than a century, the pipefitters had called the robots that cleaned and inspected the pipes "pigs" because of the squealing noise they made as they ran through the lines. Out here in space, smart pigs inspected both the outside and inside of the pipes, and even though no sound carried out here—unless you put your helmet right up against the pipe, anyway—the name stuck.

Feng Wu nodded approval. "The stuff no react with H3."

Raheem scoffed. "Yes," the darker-skinned man said, "and, if we're lucky, it won't react with anything *inside* the bomb either."

Wu and Raheem closed the airlock behind him, cutting off the rest of their debate. Rico pressed the sequence to open the emergency outer door, and there was a rush of air out into space. He stared out at the central axis. Radial arms stretched from that central point out to the ring, which housed the refinery processing units, living quarters, loading bays, and everything else. Sweat prickled his skin. He was about to launch himself out into nothingness without a lifeline.

He swallowed and steeled his nerves.

Before he pushed off blindly and wasted time scouring a city of pipes for a bomb, he stopped and tried to puzzle out the options and narrow down his search field, but the place was huge and his pulse pounded in his ears and head, making it impossible to concentrate. *C'mon, Rico, think.*

Once processed, the H3 came to the blending tank that surrounded the central axis. As it left that main tank, it entered the central node and split into a dozen smaller pipes with color-coded bands that lay along the radial arms of the station ring like spokes on a giant wheel. From there, the lines spidered off to various loading stations located at the multitude of hangar bays scattered around the haphazard layout.

To do the most damage, the bomb would be located before any automated control valves, which also served as emergency shut-off valves if the H3 flow rates went crazy for some reason. That meant it had to be between a control valve and the central node, but not too close to the node, because that would be too obvious.

If it were me, I'd plant the bomb just on the inside of a control valve. If that blew, it would take out the valve, ignite the central node, and then burn outward along each of the supply lines. It would probably take out the whole station.

Hopefully, he wouldn't have to check all twelve control valves. He'd never have time to check all twelve, regardless. They'd be dead long before then.

He pushed off and leaped from his perch on the inner ring toward the closest radial arm and valve. He could feel the minutes draining away as he drifted much too slowly across the ether of space. He used the suit's weak thrusters to keep on target, but they were not designed for speed. Sweat beaded on his forehead, and he could already feel his muscles beginning to cramp and his joints to ache. Rico tried the OptiComm. Still down. He switched to point-to-point and rehashed the plan with Raheem and Feng and the reprogramming Raheem would need to get done while Rico searched for the bomb.

Finally, he made it to the first radial arm. Nothing. *Dammit.* Even though seconds might count, he decided to take the time at each valve to manually override the automation and shut off the supply to the hangar bays. That might minimize any explosion. Maybe. He grabbed the spinner valve and cranked it as fast as his arms would go. Given the size of the line, it took almost a minute and a half. Thirty-five minutes left. Sweat prickled his underarms as he thought of the clock ticking down.

He made the long leap to the next radial arm.

When he caught the second pipeline, he checked his timer. Twenty-six minutes. It took him nine minutes to cross between lines. Not good. He searched as quickly as he could. Nothing on the second line. He checked his timer again. Twenty-three minutes. A bead of sweat ran down his temple. Swearing, he decided not to close the spinner valve. He didn't have the time. He hoped he had not just condemned hundreds of people to their deaths.

He positioned himself and pushed off as hard as he could. He glided across the void.

As he trekked across to the third pipe, doubts began to eat at him.

Martel and Khohler had outsmarted them. They must've got it all wrong. What if Martel just wanted to take out one segment of the station?! His plan could involve using one of the centrifugal compressors to increase pressure along one line until it ruptured. He was in the wrong spot! He called Wu and Kuzbari on the point-to-point in a panic, and

Raheem's voice came back.

"Rico, listen to me. It's just the oxygen in the emergency suit getting to you. We talked about this. Stick to the plan. Martel would not settle for partially taking out a target. He would go all out. You know you're right. Even if you don't, trust me. Keep going."

Rico took a breath. The air felt stale and acrid. Sweat dripped in his eyes and his vision wavered. Working for Chou hadn't been the greatest job, but he'd made a lot of friends when he'd worked over here. He was betting the life of every person on Chou. If he was wrong ....

Crap. This really sucks. Crap, crap, crap. He felt nauseous but fought it down. His joints were beginning to feel as if they'd been bent the wrong direction. A headache pulsed behind his eyes. As he came up to the third radial line, his arms wouldn't obey his brain as quickly as normal. He slammed into the pipe, helmet rebounding off the unyielding metal, and he bounced backward, out toward empty space; if he missed the pipe, it would cost him crucial time reorienting and coming back around. He snagged a hand rung as he drifted past and jerked to a stop, his body swinging around and slamming into the pipe again.

He worked his way around the pipes of the third line, but again, no bomb.

"Dammit, Wu. There're bugs in this damn suit! When was the last time they maintained these? I can feel 'em crawlin' on my skin! Those slouches at Chou should take better care of their gear."

"No bugs, Rico. Keep going."

Rico muttered unintelligibly and repositioned

himself to launch across to the next arm and valve.

Twelve minutes till detonation. One more shot. Eight to ten minutes to cross. That left less than four minutes to find and deactivate the bomb? He resisted the urge to laugh. It was insane, but insanity was their only option at this point. If the bomb wasn't on the fourth gas line, they were done. Once more he hurled himself across the divide, but his right foot slipped, as he tried to give an extra-hard push. Not only did he lose valuable momentum, but his body also twisted ever so slightly as he flew, pirouetting slowly as the giant spoked wheel of the processing facility cascaded around him. Vertigo made him nauseous as he drifted toward the distant line. Icy fear gripped him. He'd been doing space walks since he turned seven, and never once had vertigo. His mind recalled the image of a seedpod floating in a botanical ring back on Axion.

Shaking his head, which only aggravated the dizziness, he said, "Wu, get pig to dark green pipeline. Not … light green. If bomb's … not there … won't matter." Man, his head pounded.

"Already moving, boss," said Wu.

"Raheem … Set?"

Raheem's voice came into his helmet, tinny and sounding much farther away than it actually was. "Yes, Rico. We are ready. Safety protocols are off. It'll be a piece of cake."

Cake. Pig. Green. Rico tried to remember the plan he'd come up with, but the details skittered around his brain like cockroaches avoiding the light in a cargo hold, and the team lapsed into silence as Rico floated between the cold arms of a metal monolith.

Despite his mental haze, he knew the bomb the instant he saw it. A gray box, similar to the one in Martel's station berth, only longer, had been stuck to the side of the pipeline with cable ties and adhesive putty configured for use in space.

He had three and a half minutes left. Sweat prickled on his forehead and his vision swam.

"Found … it. Wu, where's that … damn pig?" Talking was becoming almost as difficult as thinking. He did not have much time left.

"Coming. Almos' there, boss.

Raheem said, "I suppose you've done this numerous times, of course?"

Rico gave a dry chuckle. "No. Took …" He lost the flow of his thinking for a moment. He shook his head and got it back. "I, uh, took a … mail-order course. They said … never do this." He licked parched lips. "Ready?"

"Of course," came Raheem's bland reply. "What could go wrong? Where exactly will you be?"

"Behind axis. If it blows, and the whole …" he swallowed painfully, "… station doesn't, then maybe … I'll survive."

"Wonderful."

Rico kept glancing at the time on his wrist-comm, waiting for something to happen. Finally, the pig trundled into view, spiraling around from the other side, articulated limbs making its movements more resemble a lizard than a pig.

The pig, however, stopped three meters away.

"Wu? Bring it … over."

"I cannot. Some signal blocking pig. No respond."

"Rico," Raheem said.

"Try–"

"Rico," Raheem said more forcefully, but still with that same reserve.

"What?"

"Check your time."

Twelve seconds until detonation. *Too late. We're too late.* He inhaled deeply, closed his eyes and exhaled.

"Been … a good run. You did fine." *Sorry we didn't get farther.*

Rico watched the seconds tick down:

00:00:03
00:00:02

Rico squinted, bracing himself, although he knew he would not feel much, if anything, this close. Death would be instantaneous.

00:00:01
00:00:00

- ELEVEN -

Rico opened his eyes and blinked. Unexpectedly—very unexpectedly—the timer kept going, counting off the seconds into negatives: -00:00:01, -00:00:02, and on it went. Either Lara had been wrong, or she'd been messing with them. Rico barked out a laugh, gave a loud whoop, and bit down on the next guffaw before he lapsed into hysterical laughter and couldn't stop. He contented himself with a broad grin.

"Borrowed time, boys!" Rico said. He started humming a popular tune about borrowed time, his thoughts scattered and drifting as wildly as he was. He sprang over to the pig as quickly as he could in the zero gravity. On the way, he suggested Wu try relaying through Rico's point-to-point comm.

"No spin, guys." We're running out of luck.

Rico pulled up a command interface on his wrist-comm and tried controlling the pig that way. The maintenance robot shuffled forward.

"Going to have to … stick around … for the show, boys."

Silence for a moment, and then Raheem said, "I take it there's no other way?"

"No. Got to be close. To it. Override the–" he couldn't find the word. What was that word? Oh, right. "The interference." He wished he could rub his eyes. If he could just take off this suit and rub his eyes. Dry. They felt so damn dry.

"The interference must be specific to the channels bots use, or we wouldn't be able to talk either," Raheem mused.

Rico heard him talking, but didn't respond; the words didn't really register. He heard them; they just didn't make sense. He needed to focus. *C'mon, Rico, buddy. Focus!* "Uhm, cut wires, now. Right?"

"Rico, you made it. Listen now. Almost there. You're going to use the pig to x-ray inside the bomb. Do that now. X-ray the pig."

His head felt like lead, but he punched commands into the wrist-comm, and finally pulled up the right interface. He keyed it and the screen showed the internal configuration of the bomb. "Got it."

"Good, Rico. Good. Find the detonation device."

"Right, right. I see it," Rico felt excitement cut through the haze in his mind.

"Use the pig's power-cleaner at maximum blast. I already reprogrammed it to go past the redline. You're good to go. Just cut through the detonation cord and shear off any kind of firing pin."

And pray. You left out the part about praying, Rico thought.

"We're ready when you are." Part of Rico's brain sensed a tightness in Raheem's voice.

He should have written his grandmother a letter. She worried about him, and she turned 93 last May. She makes the best shrimp mofongo. What he wouldn't give for some of that, right now. He should go visit her in Puerto Rico. Maybe when–.

"Rico. Go ahead. Rico. Cut the wires."

"Hnh?" Rico said. He shook his head vigorously, and immediately wished he hadn't done that. Hurt. Sonofamartian. "Oh. Right. Okay. Give me a count."

Raheem's voice came from far away, "On the cou–" Rico's mind drifted. They'd been talking about something, but he'd lost the beam on it. Blackness crowded the edge of his vision.

" ... Two ... Three."

He could hear Raheem talking but he wasn't sure why. Then he remembered. He had to push the command on his wrist-comm to activate the blast of cleaning solution from the pig. Like a water cannon. Which would hopefully cut through the detonation wire and not take out the entire neighborhood. And him with it.

He took in a deep breath and blew it out in five rapid exhalations. He felt a rush of energy course through him, and the dimness crowding in on him receded a bit.

"Here goes the neighborhood." He laughed.

"Rico–." Raheem sounded concerned, and a bit as if he might scold him.

"No, no. I'm okay. Time to ride the pig!"

He pushed the command to fire. He watched the robot-pig fire a blast at the bomb attached to the pipe. It cut through the outer casing as if it were a chef filleting a fish in front of your table at the big ring.

The big ring. Maybe he should take Inés there. If he didn't blow up.

He didn't think he did. Blow up, that is. But he

felt his hands and feet slip loose of the rungs on the axis. He began to drift out away from the center column and out toward the vastness of space.

Did we do it? he wanted to ask, but couldn't find the words.

As his body rotated in slow motion, his vision tunneled again, and this time everything went black.

- TWELVE -

Rico lay in a hospital bed on Chou Station. Raheem, Wu and someone upper level guy from Chou Station that Rico did not know had been in to visit him, but the visits were gray-washed memories. Rico's joints still felt as if a ball-peen hammer had been smacking them around, but the nan-bots were speeding along the elimination of nitrogen bubbles from his body. His headache no longer pulsed, but lingered as a clanging ache in the background. He could see again, although he felt woozy. The emergency space suit was gone, but the special solvent for removing the foam sealants had also taken off a layer of skin, which now glowed a scrubbed pink color. Since he still had all his limbs, apparently they'd gotten lucky.

Raheem came back in, green suit still crisp and pressed. Rico swallowed dryly and said, "Nice to see you so fresh and dapper. How long have I been in here?"

"Nine hours."

Rico groaned.

Raheem shrugged, as if to say, "What are you going to do?"

"The plant manager, Yi Lin, was in. Do you

remember?"

Rico waggled his hand. Sort of.

"Offered you your old job back, with a promotion. He was impressed with how you disabled the bomb. Ah, and saved the station. He appreciated that."

Rico nodded. "Old school. High-pressure has been used for centuries, although that may have been the first time a cleaning solution was used."

They both grinned at that.

"Martel?"

Raheem shook his head. "No sign, amigo. We're assuming they took off for the Belt. Fortunately, no other bombs were placed. Unfortunately, Martel, Lara Kohler, and Pedro got away."

Rico wanted them all rotting in a cell.

"There's more. While you were out, they found Holt's supervisor in the hangar bay where the Qátala-class ship had been assigned. His body had been disrupted and sealed inside a plas crate."

Damn. He pursed his lips in frustrated anger. Rico had met the guy a few times. Bahru Wagle. Poor guy. Three kids. No, four. His wife had had a baby last year.

They had saved Chou Station. That was something, anyway, and they *had* solved Malik's murder, and Tiago's as well—and now the Chief Security Officer's as well, apparently—even if the fugitives were still on the fly. But it just didn't sit right. Martel had a lot to answer for. True, he was a fugitive, but he'd been a fugitive before all this. Martel had simply been good at skirting detection.

Rico took another sip of his rejuv-juice, leaned back against his pillow, and tried to think of options.

The answer—or at least part of the answer—came to him in a flash. He stuck the drink pouch to the magnetic holder, tipped his tray upright, and opened a comm on the plas surface. When Kita Useugi appeared on the OptiComm, he said, "Dr. Useugi. I think its time we give *The Amazing Grace* a real test run. With your permission, I'm taking her out, and I'm bringing company."

He filled her in on what he had in mind.

- THIRTEEN -

The trip back to Axion on his shuttle had seemed even slower than his trip to Prime Station had been. Despite feeling a bit weak still, he wanted to take action. The good news was that his legs did not feel as rubbery by the time they docked. Uesugi had cleared Raheem to enter Axion Station, and Candra had verified he carried no unauthorized spybots. Now, however, Rico sat across from Useugi's desk, and concern drew her mouth into a flat line. The topic of their conversation sat at the conference table outside her office.

"I understand that he's been helpful, Rico-san, but are you sure you can trust him? You know that Martel is connected to Adala and that he escaped. Are you certain Dr. Kuzbari did not help him?"

Rico considered this, but it didn't add up. He shook his head. "He saved my life. He could have let me die after I power-washed the bomb. Even with Feng Wu there, a few minutes delay and I would have been burnt bacon."

Uesugi stared off, toward the pictures on her office wall, lost in her own thoughts for a moment. "And the prize, Rico? If you take Raheem you create a conduit of tangled cables."

"Have him sign a waiver and nondisclosure." Rico leaned in and held his old commander's gaze. "He deserves to go after Martel with me, Kita. He's earned it. For the time being, until he proves me wrong, I trust him. That might be crazy, but I do. At least enough to let him come along. I'll give him enough tether to see if he hangs himself up on it."

Now it was his turn to rummage through old trunks, lost in the past for a moment. What he'd said wasn't entirely accurate, but he couldn't quite grab hold of what he wanted to say. He tried again. "When you deal with the worst in life, and you get burned, the way we have, you have to consciously make a decision to trust. I've been sunblasted before, Kita, you know that—"

On a particularly dark and angst-driven drinking binge, Rico had told Kita his whole story. About the deaths of his parents, the murder of his cousin Jackie, about how even before that—how his high school sweetheart and fiancé, Karen Dewer, had slept with one of his high school buddies, Trigger.

Trigger "Attaboy" McAboy. Best friend and arch-nemesis.

Rico's two closest high school friends had both betrayed him in the end.

In their last fight, Karen had called him emotionally unavailable and obsessive. The kicker was that she'd said he had trust issues. "Trust issues. Really? Well, who the space could blame me? You were, after all, banging my best friend."

And Karen, the bitch, even took my first edition Cometallion. He gave a wry grin at his attempt to lighten his own mood.

Rico considered this in light of his thoughts about Inés lately. Maybe his ex had had a point. He set that aside to deal with some other time. Right now, he had to focus.

"Trusting Raheem is a risk I'm willing to take. I'll

keep my eyes on him, but my gut is telling me to take a chance. I have to trust my instincts. For the case and for myself."

She returned the gaze for a long moment, then gave a short, tight nod.

Candra spun out a waiver of any claim on the prize money related to the performance of *The Amazing Grace*. Raheem signed it, and they headed to the bay where the ship gleamed under Dionysian lighting—sleek and practically alive. White, black and red waves of color complemented her sensual curves. They had built not just a machine, but a work of art. *The Amazing Grace* had been, and still was, a labor of love. She sat in the hangar, waiting to be awoken, a tribute to the human spirit and all humanity could accomplish.

They had talked about the ship, the failed simulations, and the risks. Rico asked him one more time as they stood outside the ship, "You sure you're up for this, Raheem?"

"In for a potato chip, in for the bag."

Rico laughed and clapped him on the shoulder. "All right. Let's burn some ether."

Jane emerged from the ship, tablet in hand, along with a couple of other techs.

"Is it here, yet?"

"Yes, it arrived a little while ago, but Rico—"

"Jane, don't."

She stopped and he peered into his eyes. A dozen thoughts ran through both of their minds, many of them the same. One of the cardinal rules is never talk to a team about the risks before a flight. Jane bit her lip and tapped a fist against her thigh. Her eyes got watery, and he held up a warning finger.

"Fine," she said. "But you better bring some champagne back with you. And I want the real stuff. None of this knockoff crap." She took the fist that had been hitting her thigh and punched his arm.

"Ow. Hey, still recovering here."

She rolled her eyes. "Yeah, right."

"Hey. You," an angry voice said, and they turned to see Zavier Sorrenguard as he walked up and pointed at Rico. "You know this is bull, man. Talk about a cobbled together piece of excuse for taking the seat. This test run is supposed to be *mine*. You are security. You're not a test pilot." Anger made the man's usually fair skin a hot red.

"It's got nothing to do with that, Zavier, and you know it." Rico turned, ignoring him and continued on toward the cockpit.

Behind him, he heard, "Wha–. Hey!" followed by what sounded like people slapping at space mites. When he turned around, Zavier and Raheem had squared off and were gearing up to try and knock each other out of orbit.

"Problem?" Rico asked, eyebrows raised and his smile blandly contained.

"Your teammate appeared to be intent on harm," Raheem said. "Since your back was turned, I interceded on your behalf so that you could address him face to face." That ever-present hint of a smile played across the man's lips. "He took exception to my mediation techniques."

Jane chuckled. "He was probably just going to grab Rico's arm, right Zav?"

The tall man gave a curt nod, his face red and his

mouth turned down in a scowl.

"Raheem stopped his arm cold. Then he blocked three or four shots from Zavier. How did you do that?"

"*Kyoku-atsu.* It means 'Bending Force.' It's specifically designed for fighting in low gravity."

Rico gave himself a mental pat on the back. *I knew it.* "I think I've heard the name, but I don't know anything about it."

Raheem replied, "I can teach you some moves some time if you like." Sensing the threat of more violence had passed, Raheem stood, straightened out the cuffs on his shirt and suit, and extended a hand to Zavier. "My apologies for any misunderstanding."

Zavier shook his hand, but glanced warily between Rico and what he clearly considered an interloper, and jutted out his chin. "The first test flight is mine. You can't steal it."

Rico stared at him, annoyed, but took a deep breath and put himself in Sorrenguard's place. He'd be pissed, too, if someone stole his shot at breaking the record.

"Fine. You can pilot the ship on three conditions. One, I'm in charge; you go where I say, and you do what I say. Period. Two, if you come along, then you're in for the long haul. I have no idea how long we'll be gone. First time you complain, you get strapped to the hull for the rest of the trip. Three, this may involve being shot at—lasers, disruptors, who knows what. Several people are dead already. I can't guarantee your safety, and I can't babysit you. You got all that?"

Zavier might have a smile hidden on his face but,

if so, it was a subtle one. His eyes, however, gleamed with excitement.

"I got it. I'm in."

"Grab your gear. Thrusters hot as soon as you get back." Zavier took off at a run.

"That was pretty generous of you," Jane said.

Rico shrugged. "He's right. Besides, he'd do the same for me."

She gaped at him as if he'd blown a few circuits, and he laughed. Jane joined in. "Funny guy." She gave Rico a hug and nodded to Raheem and then the two boarded the ship.

The flight deck had six seats that could be rearranged depending on which station a person wanted to work at or what window they wanted to look out. Subflooring mechanisms locked them into place. Rico ran his fingers over one of the touchscreens and the seats shifted so that three of them were side-by-side.

Raheem let his gaze scan the control center and gave a low whistle, "Nice."

Rico grinned. "None of my doing. I'm just the heavy."

Zavier showed up minutes later, strapped in, and they cleared the station. They had to use the plasma engines to get far enough away from the space stations to satisfy the regulations laid out by the AMMATT Prize board of Trustees. Most of the Jupiter Consortium wanted to waive this annoying rule, but the AMMATT Board overruled them. Destroying a populated station if a test flight went horribly wrong would be bad press, even this far from Earth.

Rico thought he had a pretty good idea where Martel was heading. He'd been wrong on his first bet, but it was time to double-down. The asteroid belt was closer than Mars, much less earth. And, based on where the asteroids would be by the time Martel's fusion ship arrived, he'd probably head to Ceres, the largest rock – and the biggest station – in the Main Belt.

If he'd been in Martel's shoes, Ceres sure wouldn't have been his first choice. Ceres was large, but it had been under martial law for two decades now. The Cerean government took a hard line toward criminals, but it had the best infrastructure and a large enough population that he might be able to blend in and hide. Not a great choice, but the best under the circumstances.

The brutal part of space travel was the distances. It would take not just days or weeks, but months, to reach Ceres. Sure, with the antimatter engine they could get there in a fraction of the time, but unless Rico and Raheem wanted to wait for Martel a really long time on Ceres they needed to find him en route. Rico knew it would be the equivalent of searching for an ant from a moving vehicle, but didn't see any other options. They would actually have to rein in *The Amazing Grace* immensely until they could find the bastard. The thought of going that slowly with such an incredible new engine design galled him, And it would drive Zavier, as pilot of the sleek prototype, crazy.

He pulled up the OptiComm and made a call. "Command, this is Schroeder. Have you figured out a way for us to detect that stealth design yet? We won't be able to use the multiple sensors and cameras we used before."

The voice on the other end was not Holt's and sounded annoyed. "We know, Captain. We're working on it."

Rico pursed his lips in a grimace and cut the comm. "Touchy. If we can't break that stealth, we may as well go home."

Raheem didn't respond. He just typed away at his own console and hummed some classical tune that Rico did not recognize. He tried not to transfer his irritation to the man sitting next to him.

A triangular icon appeared on the main screen. The triangle was on the far side of one of the outer moons orbiting Jupiter, called Himalia. The label said Martel.

"What the heck?"

He reached for the OptiComm icon and Raheem stopped him with a gesture. "That's not from Command." Rico stared at him. "When I shot at Martel, I used a tracking bullet. Well, actually, one of my own design with nanbots I programmed, to not only send out a signal using their own transmitters, but also to infiltrate any nearby computer system and use any OptiComm they could find." Raheem pointed at the screen. "Apparently, he really is going to slingshot around a moon to gain momentum this time."

Rico stared at Raheem for two seconds longer and then broke into a laugh.

"It's the second rule of recovery. Always get a tag on your target."

Zavier raised his eyebrows quizzically. "What's

the first?"

"Don't lose track of your target."

"Schroeder to Command. Focus your sensors over by Himalia."

"Roger that, Captain."

"You don't really work for Dubai, do you?"

"I told you. I work for Dubai Intergalactic Chemical. All my credit deposits say so." Rico gave him a measured attitude. Raheem bobbed his head up and down in defeat and that hint of a smile played across his lips again. "Okay," the olive-skinned man said. "Let's say – hypothetically – that a person did work for some sort of clandestine agency, which has not explicitly made itself known already. Why would he be interested in keeping a low profile? No, not low. *Invisible*. Hmm?"

Raheem waited expectantly. Rico paused and then said, "Well, to safeguard agents, of course, but there's more to it, I think. Not many of the reasons I can think of come across as polite dinner conversation, though."

Zavier cleared his throat and said, "You know, uh, I'd give you guys the room if I wasn't, like, flying the ship and all.

"Shut up Zav."

Zavier snorted, but kept quiet then. Probably, curiosity regarding what they were talking about got the better of him.

Raheem gave him a level gaze. "We are not at dinner, Captain Schroeder. You will not offend me. Go ahead."

"Usually covert ops are involved in acquiring something."

"Stealing."

"Uh, yes. But also gathering information. Mostly that, in fact." He really was not sure where Raheem was headed with all this, but he felt as if he was on the verge of getting some answers, so he let it spin. "Or a person might be retrieving something—or someone—that has been taken."

"Extraction."

"They might strive to prevent an attack …"

"Protection."

"… or sometimes covert agents take out a person …"

"Assassination."

" … or a physical resource …"

"Sabotage."

"True. Are you telling me that is what you do, Dr. Kuzbari?"

"You still haven't told me *why* such an organization would want to operate undetected."

Rico was becoming annoyed. He didn't appreciate Raheem playing with him. Before he could reply, Zavier jumped in. "How about so they don't get freakin' killed? Hello?" Apparently, Zavier was irritated with Raheem's cat and mouse game as well.

"Fear of one's enemies, then? Reprisals?"

"Sure."

"I'm not sure such organizations are capable of fear. Individuals perhaps. Either way, they know the game that they play and the consequences. Is that the only reason, then, for a covert organization to hide?"

Rico blew out a big sigh, shrugged and refrained from rolling his eyes. "I don't know. Let's see." He mentally reviewed their list so far and then added,

"To avoid bad press."

"Interesting. Go on."

Clearly he was on to something. Bad press? And then it clicked. Bad press at home. In this case, although Adala did not enjoy widespread public support, per se, they had enough supporters. Some of their backers had to have substantially deep pockets. Any Middle Eastern group openly targeting them could face a great deal of political heat.

"So, hypothetically, an organization might be laying low if they did not want to upset one's own constituents or associates of those constituents."

Rico thought about Raheem's discussion about not being welcome at the preparation of the Hujjat Malik's body, and how Raheem's own team considered him—what was the word? Kufar. Rico added aloud, "Such an organization might even choose an outsider among outsiders, someone they could scapegoat if it all went wrong. Someone who was part of the culture, but did not follow the religious beliefs or the political winds of the time."

Raheem closed his eyes, angled his head, and bent it into a nod of acknowledgment. "That would seem to be both prudent and expedient."

He grunted. "Nice friends."

The olive-skinned man shrugged as he gazed out at the portal. "Such people are not friends. They hold to the bigger picture and use resources as they must to secure their objectives. Assets are expendable."

He spoke without apparent bitterness or rancor. Just matter of fact. Another spin around the station, dear.

Raheem changed the course of their discussion.

"If you have no objection, I'm going to work on some coding for my nanbots. If they don't have a jamming signal in place, I'll be able to send my bots some new instructions, once we're close enough."

"What's close enough?"

"Close. We won't need to scrape the paint off the hull, but close enough that their micro-antennae can pick up the signal, and close enough so that any upgrade I send won't be a beacon in the night for Martel and company."

Rico blew out air in a disappointed huff.

Raheem shrugged. "By the way, I think Lara Kohler's got the hots for you."

"Ha. Of course she does. I think Pedro's got the hots for you."

As they'd been talking, Zavier had brought the *Grace* on a path to hook around Himalia.

Prime came over the comm. "We're not seeing anything in the vicinity of Himalia, even with remote sensors pointing in-system. Are you sure he's there? Over."

Rico looked at Raheem who nodded. "There's a failsafe programmed into the bots. If they've been deactivated or dumped off-ship somehow, we'd know."

Rico hit the Reply icon. "He's there. Keep scanning."

Raheem tapped some figures into his pad. "How did he get out there so fast? He shouldn't have been able to reach Himalia in less than nine days. And look, we can see the triangle moving. He's going remarkably fast for a fusion ship."

"Oh, that is not good." Rico's intuition kicked into

warp drive, and he had an uneasy feeling in the pit of his stomach. "Command, broaden your parameters to detect photons, gamma radiation, neutrinos, and other matter-antimatter reactions."

Another long pause. "Affirmative, Captain. There's a trail there all right."

Rico swore. "Martel wasn't just stealing the teams' research. He built his own antimatter engine."

"No way," Zavier blurted out. "Right under Sistema Solar's nose?"

"He had his own hangar bay. It's not uncommon to have duplicates of experimental craft. And, they've been planning this for years."

"We'll wake acting CSO Holt," Prime said.

Rico noted the change in title but didn't comment. "Don't bother. There's nothing he can do about it. I'll report in when I can. Rico out." He cut the link to Prime Station and opened one to Axion.

"Jane here."

"Jane, we're moving up the timetable." He filled her in on the latest, and then added, "How soon can you rally the troops? As soon as you can, we're firing up the AMMATT engine. Zav's got her warmed up and ready to go."

"We're watching already, Rico-san," Uesugi said over the Comm. Nobody can sleep anyway. You are 'go' for ignition."

Rico grinned. *I guess I'm not the only one who's a little excited.* He hit mute.

"Are you ready, Zavier?"

"Living the dream, man."

"Are you ready, Raheem?"

"To smash particles of matter and antimatter

together, annihilating those particles and creating the largest bang per kilogram in the history of humanity? All while sitting on top of said explosion in the hopes of going a thousand times faster than we've ever gone before?" Raheem's mouth twitched as he maintained a deadpan expression. "Of course. Who wouldn't be?"

"Are we clearing this with Prime Station?" Zavier asked.

"Nope," Rico said. According to the rules and system regs, firing off the AMMATT engines this close was most definitely forbidden, but he had no intention of getting turned down now.

The OptiComm chimed, and Inés Villaverde's picture appeared on the screen. "Perfect," Rico said with a sigh.

"Inés, hi. I haven't–"

"Schroeder," she cut in like a commanding officer and her fiery mien practically crackling on the screen. She only got that dark and pinched expression when she was *very* angry. Uh oh, Rico thought. "What the hell are you up to? We cracked Martel's second pad. He's been syphoning off research from *all* the teams for months."

"I don't–"

"Save it, Rico. Our scans have picked up neutrinos over by *Amazing Grace. Ahead* of your trajectory. It's him isn't it?"

Rico let out a long sigh. "Yes. It's Martel. Inni, I'm guessing you guys have been building more than one experimental craft?" She nodded, "Well, he's been building a working antimatter drive under your noses."

Inés made a few scathing remarks about Martel

and his family history. Then she realized that Rico was going after Martel. Her eyes went round.

"You're firing up your AMMATT engine, aren't you?" Ever quick, she leapt to the next thought and then the next. "You've got a working drive?! You don't have clearance, do you?"

Rico shook his head.

"I want to be kept in the loop, Rico." She jabbed her finger at him, emphasizing her words. "You owe me that."

"Okay, okay. Talk to Uesugi and she'll patch you in. I'll clear it with her."

Mollified, Inés gave him a hint of a smile. Her voice took on a slower, huskier tone. "All right. Be careful, Federico. We have a lot of making up to do." She cut the comm and Rico cleared his throat.

Zavier grinned and, imitated Inés. "Be careful, Federico. We have a lot of making up to do."

"Shut up," Rico said, but his lips curled up in a smile as he put in a call to Uesugi.

Zavier and double-checked the course plot, set it on autopilot, and eight minutes later said the numbers aloud as they ticked down on his screen. "Ignition in 3, 2, 1." He pressed a large red icon.

Particles of matter teleported into particles of antimatter, annihilating each other and sending an inferno of energy through the combustion chamber, and out the nozzle of the ship. Rico'd flown more years of his life than he hadn't. He'd thought he was prepared for what he would experience. He wasn't. The thrust crushed him into his seat; he felt as if he'd just been hit by a planet. His ribs felt like they were cracking; his breath came in short, painful gasps. He glanced sideways at Raheem and Zavier, their faces distorted by the intense g-forces at work. His vision tunneled for a moment, and he thought he might black out. Finally, the compensators kicked in enough that they could breath. He sucked in a deep breath.

"Unbelievable!" Raheem gasped.

Rico didn't respond. He watched the readouts, stress factors, structural integrity, atmospheric viability and a host of other factors.

Prime Station pinged them with an incoming message. They all exchanged furtive glances and ignored the call. Zavier appeared to be having the time of his life.

"Axion, this is Zavier. We have positive matter-antimatter annihilation. Our speed is two hundred twenty-three kilometers per second and climbing. All systems are green."

A live feed came on, slightly pixelated in spite of the OptiComm. All of Axion's personnel were gathered in the hangar area, squeezed in front of the camera, and stood screaming their heads off and pounding each other on the back.

Zavier held his fist in the air and gave an answering, "Whoo-ooo!" and pounded Rico on the back. Rico grinned until his face hurt. Zavier might be a jackass, Rico thought, but he's our jackass.

After the din died down a bit, Rico said, "I know you have the specs on your computer, but let me tell ya', we need to adjust the compensators to kick in sooner. A bug being crushed by a boot would have felt more comfortable." Faces on the screen laughed and beamed back at him.

"Congratulations, Zavier and Rico." Uesugi said.

"Congratulations to us all. Now, go get Martel."

As they flew on, the thrill of successfully firing off the antimatter drive was only slightly tarnished by the thought that Martel had beaten them to it. Yet another score to settle with "TM." Raheem had enough class not to point out that the cloaked ship had beaten them to the antimatter punchbowl. Rico took a great deal of consolation from the fact that, as a criminal and fugitive, Martel would never be able to petition for the prize money.

- FOURTEEN -

Rico was not a fan of the Asteroid Belt. He had been to several habitats in the Belt, many times. He thought the phrase Main Asteroid Belt a misnomer. Asteroid Wasteland, maybe.

Belters lived too far from everything, including each other, for Rico's taste. If you were a Belter you were typically about a million kilometers from any other asteroid, and no major space stations were out here, since there were not enough patrons to keep one profitable. Nothing to see except distant planets and impossibly remote stars. Maybe someday they'd get to those stars, but that day was far, far off. Even with an AMMATT drive it would take *years* to reach the nearest star that might have a habitable planet.

In the meantime, if you wanted solitude, and to get away from civilization, then the Belt was the perfect place. Nothing to do except mine, and go stir crazy. He supposed the same could be said of space pilots, since it took months or even years to travel from one point to another, but at least you were *moving*. And you would eventually end up at a civilized station.

Rico loved to fly, but he found that, overall, he preferred spending time with people. He thrived working as a team, joking around with others and bouncing ideas off one another. He enjoyed the energy, the synergy. Even if security officers often worked alone, at least other people lived on a station.

The mining settlements in the asteroid belt were

far different from the tourist rings that orbited above Earth, Mars, and even Jupiter. The habitats in the Wasteland tended to be small, cramped, and miserable things that made even the most Spartan science rings seem like luxury stations. More often than not they were pieces of junk cobbled together from scavenged spaceships that had limped into the field and died. They were simply barnacles clinging to the side of a ship or, perhaps more aptly, lichen growing in a thin scale on the surface of a rock. A good scrape with a knife and the settlements, if they could be called that, would disappear over night. Some of them had. Whenever Rico visited one, he always felt as though the damn place was going to crack a seal, and they would get sucked out into the vacuum of space.

If not for Raheem's bugs and the trail of particles, they would have lost Martel's ship – stealthed as it was—and Martel once again did not go where Rico expected. Strike two for him. Instead, he headed in a different direction, and Rico spent a few minutes wracking his brain, querying Candra, and brainstorming with Zavier and Raheem before they came up with a probable destination: the asteroid Eunomia. In their current orbital positions, Ceres and Eunomia were only fifteen million kilometers apart. With an antimatter drive, that only tacked an extra hour or two onto his trip, and Eunomia had several advantages for Martel and his ill-gotten goods.

Eunomia was the slimiest rock in the sector. If you wanted something illegal, or had something illegal to sell, you went there. Ironic, since Eunomia meant law and order.

This particular asteroid system had another advantage for Martel. Lots of rat holes nearby to duck into. The Eunomia "Family" consisted of nearly 400 asteroids, the largest "cluster" in the Main Belt, and it had more habitats and miners than any other family of rocks out here. With a stealth ship and an AMMATT engine, the Eunomia Family was about as perfect as you could get.

Zavier had never used a LLAM before, so they killed some time orienting him to the weapon. Fortunately, they were fairly idiot-proof. Not that Zavier was an idiot, but firearms were nothing to sneeze at—even the "less-lethal" ones can kill you if you're careless. He'd come up through the private sector, both as a space racer and test pilot. Not much call for weaponry. Rico programmed Zav's LLAM so that it would not shoot him or Raheem by mistake, although a pointblank shot would not give the microprocessors time to compensate, but you can't make everything foolproof or it simply won't function the way it should.

Before they'd left Axion, Rico had pulled out three kinetic suits and brought them along; now, he insisted that everyone put them on. They fit under their regular clothes, and no one would notice the suits. They wouldn't stop a disruptor, but they came in handy versus other weapons.

"*Amazing Grace* to Harcourt's Hole, come in."

After a moment, someone replied in the heavy patois that had emerged among many of the Belters. Rico thought they had intentionally adopted the slang to annoy "baggers," their insulting term for non-Belters. "Diz da'Hole. Whod'fook diz?"

Rico said to Raheem, "Standard welcome." And then over the OptiComm, "This is Captain Federico Schroeder."

Rico had been here a few times. He wondered what kind of welcome he would get this time. The last time he'd been here, he'd barely gotten off the damn rock alive.

* * *

Charlie Harcourt and three of his men met him at the 'lock. They were a strange lot. Belters eschewed gravity and many other things that made humans, well, human. For one, they ate a lot of weird things, even by station standards. Rats, cockroaches, yeasts, and other vat-grown vegetation. They ate anything that would thrive in the harshest environments, not as a last resort, but out of a culinary obstinance, embracing the opportunities that could most easily and profitably be cultivated in space. Belters also—taking pride in being contrary—embraced zero-g in every setting, in every way possible.

Harcourt had the long, pasty-white body of a lifetime Belter, his bones and cartilage unhampered by gravity, Unlike most Belters, though, he was also fat, which gave him a tall, oval shape. A rectangular head and square jaw gave him a monstrous appearance. He brought to mind pale onions stuck on a stir stick for a martini. The others stood near him with a menacing air. Rico had learned never to underestimate a Belter in a fight. They were fast, wiry, and fought dirty.

They also each carried disruptors. They'd been

banned on most corporate and government stations, but the Belt made Jupiter seem civilized. Too many settlers too far from any authority. In the Belt, as they liked to say, "Whate'er we sez, goze."

As soon as he stepped onto the deck of the hangar bay, Raheem gave a big sigh and lit up a fat cigar. Rico did a double-take, since it was the first time he'd seen the man smoke, even though they'd spent hours together on board various ships. Zavier followed a step behind them.

"You can't bring doze in here," Harcourt said, pointing at the LLAMs.

"What? The cigar?" Rico asked with a grin. "Nice to see you, too, Charlie. How've you been? I'm great. Thanks for asking."

Charlie glared at him, which was better than the smile with missing teeth. He could have gotten them replaced easily, but he just didn't give a damn. He probably bought his women or used his own pleasure nanobots, so his appearance meant little out here.

"We're after a fugitive—a guy who's been going by Martel lately—who's killed a lot of people, Charlie. A couple of them friends of mine. We're bringing the LLAMs." He hefted the weapon for emphasis.

"I know yer not in d'Core no more, Jupe. You got ner authority ner more, Schroe-deer."

Rico gave the man a shark-eating grin. "Stow it, Charlie. Skulking around out here in the Wastelands, you may not've heard. I was reinstated because of the murder. This Martel guy has Adala connections. Are we going to play nice, or do we have to replay my last visit here?"

147

The man's pale, pockmarked face turned a shade of purple. "Whod'fook you dink you are, Rico? Dis my 'hole."

"That it is. And, you are da'king of diz'hole. But my friends and I have business on your station. Now, I don't think the authorities on Earth and Mars would bother you way out here – unless, of course, they found out you're shipping pleasure nanobots back there. That might upset them enough to send a military cruiser out here to scrub this rock of yours. They get upset when their citizens stop eating … or orgasm themselves to death, you know?"

Harcourt gave him a greasy, sideways glance and leer. "Is not so bad a'way'ta go, ya?" His raspy chuckle seemed lost in the docking bay.

Raheem tapped his cigar and a large section of ash fell to the deck floor. He smiled his most charming smile.

Harcourt snarled, his mood quixotic at best. A palm-sized set of nerves pulsated and jumped on his cheek. "Fook you. Dam baggers. How much, ya? Dockin' fees, station access fees, finders' fees? Eh, how much?"

"One thousand. Ten thousand if I get him. Ya?"

"Five d'ousand. Twenty d'ousand eef you bag 'im. Git off right quick, ya?"

"Two and twelve," Rico countered. "Right quick, ya."

"Four d'ousand and eight'deen. Took me months ta clean oop af'deer da las' dime."

Rico shrugged and nodded. Turning to a Belter with skin the color of dark brown beer and shocking orange hair, Harcourt said, "Take dem to da'dam'ship."

The Belter did not volunteer his name, but there was a flicker of the eyes that passed between Charlie and "Red" that made Rico suspicious over this sudden cooperation. Actually, *more* suspicious would be more accurate. When it came to Charlie Harcourt, Rico did not trust anything the schemer did or said.

Red nodded at Charlie, snarled at them, and led the way to the bay where Martel's ship was berthed. Rico made sure the man was in front of them, and he watched the other doors and corridors for unexpected company along the way.

The Eunomia asteroid housed several attractions in the stark emptiness of the wasteland—an oasis of brutality and depravity. A small space station stuck out of the end of the asteroid as if someone had stuck a pinwheel on top of a cake that had toppled over onto its side. Ships could dock there, and it provided around forty-percent earth gravity as a concession to baggers. One of the really big draws for baggers and Belters alike was Harcourt's showers. The rooms had *real* showers. Since a lot of the rockhoppers did not have centrifugal gravity, showers were not possible. In microgravity, the water would float around and could even drown you. So some of the miners would be pretty ripe by the time they came in, once every few months or so, and they were willing to shell out the credits or barter away some of the ore they'd mined for a hot shower.

Eunomia had two bars. In the pinwheel, just off the hangar bay was Charlie's infamous Hole, where most of the "baggers" socialized. The asteroid proper, if you could use that term for such a nefarious piece of rock, was zero-g—or close enough not to matter—and just the way Belters preferred it. Zeros, named for that very reason, catered to Belters. Both bars were small, one-room affairs where booze and other drugs could be purchased. In the back of each establishment were smaller rooms where sexual encounters could be bought from robots – or even real people if you were willing to pay the premium.

As they followed their escort, Raheem handed Rico his pad. Rico cocked an eyebrow up but took it. Text scrolled across the screen.

"One: D'you want us ta set up an ambush, boss?"

"Two: Are you crazy? And bring all kindsa hell down on m'rock? No. Leave da baggers be. Martel weel take care of dem."

"One: Are you tipping Martel den?"

(No transmission 3.2 seconds.)

"Two: Temptin', ya. Martel pays well, and he's no'un to piss off. But no. Too risky. Rico ez side-by-each. C'mon. Let's go'watch der d'rowdown."

(No transmission 3.0 seconds.)"

The timer continued upward. Rico handed the pad back to Raheem and, with knitted brows, mouthed, "How?"

Raheem winked and pointed at his cigar. Damn, Rico thought. Now, that's a cool toy. There must be fire-resistant nanobots with short-range transmitters inside the cigar. Rico laughed silently and shook his head.

"Stop one bay before Martel's ship," Raheem said to the henchman's back. The guard surveyed them over his shoulder, and his eyes conveyed some emotion between boredom and contempt at the obvious directive. He did, however, stop at an old barrel-shaped rock hauler and wave at the empty bay next door.

"Der she ez."

The guy started to leave and Rico said, "Hold up. You're our guide now. If they're not on the ship, you think Charlie will want us wandering around unescorted?"

Orange-hair made a face and then shrugged. "Right quick, ya?"

"You know my name. Rico. And this is Zavier and Raheem." Zavier gave a thrust of his chin in greeting. Raheem, who was now sitting on the floor and tapping furiously away at his pad, waved but kept typing. "What's your's?" "Louie."

"Okay, Louie. Wait here. We'll make it worth your while. If you want to make even more credits, you can come along for the ride. No disruptors, though."

Rico had seen too many innocent people taken out by the gruesome weapons. They were indiscriminate and could take out certain walls like butter. Maybe it was because he'd grown up on a space station, where windows and walls preserved life, but he preferred the less lethal options.

Louie smirked. "No denks."

Raheem stood up and racked some bullets into his LLAM, held his pad out in front and watched the screen.

Rico double-checked his own weapon. ShockGels loaded, safety off. He flicked on his sight laser. Zavier flexed his hand on his own weapon and Rico said quietly, "Fingers off the trigger until you're ready to shoot."

"I'm ready to shoot now," he whispered, half-serious.

"Not until your target's in sight. You'll do fine. Let us take lead." He asked Raheem, "What are your friends up to?"

"Wait for it." He kept his eyes on his pad. "Two people on board. One female, one male."

"Martel?"

"Can't tell. The digital feed was not clear."

"Then how do you know it was a guy?"

Raheem raised his eyebrows. "He was taking a leak."

"Oh. All right then."

Louie chuckled.

The entrance was on the port side of the ship, closest to them and off the centerline. Before Rico could count to thirty, the hatch opened and the ramp lowered to the ground with a quiet whir.

His eyes fierce and his face drawn in determined lines, Rico said, "Let's burn some ether." They moved forward, and Rico ignored the itch between his shoulder blades as they left Louie behind them. If he were going to burn them, now would be an opportune time. They made it to the ramp without incident, however.

The ship had a butterfly shape to it—wide and curved as a bow along the front, as if the butterfly had folded its wings back slightly. Those front "wings" circled around and gracefully arched around into a second, smaller shaped bow in the rear. He hadn't had time to appreciate the beauty of the design the first time he'd seen it.

The three of them ran toward the ship with the short, bounding leaps of lower gravity. The forty percent gravity of ship's bay was substantially more than the moon, but far less than they all were used to. They moved quickly in and up the ramp. This time, no disruptors greeted them. Raheem fired his weapon twice, and the bullets made a *thwoop* sound as they shot out. A gooey orange substance hit each of the ship's mounted guns with no other apparent effect.

"Nan-bots?" Rico mouthed.

Raheem nodded. Rico pointed at Raheem and then to the right. He pointed at himself and Zavier and indicated they would go left.

When they came to another split, Rico hesitated and then sent Zavier to continue leftward. Rico veered toward the front of the ship where the crew cabin and flight deck would be located.

Tense minutes ticked by as he moved cautiously along narrow corridors. He rolled his shoulders, aware of the tension gripping his muscles. He went through a hatch and turned a corner, and there stood Lara Kohler, her tight cabin suit showing her every curve. She held a wrench as long as her arm, which she promptly launched at him. He ducked, firing off a shot as she ducked around the corner. The jellyfish-shaped ShockGel curved around the corner and he heard a thud and an electric fizzle as the bullet hit. He bounded forward, pushed off the wall, and almost crashed into the closed hatch. His dead ShockGel lay on the deck.

He pushed, and the hatch creaked open. A flurry of non-lethal viber bullets came through the opening, a swarm of angry bees. The synthetic rubber made the bullets ricochet around the corridor. A few of them slapped at him after bouncing off the walls. They stung pretty good, but no more than that. At least she wasn't trying to disrupt his cells, turning them into cytoplasmic jelly. Rico fired two more shots himself and heaved the hatch shut. Maybe the LLAM targeting had established a fix on her DNA. If he got lucky, he'd nail her.

Rico tried the hatch again. This time no viber bullets came zipping through. He pushed the hatch open into a deserted hallway. Moving as quickly as he dared, he followed after her.

If he were Kohler, he'd make his way to the upper level of the crew cabin above him, and double back around behind him. That way, she could try and catch him unaware, pummeling him with the concussive viber bullets until they knocked him unconscious—or hit him with something worse.

He looked for a ladder with an opening to the upper level. When he found one, he leapt up, skipping the first four rungs, and pushed off, soaring the rest of the way up and through the opening like Cometallion, an old comic book superhero he'd read avidly as a kid. Rico pushed distracting thoughts aside.

Kohler was there, but not straight ahead where he'd expected.

The upper level was a plus-shaped intersection, and they ended up surprising each other. She was off to his right side. If he hadn't startled her, she'd have blasted him. As it was, she got the jump on him. She blocked his weapon with one hand. Then she raised her pistol toward his stomach.

Never let go of your weapon was drilled into every soldier. Rico held on tight to his and kicked out hard. Lara's handgun spun away in the low gravity. Kohler's arm slammed into his jaw and pain exploded across his face. He pivoted and brought the LLAM around. Before he could fire, she knocked the nozzle aside. She came at him with a flurry of blows. Rico blocked and ducked. Her blows connected but barely registered. He threw punches and the used the butt of his barrel as well. She brought her right knee up for his groin, but he blocked her with the LLAM. She gasped in pain as her knee hit, and he grabbed her forearm. With a pivot and heave, he tossed her down the opposite corridor. Before she could move, he shot her. Her body jerked from the ShockGel and then settled slowly to the floor.

A few minutes later, Zavier joined him in the flight deck. He hadn't found anything.

A bit after that, Pedro came in with his hands up, Raheem behind him.

"Pedro! My old friend! *¿Qué pasa?*" Rico gave him a warm smile, but the short, round fellow only glared at him. "Lara has been waiting for you." He indicated the unconscious woman drooling in one of the deck chairs. Pedro's eyes widened, but he still kept his tongue from moving.

Rico walked up to him and, shifting from friendly to no nonsense, said, "Where's Martel, or whatever the hell his real name is?"

Pedro considered the question. Then, he probably reviewed his options. Not seeing many, he shrugged. "You got nothin'."

Rico chuckled. "Pedro, Pedro. Nothing?" He

leaned in and his face became a mask of hard lines. "You are implicated in three murders, possible terrorism, corporate spying, and the manufacture and use of universally banned nanobot assassins. You'll be lucky not to get spaced. Think about that, Pedro."

Raheem pushed him into a chair and tied him down with maintenance cables. Rico gestured his two companions into the hallway. They could see both of their captives through the window.

"What's the plan?" Zavier asked.

"For now, we let him sweat. Uncertainty works on a person's brain pretty well. What are you going to do with your share of the AMMATT Prize money, Zavier?"

The big blonde gave a laugh matching his size. "Take a vacation someplace warm, with lots of sand."

"You're going to Mars?"

"Ha, funny. Jamaica or someplace back on Earth. Maybe bring two or three friends. You?"

Rico blew out a breath. "I've always wanted to see the floating cities of Venus. Think I'll head over there." He turned to Raheem, still impeccable in his green suit. "What will you do once this Martel business is done, illustrious Dr. Kuzbari?"

"I shall return to my flat, unplug all the electronic devices, and read fiction for a month. Maybe two."

They continued chatting, and after fifteen minutes, Rico led them back in. A sheen of sweat dotted Pedro's forehead.

"Thinking about being in that airlock, Pedro? The air being sucked back into the ship or station, then the outer doors open into the biting chill of black space." Rico moved out of sight, behind the man, and leaned close to his ear.

"You can't hold your breath, or you'll damage your lungs, so you keep breathing; but you're not taking in any oxygen because there isn't any. You're just breathing it out. Soon, the water around your eyes and on your tongue begins to boil. That's quite uncomfortable, Pedro. Take it from me. I know first hand. Your body begins to ache like it never has before. Your hands will swell to three times their normal size."

He stood up and added in a conversational tone, "But, hey, at least it'll be over quick. Less than a minute once the doors open. You'll pass out. And then you'll be gone. Dead."

Pedro swallowed but kept silent.

"Martel plays his cards pretty close, it seems. You wouldn't be in the picture if he didn't trust you, Pedro. So that tells me you're in this up to your elbows. We've got the nanobots from Hakim's murder and from the station's. We've got the comms between Martel and Lara, we have his fake IDs, and the transactions between Sistema Solera and Vargas. That's just some of what we have, Pedro. You sure your name won't turn up in any of that?" Rico walked behind the captive man and back around to the front. "The best you can hope for is a long, cold stay in Surrentis with the meager hope of parole some time before replen can no longer keep up with the collapse of your body."

Sweat beaded the round man's forehead and trickled down his neck. Rico turned to Raheem and asked, "Dr. Kuzbari, what's the average life expectancy of people these days?"

"Depends on the locale. Close to 200 years. Since the humanitarian accords now require prisoners receive laboratory organs, replen treatments and nanobot preventative care, well, a life sentence can go on longer than many nations last."

"Rico. Please. Man, I can't do that kind of time."

"Well, then, I suppose we could arrange a mindwipe." He watched the color of Pedro's face shift to gray. "Of course, that's a pretty grim prospect, isn't it? I've seen mindwipes. Strange thing. You get a truly fresh start. *Tabula rasa.* A clean slate. But then you won't remember anything except the memories they decide to give you – what they program into your brain. Were you close to your family? Your *mamá*? How about girlfriends? Have you had lots of lovers, Pedro? Did you have a first love? A first kiss? Friends growing up?"

Rico knew he was pressing hard, playing on Pedro's fears. He had no regrets. He wanted Pedro terrified. The man had chosen a life of crime, and they needed to stop Martel.

"Those will all be gone," Raheem stepped smoothly in. "Truly, it is rather amazing how complete the process is. Pretty much everything is gone except for oddities, such as food preferences. An anomaly they ascribe to physical taste receptors. One of the programmers told me that they enjoy downloading their own memories into mindwipe convicts. She told me it gives her a rush and quite the feeling of immortality."

"Most mindwipers get programmed to be boring, meek little sheep, though, don't they, Dr. Kuzbari? Cheap labor for the gas miners and rockhoppers. My understanding is that they're even programmed to enjoy the work."

"Yes, yes," Raheem nodded. "Indeed. There is something about the cheerfulness of a mindwiped individual that makes others both envious and uncomfortable at the same time."

Rico tapped his chin and gazed up at the ceiling. "They call 'em 'government work personalities,' as I recall."

Zavier had turned a little pale at the topic of mindwipes as well. Rico could understand. He couldn't think of many things more horrifying than having his sense of self wiped or scattered or suppressed – whatever the heck mindwiping did. That didn't stop him from pressing Pedro, though. "True. They never seem quite … normal, I guess, after that. I understand there's some theological debate as to what happens to the soul of a mindwipe as well. If the personality, thought, experiences, and emotions of a person are completely overwritten, does the *soul* of that person still exist? Heck, the courts even declare you legally dead, so your heirs can write you off and then inherit."

"¡Jesús! Rico. For the love of God. Don't let 'em mindwipe me. Throw me out an airlock first. Ain't no point in living if I'm not me anymore." He hit his chest with his fist. "I want to die a man, not some zombie." The man wrung his hands and his machismo collapsed back into fear. "Get me parole if I help you, okay, man?"

Rico gave him a dead stare and waited him out. "Please!" Pedro begged.

"Raheem, would you record this on your pad?"

Raheem pulled it out and set it on a console.

Rico nodded at Pedro. "I'll see what I can do. No guarantees. Start talking."

"He's meeting a buyer. In in one of the private rooms. We come here a lot."

"Which bar? The Hole or Zeros?"

"Zeros. In the back rooms. In the Floaters' rooms."

Floaters was slang for Belters, and one they might well kill you for using. Floaters had an Earth slang definition of "drowning victims," and the negative connotation had carried over into space. Funny, though, how Belter's would sometimes call *other* people—outsiders—floaters.

Pedro kept talking. "Guy's a regular. He bought some of our … I mean, Martel's military nanobots last year. Now he wants the antimatter."

Rico kept the same expression on his face, but mentally cringed at the revelation that the nanobot assassins were out in the criminal world, but he supposed it had been too much to hope for that such a potent weapon could be kept under wraps. That was going to change the playing field quite a bit.

"Is he part of Adala?"

"Martel? No. He's a businessman. A freelancer. He sees opportunities and he takes them."

"He's got enough cash to front this whole enterprise?"

Pedro shook his head. "No, Adala fronted the money."

Rico lip curled up in irritation, and the shorter man hurriedly added, "He's worked for Adala, but he's not part of them."

Raheem broke in, "If Adala fronted the money, why is Martel meeting a buyer?"

Pedro shifted his feet, glanced sideways, and then said, "He's, uh, making a little side transaction."

"Brave bugger," Zavier mumbled.

Rico agreed. Pissing off Adala was either incredibly brave or crazy stupid. "What's Martel's real name?" Rico asked.

Pedro shrugged. "Dunno."

Rico didn't buy it. "Seriously, Pedro? You fly with the guy, and you don't know his name? Quit venting oxygen."

"I don't, man, I swear. I've heard him use at least six names, but I couldn't tell you if any one of them is his real one."

"The buyer's name?"

"Santiago Smith."

"All right. Raheem, can you keep the ship and these two under wraps, and see what else you can find out?" He wanted to bring Raheem instead of Zavier, since the former man's martial art skills would be better in a low-g fight, but he knew how dangerous – and valuable – Lara and Pedro were. He didn't want to risk them getting away.

Raheem paused, weighing the scenarios and options and then gave a nod. "Indeed."

"Zavier, buckle up."

- FIFTEEN -

Rico and Zavier picked up Louie outside the ship, and the Belter led them out of the pinwheel; they rode a pneumatic tube from the station into the asteroid. The pneumatic tubes, incredibly efficient in space, always reminded Rico of giant slides or a frozen lasso.

When they entered Zeros, the bartender, a metallic green hospitality robot, nodded, photoreceptor lens reflecting garish colored lights. "No weapons allowed without a permit, gentlemen. You can pay the fees here."

Rico ignored the 'bot for the moment, taking in the room first. Lights bolted into rough-hewn rock provided a kind of emaciated illumination. Most of the light came from a mic-rel coating that made one wall shift colors and scenes. Snow covered mountains followed a beach on earth, then Rico recognized one of the moons of Jupiter.

The room was basically a large tunnel, a straight shot carved through the rock by an asteroid borer. The tunnel had never even been squared off, so the rounded floor and ceiling, at least from Rico's perspective, gave the impression that the room had no "up" or "down."

From his last visit Rico remembered the tables sprouting from every angle of the tunnel like mushrooms. A grizzled-looking fellow halfway down the tunnel glared at them with open hostility. He appeared to be seated at a table hanging upside down.

Each table had a movie or news show playing across its surface. Smells assaulted the senses – old puke, piss, space-dry rock, the heavy musky-sweat of unwashed miners, the pungent smell of various smoked drugs. The sick-sweet scent of spilled booze, sweat, and smokes floated like an oily mist that the filters couldn't quite expunge. Probably why Harcourt had a robot bartender. No one else could stand the cloying-sour stink. Even nanobot cleaners never seemed to get the smell out of a Belter bar.

There were more than two-dozen people in the room, a lot for a Belter establishment. Harcourt sponsored fights in a small arena the first week of each month, and everyone within range knew about it. There would be a lot of drinking, drugging, betting, and bedding going on over the next week. He noted that several of the patrons carried visible weapons.

The rest probably carried weapons as well.

"Belters," Zavier said. "Crazy as damned grease-rats."

"Space-you-too," Louie said.

"Cool it, both of you. We don't want any trouble in here. Got it, Zavier?" The last thing they needed was Zavier antagonizing a room full of armed rock-jocks.

The Thor-lookalike snarled, detracting from his chiseled features. "Yeah, yeah," he said. "Let's get on with it."

"Louie?"

"Side-by-each."

Same phrase Harcourt had used a while ago. He'd never had it explained, and it seemed to have multiple meanings. It always came up in situations where it probably meant, "in alignment," "in agreement," or simply, "okay."

Perpendicular to the tunnel, a smaller indentation had been carved out as well. In typical irreverent manner, the Belters called this the chancel. The chancel held a circular steel cage, like a giant gerbil wheel. With mag-shoes, the bartender could stand on the floor, sides, or "ceiling." In the center of the gerbil wheel, a smaller bar-wheel with magnetic bottles held the booze. Glowing nanobots made the bottles of liquor shimmer and swirl with light and patterns. The gerbil wheel and the bar-wheel could both be moved by the bartender, and some of them, human and robot bartenders alike, could entertain with their theatrics, spinning and mixology.

Rico answered the android. "Talk to Charlie Harcourt. We already paid."

"Is'okay, Moriarty," Louie said. "Dey'z wid me. Charlie sez dey can 'ave der'run of da'sheep."

"Ship. Not sheep," Zavier muttered. "I'm not interested in any electric sheep. Thanks, though."

Rico tensed, expecting some explosion from Louie. A Belter could easily take offense over such a smartass remark. They were a touchy lot, but they also had a sense of humor, so you never knew which way they might float.

Louie, fortunately, just laughed, and asked, "Dat mean you like real sheep?"

The robot, programmed to accommodate, said, "I'm sorry, sir. We have no cybernetic or biological sheep available."

Zavier turned red and sputtered. Rico laughed. Even a few people nearby chanced a smile. Robots.

The perfect straight men. Rico watched the humanoid 'bot and the rest of the crowd as he crossed the room, and they watched them in turn.

"My apologies, sirs. Your fee was not applied to weapons. That has been corrected."

At the far end of the room, a round vault blocked their way. Louie touched an access lock, and the door opened with a hiss.

Another round corridor waited on the other side, but narrower here. Handholds and footholds spiraled along the corridor from "floor" to "ceiling" assuring some sort of anchor or leverage point every meter or so. With an occasional pull or kickoff, they floated down the hallway, wraiths in search of victims.

When they came to the first door on the left, Rico gestured for Louie to open it up. "He'z down'dere. He rented the last du rooms on da'right."

"Great," Rico said. They moved down to the last two hatches. "Open this one."

While Louie moved up to the touchlock, Rico nudged Zavier's arm and pointed at Louie's back and then his own eyes. Watch him, he mouthed. When Zavier nodded, Rico pointed up and down the hallway and again at his own eyes. Zavier gave him a thumbs up.

The hatch opened into the corridor and Rico pulled himself into the threshold. He knew immediately that he had the wrong room. All kinds of straps and fasteners attached to the walls, and some stretched across the width of the round room. The cords spread out as if he'd entered a giant spider's lair, designed to entertain and entrap copulating acrobats. A naked client hung in what looked like an incredibly uncomfortable position.

Beneath him, a syn-skin, lying on a bed floating in the center of the room and adorned with red silky sheets, turned her head and met Rico's eyes. She looked perfectly human. Emphasis on perfect. Her pearlescent lingerie concealed just enough to stimulate the imagination. She wet her lips and said, in a husky, sexy voice, "Hello. My name is Rhondell. What's *your* name?"

Amused, Rico said, "Hi. Sorry, wrong room. My apologies for the interruption. The next six hours are on the house." He closed the hatch and then locked the pair in with Louie's employee access code. Personally, Rico didn't go in for syn-skin androids; he preferred his women real – and not paid for with credits.

"Six hours? You probably just killed that guy, you know," Zavier said, and Rico heard the nerves behind the joke.

"Nah. The 'skins have safety protocols. I think. Next," Rico said, pointing to a doorway that, from their perspective, was directly overhead.

"You sure? Martel's ner gonna like youz inter'rooptin' him and hez clientz."

Rico gave him a flat smile and gestured at the door. Louie shook his head as if to say, "It's your ass on the line." He unlocked the hatch with his palm and then pulled it "down" and open with a push-off against the wall. He swung down and to the side like a kid riding a swing. The door pointed down now, with Rico and Zavier staring "up" and into the room. Nine sets of eyes gaped down at them. Eight men and one woman waited inside with an assortment of weapons. Smoke from various 'rettes filled the air. Tobacco, pot, and rojo were most evident.

Rico spotted Martel at the rear of the room. "Air and Space Corps. We only want—"

Apparently they didn't want to listen. Someone yelled, "Hey!"

Everyone opened fire. Bullets slammed against Rico's kinetic suit, and he fired back. He heard the sizzle and crackle as one or more of his ShockGels made contact.

Louie had strategically placed the heavy door between himself and any ruffians inside. He also wisely kept his hands in view, so Rico and Raheem would not shoot him.

"Close it!" Rico yelled.

As Louie pushed against the "ceiling" to close the door, the greasy ripple of a disruptor beam narrowly missed Rico.

Zavier wasn't as lucky. He started screaming, his pain shredding the air more than gunfire. Rico had been in firefights before. Nothing compared to the devastation of disruptors. Rico couldn't spare a glance. Had to move fast. He flicked a switch on his LLAM. He selected Doppel-banger and pulled the trigger. The rifle slammed into his shoulder and fired up into the room. Rico heard swearing in multiple languages. Then the door slammed shut with a loud click.

A muffled explosion inside the room vibrated the walls. Dust shook loose and drifted around them.

A dark red globe—perfectly round to the human eye—floated into his field of vision. He knew instantly who it was from. As he turned to see the source, Zavier's silence filled him with dread.

Zavier drifted, slack-jawed, most of the hand and part of the wrist missing. A bubbled, charred lump with bone stuck out, along with the thumb and index finger. Rico felt his gorge rise and clamped down the reaction. Zavier'd been lucky. The disruptor must have only grazed him before eating away a sizable chunk of the stonewall. The cellular failure had stopped, but blood still squirted out with every heartbeat, and he would die if Rico didn't seal it. He popped a filler-pad from the base of his LLAM and kicked off the wall to get to Zavier, stretched the pad over the wound and activated it. The putty-like substance quadrupled in size in seconds, and the compressing, numbing, and antimicrobial agents went to work. Still unconscious, Zavier moaned in relief. Zavier also had a nasty gash on his forehead where a bullet must have grazed him. Rico patched that up and then examined his own body.

Several anchor bullets clung to his outer clothing as prickers would. The barbed legs that had flicked out like miniature harpoons just before impact were bent and twisted in his clothing. Although they were ideal for preventing bullets from passing through a body they were mostly ineffective against kin-suits. Unless of course, they were rigged to explode. If these had been, though, he'd be dead already. He shed his outer clothing, just in case the flattened anchors had poison in them.

"Hang in there, Zavier," Rico murmured.

Louie helped Rico strap Zavier to an indent hold, and then they opened the hatch to sort out Martel, Smith, and the lackeys. As expected, the room was a mess of vomit and noxious smoke from the Doppel-banger. One of the guards made a move for his disruptor and Rico zapped him with a ShockGel. A quick survey of the room revealed seven people. Martel and one other person had disappeared.

#

The room had a back door, through which Martel and Santiago Smith must have escaped.

"It would have been helpful to know about the back exit before we went in," Rico said.

Louie shrugged. "You didna ask. 'Sides, dey all got exits, ya?"

"Where does it go?"

"Anywhere you want."

"That's not an ans–"

Screeching alarms cut him off, and a smartwall nearby flicked on. Martel's face came online, and the visage of a disapproving parent filled the screen.

"Attention anyone within range of this signal. My associate was supposed to input a security code into my ship every fifteen minutes. He has failed to do so. When he didn't, it started a timer. In less than fourteen minutes, a matter-antimatter explosion will destroy the ship, the docking bay, and anything attached to the docking bay. That includes this asteroid." Martel leaned towards the camera and, in a stage whisper said, "That means it will go boom." He mimed the explosion with his hands and made a 'Boucch!' noise. "Oh, and once the countdown activated, the security code changed, so my associate's code will no longer work. He won't be able to help you."

Martel smiled. "We apologize for any inconvenience. Have a nice day." The screen went blank.

Rico set the timer on his wrist computer for thirteen minutes. As he was finishing, his wrist comm chirruped. "Yeah, Raheem. We saw it, too. On my way," he said and cut the link. He started unstrapping Zavier.

"Wait," Louie said.

Rico paused and glanced at the Belter.

"Martel. I recognized the conduits behind heem. I dink hez goin to his odder sheep."

"Other ship? Where?"

"Lower berths."

"Son of a Martian."

Rico knew about the lower berths. They were private bays for smuggling out the pleasure bots. Even way out here, it paid to protect your assets.

Rico thought about it but didn't see many options. "Take Zavier back to Raheem on the *Scimitar*." Then he added, "You'll probably want to evacuate the station."

"You dink?" Louie gave him a dry look. "Ya."

"What about these guys?"

Louie punched some numbers into the touchpad. "Lockdown."

Harsh, but fitting. If the asteroid blew, they'd go with it. Rico didn't have time to argue the niceties of ethics. He took off at a run, trusting the tall Belter to drag the floating and unconscious Zavier back to Raheem like a barge towing a cruiser.

A moment later, he called Raheem as he bounce-ran through the corridors. He filled him in on Zavier and Martel, then asked, "Any ideas for handling that bomb?"

"I don't suppose you've got a working teleport device?"

"Not quite, spy-man."

"I was afraid of that. Guess we'll have to do this the hard way. You're not going to like it."

Rico grimaced. "Hit me."

"We'll thruster out and then couple the *Amazing Grace* to the *Scimitar*. We'll fly out as far as we can, and then I'll try to separate the two ships. Hopefully, we'll be far enough away so that Eunomia won't become a charred husk, and we'll still have enough time to get away from the *Scimitar* as well."

Rico shook his head. Their odds were not good. Without any atmosphere, they should be able to separate without incident—unless the ships rotated and one impacted the other. If that happened, then Martel's antimatter bomb would be a two-for-one, and *The Amazing Grace* would be an amazing new star instead. "Who's flying?"

"Me ... and Zavier."

"Great." Zavier would be stoned out of his gourd on stims and painkillers, but what other choice did they have?

Rico cut the comm and ran on in the gazelle-like style mandated by microgravity. He followed the guide lights Louie had called up on the wall panels. There were not as many as on a real space station, and he lost valuable time at intersections finding the next panel.

Finally, he reached the hangar where Martel's

second ship should have been. He was too late. Only an empty hangar bay and the vacuum of space waited on the other side of the hatch.

Rico clenched a fist and resisted punching the door, since it would only hurt his hand. He went to a wall panel and hit the comm. "Schroeder to Harcourt."

"What?" came the abrupt reply.

"I need a ship. Lower berths, right now."

Harcourt glowered at him with hooded eyes. "Dis your fault. Should vent you now."

"Charlie. Eighteen k, remember? Plus, you can keep any credits we get off Martel."

Harcourt considered. "Da'bomb?"

"Raheem is going to fly it out as soon as Louie gets back to him."

"Thirty thousand credits, plus all Martel's, ya?"

"Thirty k. Deal." Rico said immediately. Thirty thousand credits would put a big dent in his savings, and he had no idea if he would get it reimbursed, but at this point, he didn't care. He wanted this guy.

"Ya, deal. Bay eight."

Harcourt cut the link. Rico felt a grim satisfaction. He wasn't out of it yet. *I'm coming for you, Martel.*

#

The ship, called the *Red Beetle*, was an old core sampler meant for grabbing hold of an asteroid and drilling into it. Since it needed to find candidates for further mining as quickly as possible, it was reasonably fast, despite its age, and loaded with sensors.

Martel's backup-ship would undoubtedly be stealthed, but at least it wouldn't have an antimatter drive. Probably. Rico had a hard time imagining how he might have pulled that off. When he arrived at the hangar, a droid had the ship warmed up and ready. Harcourt had already sent him telemetry on Martel's escape route. The hard-edged Belter had apparently put a tracker on the ship.

"Does everybody tag ships these days?" Rico said aloud.

Raheem's voice came over Rico's wrist comm; he had looped him in. "*Scimitar* to Eunomia," he said, using the official name of the asteroid. "Engaging engines in ten seconds."

Rico had long enough to wonder if Martel's ship was rigged to explode on ignition. Then red lights flashed on smartwalls and sirens shrieked, ripping up and down the hallways. Rico grabbed a handhold and stopped, bracing himself as much as he could. The loud clangor drilled into his head. Did the ship explode? Was the rotating station still there? Were they even now hemorrhaging atmosphere into space, or did emergency hatches do their job?

The lights and alarm stopped, leaving a ringing in his ears. Harcourt's angry voice went out system-wide over every resonant crystal in the asteroid. "Stand down. Idiot hit da'bay frame on da way out."

Probably Zavier. The effects of the drugs were dragging him. Rico switched to system map view on his smartwall to check their progress. He watched as the ships merged and then shot across the screen, impossibly fast.

Rico turned his attention back to his own

problems. He was closing in on Martel's second ship. The display listed the ship's name as the *Kukri*. This one was smaller, and normally wouldn't have any weapons to speak of. With Martel, he wouldn't bet on it. Unfortunately, the driller definitely had no weapons, which left him with limited options for making the fugitive heave to.

He came in above the ship and used the short range comm. "Martel this is Schroeder. Cut your engines now. You can't hide from these sensors."

No response, as expected. This part of his plan was the riskiest part, probably. He was going to collide with Martel's ship. Not quite ramming him, but more a hard slam. If he was lucky, they wouldn't both blow up. Between Raheem's little adventure and his own, Eunomia might have quite a show.

Rico turned the ship down and into Martel's trajectory. He kept on until the ship jolted, and then he activated the grappling legs. Six articulated arms extended and tried to grab hold of what the computer thought was an asteroid. They missed. Rico, his mouth set in a grim line, eased in again until the ship hit with a loud bang and rocked sideways. He turned into it and hit the grapplers a second time.

The claws dug into the ship as if it were some predator from prehistoric earth.

"Asteroid secured."

"Power down, Martel, or I'm cutting right through your hull."

No response.

Rico turned on the robotic arms and moved the drill into position. He'd already prepared the, "Drill core sample" command.

"You've got thirty seconds to cut engines."

No answer. Okay then. Rico activated the drill and atmosphere leaked slowly out of Martel's ship as the drill cut through metal and plas. By the time the drill cut a large enough hole for Rico to board, airflow had ceased. A special miners' lockdown tube automatically sealed tightly into place.

Since he didn't want all of his air going over to the other ship, he put on a quick-skin and grabbed a helmet. He was almost at the lockdown tube when a thought occurred to him. He went back and locked out the computer controls. No sense making it easy if Martel still lived.

Rico entered the cramped tube, LLAM held out in front of him as he wriggled between the two ships as if a salmon climbing up a space station's fish ladder. If Martel was still alive, and he had shown himself too resourceful so far to not be, then Rico would be easy pickings in the docking tube. Like shooting fish in a barrel, he thought, continuing his fishing theme.

No gun appeared in the tube between the two ships, however. Rico made his way carefully past the razor sharp edges the drill left behind. The borehole brought him into the common area. Twisted curls of metal and plastic surrounded the breach. He moved slowly since the filings and shavings could cut his suit if he was not careful.

Debris from the hull and the ship floated in the airless compartment. He moved into the bow of the ship. A food tube glided past his visor. Then he saw the frozen orbs of ruby ice. Small crystal globes of blood danced a slow, macabre ballet. The drops floated along, chance collisions occurring, making them bounce off in different trajectories as if marbles, a mockery of their once life-bearing role.

The amount of blood made Rico feel like he was inside a madman's snow globe. And that triggered another thought. Something wasn't right. Why would there be so much blood? The depressurization wouldn't have made Martel bleed, at least not to this extent.

The body was strapped into the pilot's seat, head hanging down. Someone had bolted a powerful handheld rock cutter to the chair on the far side near the pilot's right shoulder.

The pilot had been bound to the chair with bright yellow cargo webbing. He noticed the hands clutching the armrests: blue, oxygen-deprived hands gleamed in the dim panel lights, and fingers dug into the soft upholstery.

Tears were frozen on the man's cheeks. Blood had burst from the eyes and nose and ears. In the zero-g, it had not run down but had simply drifted out until the heart had stopped pumping. Then the blood supply had simply stopped, leaving specks of blood visible on the edge of each orifice. Hoarfrost covered the bare flesh. Rico's heart pounded. He whipped around, alert for some unseen threat, expecting an attack at any moment.

None came, and he double-checked his first impression. The body strapped to the chair was definitely not Ted Martel's.

Rico circled around the chair. A gaping neck wound explained the blood floating around the cabin. A look at the controls showed that the ship's computer had been programmed to fire the cutter when the air pressure dropped.

Martel had struck again.

#

Rico marked the ship's location, set up an Air and Space Corps lock code and auto-message warning off anyone who attempted to open the ship, and headed back to his loaner ship. He put a call out to Zavier and Raheem, but no one answered. He recorded a message and sent it out, hoping they would pick it up.

Their silence was troubling.

He called station control, and got Harcourt himself, but the Belter had little to report. The ships had taken off, heading out-system. At the moment, the two ships were still coupled together and had not yet reached the coordinates for separation that he and Raheem had worked out.

"All right. Listen, Charlie, Martel was not on this ship. Santiago Smith is out here, and he's been iced."

Harcourt grunted. "I dink yer friends are in trouble, Schroedeer."

"Yeah. Me too."

And there was damn little he could do about it. Several scenarios went through his head, none of them good. "I'm on my way back." He cut the comm and engaged the thrusters. Minutes later, a comm came in, location blocked. He hit accept and a familiar face appeared on the screen.

"Hello, Rico. You've been a busy man," Martel said. Rico could not tell from the background if Martel was still on Eunomia or if he'd boarded yet another ship.

Rico considered what to say. He didn't know the status of either Zavier or Raheem; he did not want to put the spotlight on Zavier, if he was still alive. "Yes. Sorry about interrupting your business deal."

Martel shrugged. "My business was concluded." He pursed his lips and shook his head. "Such a shame about Santiago, though. He was a good customer."

"Why'd you kill him?"

"Me? I didn't kill him. *You* did when you boarded his vessel. Quite sad."

"Smith provided a nice distraction for you. Where are you now? Let's get together, face to face."

Martel chuckled and gave a slight nod. "I must say, I did not expect anyone to board the ship so quickly. That was quite brave. Stupid, but brave."

"Lara told me about the autopilot trap on the *Scimitar*, Martel. It's not going to work. We sent the two ships out on the *Amazing Grace's* autopilot. The *Scimitar* is not going to blow up. At least not that way."

Martel's olive complexion went flat and stony. "Don't," he said, biting at the word. "Don't insult me, Schroeder." Martel walked away from the screen and another cam picked him up automatically. He was looking down and ignoring Rico.

Rico couldn't do anything except wait, so he hit some buttons on his own screen and put the *Red Beetle* on autopilot back to the asteroid.

Zavier's face appeared inset on Rico's screen with the border, "Incoming Message." Rico checked on Martel, and he was still typing and ignoring Rico.

He hit mute on Martel and then accept on Zavier's.

"Rico, where have you been? I can't raise Raheem, and I'm going to have to cut the *Scimitar* loose soon, if I'm going to have any chance of getting away from the blast radius." His voice sounded strained.

"I sent you a message. Didn't you get it?"

"No. This comm is the first to come through."

Something didn't sound right about that. "Wait. What do you mean, 'come through?' What are you talking about, Zavier?" Rico asked, hesitating over his words as his brain tried to play catch up.

"Your comm. It's the first one to come through since we launched."

"Zave. I didn't comm you." Rico glanced down at the inset screen, and Martel smiled at him across thousands of kilometers of space. The threat leaped out at him all at once. "Zave, get out of there! Now! Martel's on the *Scimitar*. Go!"

Zavier's hands were already flying fast. "Right. Got it."

Martel's face disappeared, and the inset screen's view switched to an outside camera. From this angle, Rico could see the thrusters of the *Amazing Grace* blasting away even as the clamps were still retracting. She fell away like a whale breaching out of an ocean. He watched as she receded away from the view screen.

He watched in tense horror, knowing something terrible was about to happen. Martel's face appeared again on the screen. "Eventually," he said, "antimatter weapons will become the new standard in destruction, held by the powerful few, of course, since antimatter still won't be overly plentiful. However, for now, we'll just have to rely on old-fashioned lasers."

"No!" Rico grabbed the console, but what could he do? Nothing. He watched, horrified. He saw a flare, as if from a flash camera, come off the ship's hull, and then the *Amazing Grace* erupted into a ball of fire.

The ship—and Zavier—were gone.

Rico clenched his jaw so tightly that his teeth creaked. He glared at the screen.

Martel continued talking, the words bouncing off Rico's numb brain. "I thought you would want the opportunity to see Mr. Sorrenguard off to eternity. Don't worry about Dr. Kuzbari, though. I know you two have become such good friends. Unfortunately for you, he has been assisting us all along." Martel stepped back and gestured, and the smart screen shifted view to Raheem. Lara sat in his lap. The man he had been beginning to think of as his friend smiled at the screen.

Lara laughed and kissed his cheek. His hand tapped on her leg with familiar affection. Rico felt sick. It wasn't the first time he'd been played, but it cut deep, a thrust to the gut. He'd just started to trust Raheem. He'd even stuck his neck out for him with Uesugi. He'd been screwed over by people a few times now. It didn't shock him, just created a slow burn in his stomach.

Martel started speaking and the ship's AI shifted the camera from Raheem back to the leader of their merry little band. "I thought you'd want to know Raheem is safe and doing well."

Spots of anger flickered before Rico's eyes. Flashes of white and dark. A stabbing pain hit him behind the eye, inside of his head. Rico had never had a migraine, but it felt as if this must be worse.

Martel gaze surveyed his control room, his assembled crew, and then turned back to Rico. Martel, Pedro, Lara, and Raheem watched him, as if posing for some demented family portrait. Raheem continued to tap on Lara's leg, playing percussion to some tune only he could hear, and she wriggled sensually against him. "Well, Rico, we bid you farewell," Martel said. "We have assassin-bots and antimatter to peddle." He walked up to the screen, ostensibly to cut the comm, but really just to make his face imposingly large.

"Are you okay? You don't look so good, Rico." Martel cut the comm.

#

Rico Schroeder stared at the blank screen. Zavier's death and Raheem's betrayal left a flat, hollow spot inside his gut. He tried to think what to do, but he was stuck on a slow ship to nowhere. Even once he got back there was no way to catch up to Martel's ship. He was out of options, for now.

Eventually, though, he'd catch up to Martel and Raheem. And then there would be hell to pay.

Rico sent out a coded message. He didn't feel like talking to anyone.

TO: Kita Uesugi, Reuben Holt, and Inés Villaverde.
FROM: Federico Schroeder

Martel escaped. Lara Koehler and Pedro with him. Raheem Kuzbari betrayed us. Put out an Arrest on Sight.

Amazing Grace destroyed. Zavier didn't make it. Will comm from Eunomia once I get back there.

- Rico

He turned on the autopilot, and closed his eyes. He didn't think he would sleep, but exhaustion, the migraine, and grief won out. He slept deeply until something jarred him awake. Instantly, he jerked into alert mode, thoughts flipping through his mind like rifled playing cards. He thought what any space farer thinks under impact: collision. Meteoroid. Ship. Hull integrity. He rubbed his eyes, blinking and tried to make sense of the controls. The autopilot had docked the ship on Eunomia was all. After a few seconds, he relaxed, but with everything that had happened he felt dragged out, almost hung over.

Rico unstrapped, pulled himself around the seat and hopped in the low-g over to the hatch. A droid greeted him and started hooking hoses up to the docked ship.

Schroeder decided he needed a beer before trying to find a ride back to Jupiter system. Perhaps he could get the one along with the other, but he'd had enough of low-g for a while, so he headed for the Hole.

He had gone through three auto-hatches when the first spasm hit him. A gut-wrenching convulsion of pain doubled him over. His breathing came in short gasps. A nearby smartwall snapped on.

"Hello, Rico," Martel said. "How are you feeling?" He gave Rico a knowing smile. "Headache? Trouble breathing? Blurred vision?"

Rico didn't respond. *Couldn't* respond. Another wracking paroxysm ripped through him and he vomited. Suddenly, he could no longer breathe. His throat felt constricted. He was dying. Martel had won.

"My nanobots targeted you the moment you set foot on my ship, Captain Schroeder. Latched onto your DNA and waited for you to return to Eunomia. Now, you are dying." The smiled snapped off as if a viewport shield had slammed into place. "This is your payment for interfering with my plans. And, don't worry, the nanobots will give you plenty of time to regret your interference. Farewell."

Rico would have laughed if he'd had the air. Hysteria or lack of oxygen? He wasn't sure. He wanted to claw at his throat, rip it open. Instead, he tried to think of a way out. He needed one of those pulse things that Raheem had used in the lab, but he had no way of getting one before it was too late.

Rico closed his eyes. There was simply no justice in life. He gasped for air. Gasped again. His stomach heaved and he vomited again.

The hatch at the end of the corridor opened and through blurry vision, he saw Louie coming toward him.

"Lou–" He gave up trying to talk and sucked in a breath instead. He let go of the wall and started to move toward the tall Belter, but Louie raised his weapon and pointed it at Rico. In a reflexive gesture, Rico stopped and raised his hands to protect himself.

"Sorry, Rico," Louie said. Then Louie shot him.

A ShockGel hit him in the chest, his body arced backwards, and his muscles contracted into rigid, bucking cables. His legs spasmed and kicked rapidly. Someone had clearly stuck a vibrating knife in his chest. An electric knife that was on fire.

Definitely no justice, he thought, right before his brain short-circuited and he passed out.

- SIXTEEN -

Rico woke up in what might charitably be called a medical bay. He floated in fluid in a med pod. Storage bins were piled in one corner. Odd scaffolding frames were battened against one wall. He felt disoriented and wrung out, as if he'd been on one heck of a bender. Then he remembered that he had docked on Eunomia, and Louie had shot him. He tried opening the translucent med pod, and an alarm started chirping, low but insistent. A medical droid that was the twin of the one at Zeros, but with a metallic orange surface the color of burning embers, appeared from an adjoining area. "Please remain calm, Mr. Schroeder, and I will open the pod." Her voice had a distinct female tone. "Your vital signs are within acceptable parameters."

Rico grunted. Why would he be panicked? "I was hit by a ShockGel, not a bullet." "Where is Louie? Why did he shoot me?" The robot opened the large container and held out a flat-metal-gray hand. The dull color contrasted with the burnt orange chrome of the rest of the android's body. He stepped out of the tank, and the ambio-fluid sluiced back into the tank, leaving his clothes completely dry. His body felt akin to Jell-O.

"You do not recall the infestation?"

"Infes–. What?"

"Infestation." The medical bot's voice had a subtle and intentional electronic quality that actually made the robot more personable rather than less. "You had over one hundred thousand nanobots in your body. Their programming directed them to constrict your airway considerably and to attack the central nervous system. Apparently, the programmer wanted you to experience a slow and painful death."

Rico's brain still felt sluggish, but the memories rushed back. The assassin bots. Martel's taunting message. The pain. Rico's heart rate spiked at the memory, and the medical equipment started chirruping with an insistent alarm.

A robotic arm near the medical pod drew a blue liquid into a syringe and maneuvered toward him. Rico leaned away and spoke rapidly to the med bot.

"Easy. I'm okay. I need to keep a clear head." The arm retracted and Rico said, "What's the current status?"

"The ShockGel temporarily incapacitated the invasive nanobots. While they were inert, I removed them. You are free of all nanobots, including your normally administered medical bots."

"Great. I can live with that. Thanks."

"You are welcome, Captain Schroeder. You will want to have your regular regimen of nanobots replaced as soon as possible. When you are feeling up to it, Mr. Harcourt and Louie await you in Mr. Harcourt's private residence."

He quirked an eyebrow. However, if Louie or Charlie wanted to kill him, he'd be dead already. In fact, he apparently owed them his life. That was an odd twist.

He drifted off for a bit. He didn't know how long. His close call, getting shot, and whatever drugs the medbot had pumped into him made his thoughts fly off in random orbits.

For the second time, Martel had pulled out assassin bots. There was no way they could contain this. Once news broke, it would be on every cube in the sector. Hysteria would break out. Paranoia. Assaults. Maybe another cold war between Earthers and outworlders and spacers. Definitely increased tensions between Arabs and non-Arabs, even though all the Arab nations and space habitats had signed the Trans-Terran Protocol banning assassin-bots. That treaty had been a banner moment in human history, right up there with banning nerve gas and nukes.

There would probably be riots. Best-case scenario, a lot of people were going to die.

And that thought reminded him of Zavier, with a pang of regret. He'd miss the pigheaded giant. First time he'd met him, Zavier had said, "Hello, Rico. I'm Zavier Sorrenguard. I'm going to make you a very wealthy man." He'd been referring to the fact that he was going to pilot *The Amazing Grace*, but what an arrogant piece of work.

That led him back to Dr. Raheem Kuzbari, man of mystery and crime-fighting partner until a little while ago. Apparent spy for Adala. He had an arrogance of his own, but of a more subtle sort. Audacious, maybe? Son of a Martian, he hated misjudging people's character. He'd been fairly certain he could trust Raheem, and apparently he'd been wrong. Again.

He could count on one hand the big betrayals he'd experienced, but each had left him more jaded toward people. Rico knew people who had descended into anger or addiction or psychosis from betrayals. He hadn't, but he did have to fight harder to open up and trust after each one. You moved on. You became friends or lovers or enemies, but did you ever really trust the same way again? Hard to say.

He was angry at himself, but he was angrier with Raheem. His betrayal had led to the death of Zavier and the loss of the *Amazing Grace*. Now, both were gone, and Martel had the fastest known ship in the solar system. And, although small in comparison, odds were he would not get reimbursed the credits he'd promised Harcourt for the ship either.

Maybe that was why Louie incapacitated him, Rico thought wryly: Harcourt wanted to make sure he got his credits. Rico chuckled. Whatever the reason, Louie shooting him had saved his life. Time to find out why Harcourt had decided he was worth saving when he could have just let him die.

He thanked the droid and left the medical bay, which was right near Harcourt's entertainment arena. He made his way back to the main tunnel, out past Zeros, and almost to the rotating hangar bay. Rico had never been in Harcourt's private quarters, but he knew they were on the end of the asteroid, for easy access to Control and the hangar bay. Other than the massive security bots outside the door, it was easy to get there. The security bots, however, posed an imposing barrier. They seemed comparable to mechanized spiders fused with insane autokitchens. Appendages akin to knives and can-openers could be seen, as could muzzles for releasing various weaponry—disruptor beams and lasers among them.

Harcourt must have been waiting for him, however. One of the bots spoke with an electronic buzz. "Good morning, Captain Schroeder," and then skittered to one side to get out of his way; the others followed suit. He'd never trusted those bots. Creepy, but he supposed that was the point.

The hatch opened automatically, and Rico walked into such opulence as he had never seen on a Belter habitat before. Harcourt clearly had a good gig going here with his fighting ring and catering to the illicit desires of lonely asteroid miners. Not much else to spend money on this far out in space, and nowhere else to really spend it. And all of that was probably small change compared to his illegal pleasure-bot trade.

The first room was absolutely huge and perfectly spherical. What shocked the senses, however, was that the concentric rings of a giant armillary sphere filled the whole first room. Rico counted thirteen gold or brass rings that rotated slowly around the spherically carved room. Round cars rode those rings reminiscent of rides at a carnival. Instead of chairs, each car had donut-shaped cushions. Some of these cars had tables, others did not. Embedded in the rings were brilliant jewels lit underneath casting out subtle shards of light. Large chunks of colored glass, maybe as big as Rico's chest, had been rough-cut and inlaid into the stonewall. These, too, had lighting underneath them. Deep ruby, midnight blue sapphire, icy topaz, amber-citrine, and the green of peridot glowed at him. They were too large to be real, but they were impressive. In the center, a gold metal globe reflected the lights back out at the inhabitants. Rico felt as if he was standing inside a mad pirate's treasure chest – perhaps he was at that.

"Rico," he heard Harcourt's voice. He turned around and tilted his head up toward the sound. The large man sat on a car that had been going around above and behind the entry portal. Vertigo made him grab the hatch frame, and he thought to himself that this place would make most Earthers hurl, which was probably the intent. Decadent and disorienting at the same time.

He started up and then stopped, shocked, his heart and breathing picking up speed. There, next to Louie and Harcourt, sat Inés Villaverde. She gave him a sad smile and toasted him with a sealed flute glass. Even across the room, she had a competence and beauty that compelled him. She had a strength and determination in her eyes that reminded Rico of women from history. Joan of Arc, Amelia Earhart, Margaret Thatcher, among others. On top of all that, she had the timeless beauty of a virtual immersion star—the present VI stars and the simulations of actors long gone and "resurrected" through programming and making new movies and music. Something about Inés reminded him of Ingred Bergman.

Her beauty, her composure, and her very presence sitting in Harcourt's lair threw Rico off. He didn't know what to say, and when he did speak, his words reflected his befuddlement.

"Inni? What the heck?"

She patted the seat next to her, and he joined them. For the next hour, they exchanged stories, updating each other on recent events. Inés was the big surprise. When she filled in Sistema Solar's team leader on Martel's web of deceptions, they'd started digging into what records they could find. Martel had stolen a lot of sensitive research. Inés'd gotten the green light to go after him. Sistema Solar's own antimatter drive had been farther along than she'd let on. She gave Rico a sheepish smile, which made him laugh. Solar's progress also helped explain Martel's own working drive. He'd been stealing from Solar and everyone else.

Harcourt did not have much to report. After the explosion of the *Amazing Grace*, the *Scimitar* had just disappeared. They had scanned for some sort of antimatter signature, but Martel must have figured out that was one of the ways they were following him. He had made overlapping looping patterns to cover up his real destination.

"Any sign of an escape pod?"

Harcourt shook his head. Rico had figured as much. There hadn't been enough time for Zavier to get out.

Inés put her hand on Rico's and he took it. The familiar softness of her skin was bittersweet.

"Hey," Rico said, turning to Harcourt, a sudden question occurring to him, "How did you know Martel had infected me with nanobots?"

Charlie Harcourt grinned. "One"—he pronounced it "woon"—"of my assistants happened ta'overheah Martel's conversation, wheech is jus'between you and me, Rico, ya? My clientele like'ta believe der transactions're private, and it would hurt business if dey knew otherwise. On a prior visit, maybe two years ago, Martel and Smith started talkin' 'bout nanerbots. My system flagged it. We reviewed the transcript and figured out he was making nanerbot assassins. We'th a little effort and a free visit to da pleasure suites for Santiago, we get a sample of da nanerbots and download the code we'th out him even realizing. Turns out Martel had stolen a boonch of my code and manufacturing specs from my'pleasure nanobots and reworked it. Since he had a beef we'th you, it seemed sunrise-sure that if you weren't dead already, you'd be infected we'th assassins."

Rico quirked a half-smile at sunrise-sure. He'd forgotten about that colloquialism. "Sorry 'bout shooting you," Louie said.

"Side by each, man. You saved my life."

"I don' like it when people steal from me," Harcourt continued. "We've been keeping an eye on him eveer since."

"Why let him on your rock at all then?" Inés asked.

"Money," Harcourt and Rico said at the same time.

Charlie took his empty drink flute and flung it casually toward the gold globe in the center. One of several hummer bots hovering on standby throughout the room flew over, and snagged it deftly out of the air. The bot placed it in a storage compartment in what would have been a person's abdominal region. A different robot, this one a hospitality droid – golden orange, matching the rings of the armillary sphere – waited expectantly. Harcourt held up four fingers and the droid quickly created new drinks for them. Another hummer delivered them, hovering as they took their drinks.

"So what do we do now?" Inés asked. "We have my ship, but no idea where Martel and the others have gone."

They sat in silence, each thinking their own thoughts. "What about your monitoring activities, Charlie? Anything?"

Harcourt shook his head. "We've checked. Ner clues as ta other bolt holes or hiz next stop."

"What about triangulating from his last two comms with me? Can you figure out his heading based on this location signature?"

Again Harcourt shook his head. "Martel iz smart enough ta strip out his comm location – and even if he didn't, the last message from him, just before Louie shot you?" Rico nodded. "Dat was a prerecorded message. Your proximity to the station, or perhaps docking, must have triggered the assassin bots."

Louie added, "You was lucky he wanted you to make a dramatic exit … and dat we were ready for nanobots."

"I'll say."

"And, before you ask, ner, we did na put trackers on his current sheep. Dat's very risky, and has to be done under just d'right circ'oomstances."

"Such as?" Inés asked, eyebrows raised.

"Either da owner has to be in a coma or off station. It takes a while." Harcourt said with a wry smile. "Since Martel berthed the *Kukri* heah, we had plenty of time ta plant the tracker carefully, and den hide our own tracks. Martel iz an excellent hacker. I'm better."

"Do you have the feed from my comm with Martel?"

"Candra, comply we'th Rico's request."

The artificial intelligence complied. A clear screen, which Rico had not noticed before now, rested inside one of the inner rings; it turned opaque and the hummers maneuvered it over in front of their car with the help of built-in thrusters. His conversation with Martel played out as Rico remembered.

The video paused. "Mr. Harcourt," a disembodied voice said.

"Go ahead, Candra."

"There is unusual data embedded in the recording starting at two minutes thirty-three seconds."

"Elaborate."

"A burst of additional data in the ultraviolet and infrared ranges, outside detectable human sight. More than would be found in a normal transmission."

"Could it be a spectral analysis transmission?" Inés asked.

"Negative," Candra replied. "A full spectral recording would be substantially larger in size."

"Pattern?"

"It appears to be a message. No malicious programming detected."

"Shift, display, and translate."

"Shifting light patterns into visible range and transcribing." Raheem's face appeared on the screen again; however, where his eyes should have been, a chaotic storm of light in hues of purple and red flared across the screen in pulsating color patterns.

A distorted voice filled the air of the spherical room. As it continued, the AI compensated and Raheem's voice came through with minimal distortion. "Rico. Martel got the drop on me. Access my bots. Still on. Take him out."

The playback returned to its normal state, with Martel taunting him as before.

"Um, what the heck was that?" Rico asked.

Harcourt drew a hand over his face, pulling on his chin. Surprise lingered on his visage as he stared in amazement at the vid.

"Sumgum. Dat be crazy. Nanerbots in his head, sending light out through his besotted *eyes*."

"That's impossible," Inés said.

"Why? Because you neveer thought of it, ya? Baggers," he scoffed with disgust. "Light goes in, why not come out, eh? Brilliant."

"How did he even do that with them watching?"

Harcourt shrugged. "Not much different dan gameware jacked into yer head. Software transfeered into brain patterns. Thoughts are electro-chemical signals. Dis just da reverse, ya? Instead of sending in, nanerbots read dem signals. Interrogators and courts already do dis. Dey read thoughts and transfer dem out. Although for d'law, usually transfer using text-audio-visual. *Non*-visible light, dat's …" Harcourt fumbled for the words … "covert genius."

"Hey, check this out." Inés pointed at the megascreen. "Watch Raheem's hand. "

Rico remembered their seeming intimacy, Lara sitting on Raheem's lap; but now Rico could see the flatness of Raheem's eyes, and he saw the Middle Easterner tapping on her leg, not in an affectionate way, but as if he had a nervous twitch.

"What?" Charlie asked, just as Rico realized what Inés had spotted.

Inés thrust her pretty chin toward the image. "It's Morse code. He's tapping out C-E-R-E-S."

Raheem had left one additional signal, in case the AI did not trip on the data burst he'd sent out via his nanobots. He'd done everything he could to tip them off.

Now, they needed to make good on the tip.

#

Hopefully, thanks to Raheem's message they could hang back and not worry about Martel slipping away. They knew where he would land. However, in the vast openness of space, they couldn't be sure he would not spot them if they got too close. They hung back and took their chances.

Inés had set a course for the dwarf planet Ceres, and the engines ran smooth as silk. In spite of this, Inés glowered at the control screen and grumbled to herself. As far as he could tell, her ship, *The Indigo Saber*, seemed to be performing perfectly. He had no idea what was eating at her.

To try and break her out of her mood, he asked her, "Why do you think Martel is headed to Ceres?"

"Damned if I know. I hate that rock." The vehemence in her voice surprised him.

"You've been there?"

Inés nodded but didn't elaborate. They'd "dated" less than three weeks, most of that while being shot at, and there was a lot Inés and Rico had not asked each other. It had been a whirlwind romance, more full of passion than long talks.

The thought instantly brought up the memory of making love to her. His mind conjured up her bronze skin and graceful curves shimmering in the morning sun. Gauzy curtains the color of apricots drifted in on the ocean breeze, intermittently obscuring her naked form as she walked across the red-brown tiles of their hotel room to get them something to drink.

Rico immersed himself in the memory. Her long brunette hair shone, dark silk lit by starlight. One of her bangs had slipped out of place and down over one eye, so she appeared to be peeking out at him. She came back into the room, gloriously beautiful, and smiled down at him where he lay on the bed. She bit her lower lip—rich, sensual lips that teased a challenge, daring him to even *try* resisting kissing her.

He'd sat up and pulled her close, kissing her smooth stomach, and gazed up into those soulful brown eyes. Her oval face, with strong but not harsh cheekbones, along with a gentle swoop of a nose, seemed as if carved from a master craftsman. With a smile, she handed him a water. He drank and distractedly set it aside.

Not for the first time, he wanted her. He reached up, cupped her cheek and chin with his hand, and slid his hand around into her hair. He pulled her down toward him and kissed those lips, which promised such passion. They surrendered themselves to one another.

It had been an incredible day.

"Are you listening to me, Federico Schroeder? What are you smiling about?"

His face flushed red. "What? Oh, yes. Nothing. What were you saying, Innie?"

She sat in stormy silence, her brows knitted and her mouth pinched. Even angry, she had a beautiful face.

"I said, 'What else did ASC tell you? About Ceres?'"

"Ahh." He'd read a lot about Ceres, of course. Everyone had. Between the three incredibly violent revolutions they'd had—and then the breeding program—Ceres was infamous in the solar system.

"You want the long version or the short version?"

"Bullets please."

"Well, between the news blogs and ASC, I know that violent and prolonged solar flare storms interrupted shipments of food and supplies from earth. There had been plenty of food, of course, since Ceres supplied most of the water and food in the Belt, but then some sort of bacteria or something contaminated the hydropods. Viruses took out the fish, rabbit, chicken and rat farms. Basically, they lost everything. One faction or another had sabotaged the food supply.

"Riots erupted on the dwarf planet, and the private security firm in place declared martial law. All the management reps for Ceres Resources, Ltd. were executed. The security officers declared themselves a sovereign government. More food riots led to more executions and a reign of terror. Thousands of workers were vented out into space. It got so bad that when ships finally did arrive, they could not dock without encountering frozen corpses.

"But those ships were a long time in coming. Ceres Resources Limited blocked all aid to Ceres, and sent a new security force to reclaim the rock from the first batch. They did so, in a bloody low-g battle, and executed the leaders of the rebellious security force.

"Right around then, an infectious disease broke

out. No one knows where it came from. Adala laid claim to it. Others suspected the first security force released it as they were defeated. The disease hit the invading security forces first, so the miners on Ceres claimed that the new ship brought it with them.

"Regardless, the workers rose up again, taking out the weakened security forces. Any member of security, or anyone infected, was tossed out the airlock. The dead outside now outnumbered the living inside.

"A few more assassinations later, Shirley Holland seized power. She ruled with a firm but more temperate hand, and reestablished order and contact with the outside. She held power for a long time until eventually she got assassinated as well. Now, her daughter, Victoria Holland, rules. That about sum it up?"

"You forgot the breeding programs," Inés said, her expression flat but drawn.

"ASC didn't brief us on that much, since it wasn't part of the political tensions—at least not at the time." Rico watched her face, and saw grief there. Old, long-lived-with grief that had never been put to rest. "I know they brought in surrogates."

Inés gave a mirthless chuckle. "Yes. They did at that. I researched a lot of what happened on Ceres, trying to make sense of it. I saw a lot of feeds on it. You already mentioned that a lot of people died. After the purges, the population was really low." Her eyes, dark haunted circles, bore into his. "Dangerously low. So, yes, they brought in surrogates. Women to be breeders." The anger flashed back into Inés' eyes. "For seven-year contracts. After that, the women could stay and stake a claim on that godforsaken rock or leave, but any kids had to stay behind."

Inés stared flatly at the monitor screens, her face lit by their eerie glow. She met his gaze and said, "My mother chose to return to Brazil after her 'service' on Ceres. They bred her like a cow, and then packed her back home as if she'd done nothing more than mop the floors. They used siblings I've never even met in genetic experiments."

"I'm sorry, Innie."

"That's life, eh? Meu mãe—my mother—thanks to prolonged treatments, went on to have many more bebês." Inés gave him a brave smile. "I was the youngest."

"That explains a lot," he said with a gentle smile.

She patted his arm affectionately and then stared off into a dark past.

"That wasn't the worst of it." She gazed into his eyes and her lips trembled. Tears filled her eyes, and she turned away until her composure returned. "That was bad, but not the worst of it. They killed my brother."

"Your brother? Why?"

"You have to understand that family is very important to us, and our religion is integral to family and who we are. The Pope declared DNA manipulation and surrogacy for colonization a mortal sin. He put it up there with abortion, you know? He made an *ex cathedra* declaration, an infallible statement. If you violated it, you were going to hell. Not all Catholics follow what the Pope says, you know? A lot of Catholics use birth control or get abortions. A lot of people waved off the DNA edicts, too, but not us. I guess you'd say we're what you'd call 'strict Catholics.' For my mother to do this was very, very bad.

"Miguel was the oldest of us born on earth. At one point, he wanted to become a priest. Mãe had eight of us, just on earth. On Ceres, through the miracles of fertility drugs and artificial insemination, she gave birth to twenty-eight children in seven years. Miguel learned about Ceres. I don't know how. He was appalled and very angry. He fought with my mother. He said … very hateful things. He called her a … a brood cow and a whore and a prostitute. I still remember my mother's face. Shocked, stunned, as if he'd slapped her. He became obsessed with the siblings that had been stolen from us, and that she had abandoned and 'sold,' as he put it."

Rico couldn't imagine talking to his mother that way, but then both of his parents had died when he was young, so he'd never had the chance.

"Miguel said that she had betrayed the family and, worse than that, she had committed a great sin." Inés stared at the floor in front of her. Her eyes and face lined with grief for her mother's pain and the loss of her brother.

"He left and went to the Guiana Space Centre until he could get work there. First, he made it up to the platforms above earth, working as a lumper." Rico gave her a quizzical glance. "Uh, the guys who move freight from the space elevator to the shuttles. Then he got work heading to Mars.

"The work was tough; despite his high and mighty attitude, he fell into drinking and gambling as a way of escaping the pain. Eventually, he made it to

Ceres."

"What was he going to do once he got there?"

"He never said. I think he wanted to find them. Our brothers and sisters." Inés busied herself with ship controls that did not need to be checked or adjusted. "He found some of them. What I do know is that he apparently got in trouble in the casino. At least that's what Cerean officials told us." She sighed, emotionally exhausted from reliving the details.

"However it happened, he got into debt. Maybe he gambled to raise money to buy out a brother or sister's contract. Maybe he needed cash to bribe some officials for genetic records. I know he bought out at least one sister's time. Kids cannot leave Ceres until they turn 25. Maybe he was going to bribe his way off planet with her. Whatever. We'll never know.

"If you get into debt on Ceres, and you cannot pay with cash, you can pay with your DNA. He refused. He didn't want to—couldn't—commit a mortal sin. He would not sentence more família to life on this rock. Plus, there were all the rumors about genetic experiments. People being turned into freaks. Monsters."

Rico knew that those rumors had later been confirmed. Ceres was defiantly proud of their genetic enhancement program. Inés brushed the tears off her cheeks and would not meet Rico's eyes. He wanted to reach for her, but he knew she didn't need that from him. She needed to finish her story. "Ceres contacted us. They do their due diligence these days to placate the other world governments. We couldn't pay. We were still incredibly poor at that point. In a last comm to me, Miguel told me he still refused to willingly give them his DNA. He was proud, and he told me, 'Eternity is a very long time, irmã. They can have my DNA when they take it from my dead body. Take hope, my little irmã; I may die but I will see you in heaven. Tell mama to repent her sin, so I can see her, too.'"

Now she turned her eyes to Rico, and they were red from crying but also from fury. "They vented him. Put him in a special chamber, and then opened the door to space.

"They killed him. And then those retros took his DNA anyway. Meets the letter of the law. They cannot take DNA by force, but once a person dies, the body becomes the property of the state. They strap the person into an airlock against the station wall, they suck the air inside, and simultaneously open the 'lock to an unrestricted view of the Cerean landscape. Of course, sucking the air out would be enough to kill a person, but they vented him. Why? Because nothing terrifies a spacer more than dying in the vacuum of space. Ceres is an evil hellhole, Rico. Nothing is as it appears, and they incubate horrors under the guise of science and progress."

Rico didn't know what to say to that. Inés' tension filled the cabin like a live wire. They rode in silence for a long time after that, each lost in their own thoughts.

Experimental craft did not build in many amenities, and the *Indigo Saber* was no exception. The ship held no sleeping quarters, no galley, and only a small head with a utilitarian sink and no shower. She brought out the only food available — squeeze packets and recon bars—but then she produced a bottle of silver tequila. Rico arched an eyebrow at her. "Innie, are you trying to get me drunk?"

"I'm trying to get *me* drunk, Chico, and I'm taking you along for the ride."

They took turns taking pulls from the bottle, and Inés put an old movie on the screen, some romantic comedy from the last century that he didn't recognize. In time, her fingers reached out, traced and clutched his. She moved her fingers from his palm up to the tips and electric fire ran through his body. He wasn't sure this was a good idea, especially since he'd been thinking in the back of his mind of trying to rekindle the relationship they'd started back in French Guiana, if they lived through this assignment.

Inés kissed him, and his misgivings scattered in the wind. Who was he to argue if a beautiful woman who knew her own mind wanted to make love to him? He told his overactive brain to shut up and kissed her back, teasing her with his tongue.

Her full, passionate lips tantalized him, and vivid memories came flooding back, making the blood roar in his ears. He ran his hands up her arms, around to her back, and pulled her close.

She took a swig of tequila, and then she climbed on top of him, putting a hand against the ceiling to keep from whacking her head as she straddled him. They laughed as he pulled her down on top of his hips. Inés took his ear between her lips, and then bit at his neck, just enough to make his nerves sing. She took off her shirt and set it floating freely around the cabin. His hands wandered, caressing and doing his best to distract her from the ghosts of her past.

Rico kissed her belly, relishing the beauty of her subtle curves, and moved up from there. She moaned and clutched his head. He ached with passion for her, and wanted her right then. Instead, he immersed himself in the torturous anticipation.

By the time they were done teasing and finally pleasing one another, cool sweat clung to their naked bodies, clothing floated around the cabin, and the movie had long since ended. She nestled on his lap and dozed. Rico drank in the scent of her hair and lightly perfumed skin until he, too, drifted off to sleep.

- SEVENTEEN -

An automated alert beacon chirruping in the cabin woke them both up. They had entered Cerean space. Inés, not bothering with any clothing, checked various screens. Rico admired the curves of her body while she worked.

Long-range scans showed Martel's ship as it lined up with the docking station known as Centri—short for centrifuge. Centri spun in orbit above Ceres and provided a heavier gravity than the asteroid could provide. Earth's moon boasted six times more gravity than Ceres, which made moving around on the asteroid akin to those old martial arts movies from previous centuries. Visitors found it fun for a while, but their bodies soon yearned for gravity, unless they were true Belters.

After they were sure Martel's ship had docked, Inés shut down the AMMATT drive on the *Indigo Saber,* and switched to fusion drive. At this distance, reaching station would take a lot longer, but they definitely did not want to cause a stir by coming in on an experimental engine. And they absolutely didn't want Martel getting tipped off and slipping away again.

They had time to kill, so they made love again. This time, less frantic and more tender.

Inés cuddled up against him, nestled in his lap, her face against his shoulder. They sat in the dark, lit only by console lights, for a long time. The smart screens had all gone into sleep mode. When she spoke, her voice was muffled by his shoulder and, perhaps, uncertainty over what he might say in turn.

"What happened, Rico? After French Guiana. We have good chemistry, no? Why did you run away?"

Her voice was quiet, husky. Tender and sexy all at once. Perhaps she sensed the precipice they stood on as well. It was a risk, just asking that question. Would he bolt? A lot of guys would, when pressed for an explanation of why they hadn't called. Over the millennia that much had not changed.

Why *had* he run away? It was a good question. A legitimate question. He'd wondered the same thing himself. Still, he gave a mental sigh. He didn't want to have this conversation with himself, much less with Inés. If he opened up to her, there would be no turning back. They would move forward, or it would be gone, water vapor exposed to vacuum. More than that, however, were the demons waiting there in the dark for him—waiting to dig their talons into his psyche.

As he often did, more as a reflex than as a conscious thought, he used humor to deflect and dull the pain. "I had to see a man about a horse."

"Oh, really?"

"Okay, okay. I had to see an alien about a spaceship."

She pulled back, her hair waving lazily in response to her movement. "Fala sério." With her face wreathed by her hair, she looked like an angel or a mermaid.

He gave her a half-smile. "I always talk seriously."

Inés punched his arm and her body moved in

pleasantly distracting ways. He kissed her, and she responded in kind, but then pushed back again. And hit him again. She gave him her patented Inés look.

"Let's just say that things have happened. Trust is a tough commodity to come by, you know?"

"Everyone has baggage, Rico. And what do you mean trust is a commodity, eh? Am I just a commodity, too, Rico?" She ran her fingers through his hair and grabbed the back of his head. She gave his hair a playful tug and then kissed him on the mouth, long and with great passion.

He drew back and quirked a smile at her. "No, Innie." He kissed her hand, then the inside of her forearm. "Never, Innie."

"Then give, Rico. I can handle it. Something is holding you back. I like you, Chico, more than anyone I've ever met. I want to give us a shot, if you want that, too. Hey, we're living at the edge of inhabited space, on two separate space stations, and competing on two different teams for the largest prize in the history of humanity. How bad can the skeletons in your closet be?" She grasped his chin and turned his face toward hers. Gazing into his eyes, she raised her eyebrows and waited.

"All right." He made up his mind. He had to take a chance. He sighed again, this time out loud. "You asked for it. There's a lot I've never told you, Inés. A lot we never had time for in French Guiana or that I simply avoided going into. I don't talk about my past much. Trust is ... hard for me. When people—" he faltered, stumbled to a halt. He shrugged and swallowed hard.

Inés waited, and when he didn't reply, she said,

"Rico." She wasn't angry; she didn't chastise him. She simply cupped his cheek with her hand and leaned toward him. "Keep going," she said. "What happened?"

Her tenderness disarmed him.

"It's a very long and depressing story." His voice was a whisper in the small cabin, and it sounded hollowed out to him.

"I'm not going anywhere," she said.

For the first time ever, he found that maybe he actually wanted to talk about what had happened, actually wanted to trust someone and open up. He just didn't know how to start. He decided to just rip the band aid off.

"My parents died in an explosive decompression back on Branson Station, two weeks before my ninth birthday.

"That was just the beginning of some very bad mojo. If I were you, I would definitely get as far away from me as you can. Death has been my constant companion since I was eight years old." He quirked a half-hearted smile at his attempt at melodrama.

"You sure you want to hear the tragic tale of Federico Shroeder?" Rico's voice was flat, and part of him—clinical, analytical—recognized that in himself. He reported the events as if he were debriefing a case, holding the torrent of his emotions at bay, refusing to even acknowledge that they might be there.

Inés just nodded.

"After my parents died, I had to leave Branson Station and go live with my abuela down in Puerto Rico. There were some great parts to that. My grandmother was very affectionate and funny, but she died when I was twelve."

"So...back up to Branson Station. This time with an uncle. Uncle Janiel. My uncle was a maintenance worker for the microwave transmitters that beamed power back down to Earth. He was out on a ship, doing a space walk when an unexpected solar flare went up. Uncle Janiel got tangled in some equipment. The solar storm hit, and he died of cancer less than a year later." Rico remembered the rest of it, but he left it out. Not much point in telling Inés that his rookie partner panicked, rotating the ship to protect himself from the flare and that that was why his uncle had gotten trapped. If they guy had kept his cool, his uncle would probably still be alive.

Rico stared through the blank smartwall into the blackness of space. "You sure you want to hear all this? It gets worse."

Inés caressed his arm. "Stop dodging."

Rico gave a curt nod and pressed on. "They put me with a foster family. Eventually, me and another kid were adopted. My adoptive sister, Nikki.

"I ran with a tough crowd back then. Had a lot of anger. They called us 'Tunnel Kids,' because we would run rampant through the maintenance tunnels of the station. Me, Trigger, and Topper were the most tight. We did everything together. Mostly, we got in trouble a lot."

A rash of escapades, ranging from the funny to vandalism, flashed through his mind. One event stood out more than the others. Rico gave a humorless chuckle. "One time we made a chem bomb. Almost took out a whole section except the fire controls kicked in. My adopted parents grounded me, talked to me a lot. Got me into counseling, Space Scouts—back into sports. I fought it all quite a while.

"After another incident involving some shoplifting—they shipped me over to another ring of the station to stay with my adoptive grandmother and grandfather. I think they wanted to get me away from some bad influences."

Rico considered his grandparents. They had all been a big, counter-balancing influence. All his family was, really. Even Nikki's good natured teasing and cajoling. Kind, persistent, and patient. Mostly, they had been loving and encouraging. Without them, he was not sure where he would have ended up. Well, maybe he did, since Topper was dead and Trigger had been mindwiped. The love of his family had saved his life.

"Somewhere along the line, something sunk in. Partly, it was that Trigger and Topper both flunked eighth grade. I started hanging with a different crowd. Then Topper died of an overdose of hero-spike." Even at the time, that had left Rico stunned with disbelief. They had never done the harder stuff.

"For awhile, things seemed almost normal, whatever the hell that is. I competed in in track and *kyoku-atsu* and did pretty well. I was still a loner and not into team sports, but I was doing okay. I started thinking about college and the future."

He left out the accident Nikki had had that left her laid up for four months, even with rapid healing. She'd broken several bones but her life had never been in danger—or so they thought at the time. The fact that she hadn't been killed had simply been dumb luck.

"Then some bastard killed our family dog. We had a sweet curly-haired mutt named Rosco. She was poisoned—we had no clue by who—and the vet couldn't do anything to save her. It was just a damn dog, you know? But I loved her, and when she died, it brought everything back. It was my senior year, and I went into a tailspin. Almost didn't graduate. Refused to leave my room, quit the track team and martial arts."

Rico let out a shaky breath, and took in another one, stalling a bit before telling the next part.

"My family flew my biological cousin up from Puerto Rico. Jackie and I had always been close, even over comms. We got really tight when I lived Earth-side, spending every day together playing and exploring."

Jackie had come up to Branson, and even transferred schools, sacrificing her own senior year because she'd known he needed her support. Even in his black despair, he'd recognized the generosity of her gesture, and he'd loved her even more for it.

"It worked. I gradually rejoined the world of the living. I started socializing more than I ever had before. Jackie was a naturally warm and friendly person. I got invited to more parties with her around than I had the entire three years prior. She was something else. Special." Rico gave another chuckle, this one with actual humor in it.

Jackie had even introduced Rico to his first real girlfriend, Karen Dewer.

"One night, some of us were out at a club, and we came across Trigger. Even though he was a year behind me now, we still saw each other once in a while in school. He'd changed quite a bit, just as I had. He was smoother, more charming, but with a live-wire edge. Jackie fell for him instantly. I tried to warn her, but she was hooked. For the next two months, we all hung out together." For awhile, Trigg had even charmed Rico, and he thought his old co-conspirator had truly changed, but it had all been a ruse—a very elaborate ruse.

"I joined the Air and Space Corps Reserve Officer Training Corps for the scholarship money. Trigger followed suit. We went through Basic Training together, renewed our friendship, and had a few laughs together.

"We'd go play space ranger once in a while, and ASC paid for our schooling. Jackie had already received a free scholarship to Mars, so she had already left by that point. Trigg and I were both enrolled at Hallsworth University, and planning to become hotshot pilots. We were thick as thieves again.

"One day, I came home unexpectedly—one of my classes had been cancelled—and found Trigger in bed together with my girlfriend." His first girlfriend. Karen Dewer. His first "true love." And she even took my first edition *Cometallion*. Old joke. But a goodie.

"That was the end of that. Didn't even fight. Just took my stuff and left."

He'd been devastated at the time, but the shock and depression had only lasted a few days this time. Mostly, he'd been hurt by the betrayal. "Maybe I'd just expected things to end in the crapper, since everything else in my life had."

Rico paused, holding Inés by her arms as he looked into her deep brown eyes. "You might not know this about me, but I have to work hard to hold onto my sunny disposition."

Inés gave a laugh and put her forehead against his. "You do have that, Chico. That's for sure."

"Trigg dropped out of ROTC and Hallsworth. That was the end of my freshman year. That summer, while I was attending my summer ASC ROTC training, my cousin Jackie was murdered on Mars."

Inés gave a soft but sharp intake of breath.

"Mars had no leads. I was supposed to be locked into maneuvers for the whole summer. I told my commanding officer what happened and asked for a leave of absence. She wasn't going to give it to me, but she finally did. If she hadn't, I'm not sure what I would have done. I spent the next several weeks following the trail of my cousin's killer."

Rico set his lip in a firm line and looked at Inés, and this time his eyes were hard shards of flint. "It was Trigger."

"*Ni pa!*" Inés whispered.

"Oh, yes way. He was a sociopath. He'd been plaguing my life since we'd met as kids. In the end, he told me everything he'd done. He'd killed Topper. Made it look like an overdose. He killed the family dog, Rosco. He caused the accident that almost killed Nikki. He killed another friend of mine as well."

And that had been the end of his first love, Karen Dewer. He hadn't even known she was dead until Trigger had told him.

"He followed Jackie to Mars for the sole purpose of murdering her."

He'd done so in horrendous fashion. The crime scene photos started to pop into his mind, and he violently slammed the door shut on *that* room. No way was he going there.

Inés stared at him, nonplussed. "But...why*?*"

Rico gave a bitter laugh. "I told you. He was a sociopath. He thrived on my grief, on knowing he was causing me incredible pain. He was like a stalker. He wanted my attention. The fact that we were 'friends' only heightened the excitement for him. The danger of playing mind games with me gave him an adrenalin rush It helped his dead soul feel alive."

"So then what happened?"

"I found him, finally, in a back alley in the slums of one of the dome cities of Mars. We fought. I chased him. Eventually, I caught him. He laughed at me. Mocked me. Dared me to pull the trigger.

"I had an illegal blaster, and I held it to his head. I wanted to pull that trigger more than anything I've ever wanted before or since."

Still, Rico had not pulled the trigger. It had been almost physically painful, not taking revenge, not taking the law into his own hands and handing the killer the justice he so undeniably deserved, but the wisdom of the ghosts of his past had saved him, and he'd found the core of who he was that day.

"I didn't want to just kill him. I wanted to destroy him for the pain he'd caused me, for the lives he'd taken and for the shitty deal the universe had dumped on me."

Rico stopped talking. Adrenalin pumped through his body as he remembered that pivotal moment so many years ago. His breathing was shallow and fast.

"What did you do?" Inés asked. There was no recrimination in her voice, only curiosity.

"I pulled the trigger." Inés gave a soft gasp of surprise. "I shot and disintegrated a steel door and some bricks, and then I slugged him a few times."

Inés laughed and then covered her mouth as if embarrassed that she'd laughed. He gave her a wan smile.

"It was one of his own taunts that stopped me from killing him. He bragged about how many people he had killed. It was all those families that kept me from killing him. They needed closure."

Trigger's words still made his blood run cold. *Go ahead and kill me. The families will never know what happened to their loved ones. I'll savor the wine of their anguish while I'm in hell.*

"Then what happened?"

Rico shrugged. "Scott 'Trigger' McAboy was found guilty of eighteen counts of murder. They pulled all the details out of his head before he was mindwiped. He was relocated under a new identity. I went back to school, changed my major to criminal and investigative psychology, finished ROTC, enlisted full-time, and got myself assigned to the Office of Criminal Investigation."

Rico pulled her close and nibbled on her chin and then her neck. "And, that, dear Innie, is why I have slight trust issues." He held his index finger and thumb a little but apart and she laughed.

Inés turned serious again, brushed the hair away from in front of his eyes, and gently ran her fingers along his cheek, and then traced his left eyebrow.

"Thank you," she said, her voice husky with

emotion. "I promise I will do my best to never violate your trust in me."

Rico grunted. "You better not, woman. Even a blaster-proof fellow like me can only bounce back so many times, you know."

They kissed. They hugged. They made love for the third time since they'd embarked on their journey. And the third time was by far the very best.

Inés slept. Rico stared at the ceiling, wide-awake and trying not to wake her. Despite making love, his mood was somber after sharing his story with Innie. Too many memories, too many brutal losses. At the same time, he felt as if a small a part of his burden had been lifted from him. He lay there, pondering, trying to figure out what else he was feeling. He couldn't pin it down. Something warm and comforting but elusive. After awhile, it came to him: he felt like new possibilities were opening up for him.

- EIGHTEEN -

A few hours later, Rico and Inés were both awake when another beacon signal arrived requesting identification. Inés sent the ship's transponder signal on a tight beam to the dwarf planet.

A comm alarm chirruped awhile later. "Ceres to *Indigo Saber*, come in."

Inés hit the OptiComm, "Go for *Indigo Saber*."

"A message from the Superintendent of Security transmitting in five."

Moments later, a tall man with black hair and a light touch of gray appeared on the screen. "Welcome to Planet Ceres, traveler. I am Superintendent of Planetary Security, Tamos Oberkell."

"They know it's just a *dwarf* planet, right?" Rico muttered.

"Yeah. Try telling them that."

The message continued. "—some regulations I want you to be aware of. First, kidnapping is a capital offense on Ceres. Attempting to remove a child from the planet is punishable by death. Second, absolutely no nanobots are allowed on-planet. All ships will be quarantined, boarded, inspected, and all micro-technology sealed in our containers for the duration of your visit. This includes *all* medical nanobots, regardless of their function. *No* exceptions. If you do not agree to these terms, you must remain in quarantine on your ship. Please familiarize yourself with the full list of our laws and regulations downloaded to your AI before your arrival. Lack of awareness of local regulations will not mitigate any offenses; any and all violations will be prosecuted to the fullest extent of the law." The no-nonsense superintendent paused, smiled and attempted—unsuccessfully—to shift his demeanor to that of a beneficent grandfather. "Now, our Planetary President, Victoria Holland has a few words."

A tall woman, with reddish brown hair and a long, square jaw appeared on the screen in a prerecorded message. "On behalf of the Cerean people, I'd like to welcome you to our planet. Ceres is the leading provider of pure water and hydroponic crops in this sector. We also have several five-star hotels and restaurants. There are numerous recreational activities for you to try and, don't forget to visit our casinos for a complementary meal." The woman on the screen gave a thin smile, and the screen went black.

"Some carrot and stick show," Rico said, shaking his head in amazement. "So that's 'Rockhard' Holland, eh?"

"You've heard of her?"

"Oh, yes. ASC briefings. Seems odd, though, for a planetary president to take time to record the 'Welcome to Ceres' message." He started to chuckle, but the expression on Inés' face stopped him. He cleared his throat.

Inés looked deadly serious. "It's no joke, and they want to make sure we know it."

The trip from the outskirts of Cerean space to dock took quite a while, because Inés had switched from antimatter to plasma. That gave them plenty of time. Inés hooked them both up to portable shunt-storage units and issued the appropriate emigrate commands and authorizations to get started. A massive microscopic migration began internally, although Rico could not sense it.

By the time they docked, the bots were out of their bodies, stowed in the storage units. Two humorless security officers carrying LLAMMs came on board once Inés opened the hatch. They also carried laser pistols openly on their sides. They wore midnight blue jumpers with yellow piping, and their bodies stretched out in the typical lanky Belter manner. The one in charge was a woman with gray hair in a crew cut. The second in charge—a man with thick glasses that seemed of the sort a blind man might have worn back before eye replacements— waved in four others in slate-gray coveralls, who brought in scanning equipment and stood at attention by the portal.

The woman stepped forward, "I'm Chief Curtis. Are you familiar with the procedures?"

Inés spoke, "Yes."

"And you are?"

"Inés Villaverde, Captain of this vessel, *The Indigo Saber*."

The woman flicked a steel gaze on Rico and he answered on reflex, flashing back to his training at the Academy. "Federico Schroeder, Reactivated Air and Space Corps, Earth." The last bit was self-evident, since Mars called theirs the Mars Space Fleet, but it was tradition to add it. Chief Curtis kind of reminded him of his Military Training Leader, with her 'high and tight' haircut and her large frame. Rico figured Curtis could handle herself in a fight.

She gave a slight nod of acknowledgement and

then looked up from her pad. "You've been here before, Captain Villaverde." It was a statement, not a question. Inés gave a slow nod but did not volunteer any other details. Curtis read a few lines on her pad, but did not react to whatever she saw there.

"Permission to access your ship and AI, Captain?"

"Granted." Inés handed over her nanobot storage unit, and Rico did the same.

The officers put the storage units inside two larger containers, and then sealed those with tape and a blinking security console. They passed these off to two of the underlings in gray, who handled them as if they'd just been given radioactive waste, taking them off ship for quarantine. Talk about paranoid, Rico thought. The other guys in gray started wanding the place.

Chief Curtis asked, "Do you have any other nanobots onboard this ship?" While they were being grilled, the workers in gray connected to the ship AI and scanned every millimeter of the ship.

Inés shook her head. "No."

"Business on Ceres?"

Inés nodded for Rico to answer. Since this was her ship, protocol dictated that he follow her lead. "We're in pursuit of a system felon, wanted on Earth, Mars, and Jupiter. He's known to traffic in illegal nanobots." He knew that would get her attention, without having to mention the assassin-bots. Ceres had used nanobot assassins to devastating effect during its second purge, to the point where they were now entirely banned on the small planet. "They may also be in possession of antimatter munitions."

Curtis flicked her eyes from her pad to Rico's

face. "Names and descriptions?"

Inés tapped a screen on the console and the three faces of Martel, Lara and Pedro popped up, with details below. With a push, she sent it over to her screen.

"Why didn't you comm this ahead?" The security officer asked, her voice terse; she scrutinized Inés and Rico both.

Inés answered her. "We've got a man inside. He's undercover. We didn't want to risk an intercepted comm and have Martel end up spooked into running—or killing—our operative. He's exceptionally talented with tech."

Rico hid his smile with the practice of a seasoned security officer. Inés was good at improvising on the fly. Good for her.

"His info?"

She pulled up his specs and sent them over as well. "Dr. Raheem Kuzbari."

The woman gave her subordinate a glance, and he stepped to the side and started speaking into his wrist comm. Rico eavesdropped. "Secure comm to Superintendent Oberkell, Priority Code 999 dash 477. Eyes only. Threat imminent." Rico could not make out the reply, but the young man came back and whispered in his superior's ear. Her face darkened. She straightened and turned to them.

"I'm sorry to inform you, but the three fugitives that you're after have requested asylum."

Inés crossed her arms and stared laser beams at the woman. Rico asked, "Asylum? On what grounds?"

"State security. Asylum is granted to anyone who

requests it, for any reason, so long as they are willing to donate genetic material to the government of Ceres for unrestricted use in perpetuity." She was clearly reciting a statute she knew by heart. Rico thought that just maybe he could sense an undercurrent of distaste for her duty in this regard, mostly hidden but discernible—at least that was his impression. Maybe what he sensed was just a general distaste for Martel and company, or maybe it was a general disagreement with the coercive policies of genetic thuggery.

Either way, he pressed her on it.

"You realize that he is a known trafficker in illegal nanobots? He attempted to blow up Chou Station; he threatened to blow up Eunomia; and he is suspected in several other crimes."

"Mr. Schroeder, sanctuary takes precedence. Our laws and protocols are very clear on this. Genetic integrity is priority one. My apologies, Captain Villaverde."

"Search his ship," Inés said, her words clipped and sharp as shards of mined rock.

"Already done. That's S.O.P. here." The woman shook her head. "Nothing there. All their personal bots were surrendered and secured."

"Chief Curtis, listen, this guy is dangerous," Rico said. "Really dangerous. He makes professionals look like grade-school punks." His military background kept him standing straight and respectful, but he wanted to grab her arms and shake her.

The guys in gray wrapped up their scanning, and all but one of them left. The remaining one came over and their conversation halted momentarily. The tech gave both Rico and Inés an armband. The bands were a complicated geometric maze of hexagonal colors. His were all shades of green. Hers were green mixed with yellows.

"Keep these on at all times when you are not in a private room." The tech gave Curtis a nod, which she returned, and then he left.

Inés jumped into the void. "So justice has no meaning here?" she said, caustic and more accusation than question.

"Careful, Miss Villaverde," her eyes were cold rock. "Survival is a precursor to justice." Then she let out a long, drawn-out breath. "You have to understand that these policies were put in place during a time of great turmoil. The entire planet almost ceased to exist. Draconian measures were taken. I sympathize with your problem. We'll keep an eye on him. That's all we can do. You are welcome to Ceres, but I am required to warn you both that interference with our citizenry, even probationary citizens, will not be tolerated."

"Are these guys really the kind of DNA you want brought into your gene pool?"

Officer Curtis drew herself up even taller, and Rico and Inés had to look up to meet her eye. "We collect *all* DNA, Captain Villaverde. We are the premiere genetic researchers in the solar system. Because of Ceres, numerous diseases no longer exist and life expectancy has more than doubled. We safeguard a catalogue of *all* species found on Earth, living and extinct. While I may not always agree with our policies, I can assure you, we can take care of our own gene pool."

Curtis took a tight breath and added, "Thank you

for your concern." The platitude cut through the atmosphere like a laser cutting through a ship's hull. She and her young protégé turned to depart.

"Wait," Inés said, stopping them. "What about Raheem Kuzbari?"

"We have no information regarding his whereabouts. We'll keep an alert active for him if he turns up. That's all we can do. Now, if that's all, I really have some pressing business I need to attend to." And with that, Curtis and her aide left, leaving a palpable frost in the air.

#

"Now what do we do?" Rico asked. "Martel will recognize me immediately. Even if he doesn't, if we get caught investigating him, Ceres will turn us into part of their mad chemistry experiment. I don't relish contributing to the citizenry on Dr. Moreau's island."

Inés growled under her breath. "Me either. Come on. We need to get on Martel's ship without getting blasted. I need to make a call, but I can't do it from here."

They rode a transfer pod from the docking station, down the spiral, a giant lasso in space, rotating in sync with the station. The pseudo-gravity of the spinning station gave way to the much lower gravity of Ceres proper as the pod clicked into place and the bow portal opened.

A robot port attendant spoke as the portal opened, "Please watch your step, ladies and gentlemen. Welcome to the planet Ceres." The walls of the spiral tube made a loud humming noise as they rotated around the docked transfer pod.

"Impressive," Rico said. "A lot more hospitable than the transition at Eunomia."

Inés just grunted, her irritation back in full force. *Apparently, she's not impressed.* The chaos of a low gravity market swam before them. Booths crammed the floor but also the air overhead, with vendors hawking wares from various geometric-shaped booths. Globes, cubes, and all kinds of polyhedrons crowded the plaza. Words and graphics flitted on every side possible of each of these booths, so that no matter where you stood, you were barraged by the latest and greatest from Ceres and off planet. The scene reminded Rico of a hot-air balloon festival he'd once attended in Miami, Florida.

The sides of the booths, as well as slanted platforms positioned throughout the mall, served as "steps" or launch pads, and people easily bounced their way up to the highest levels in the low gravity. Occasionally, an offworlder would misjudge and fly off into the safety netting on the outskirts of the area to the raucous cheers and jeers of everyone around.

The mood was boisterous and jovial. Vendors who knew each other called out insults and greetings to one another. Sometimes they sent an item zipping between them with a yell of "Hey-ho! Flying!" to which the others nearby erupted with a chorus of, "Flying!" Rico saw food, beverages, electronics, articles of clothing, and other items fly between booths and from booths to customers. He had to stay alert to not get beaned. Many of the hawkers used a string to send items out in wide sweeping arcs. Even with all the air traffic, collisions were rare.

"Hey, how come no one steals any of the packages floating by?"

"If they're to other Cereans, then they're DNA tagged—a genetic mailing address. That cuts down on a lot. If they're not, and someone tries to steal a package, the others zap the thief with stun batons and kick the snot of him or her. It's not pretty."

Inés step-jumped as if a cross between a superhero and a gazelle, pushing off and then gliding over to the first booth. She bought two pairs of sunglasses, similar to the one the security guard had been wearing—oversized and wrap around. She handed Rico a pair and put on one herself. They weren't much of a disguise, but something was better than nothing.

"Why do people need sunglasses here? Fashion?" he asked, since it was not excessively bright in the market area.

Inés shook her head. "Augments," she whispered. "Freaks. A lot of the citizenry have enhanced eyesight for better vision mining in dim light. Makes normal light painful."

Ah, Rico thought, I should have made that connection. Ceres had not only embraced genetic engineering in order to help them survive when their population collapsed, they had turned it into a thriving economic commodity. People from all over the system came to Ceres for medical help. 'Better living through gen-eng.' What the ads didn't tell you was that there was often a price to pay for any mods you received, beyond just the credits involved.

A group of teens twirled and strolled past them, kicking off various booths—the "low-g" equivalent to strutting—to the protests of their owners. The teens' heads were shaved bald, which was startling since no one was bald these days except by choice. Red light panels on either side of their heads lit up in patterns of lines and geometric shapes and they laughed at jokes beamed privately between them. Their gangly bodies were as tall as Rico. Many of the adults nearby were a dozen centimeters taller than him. He felt as small as a child at a festival by comparison.

"Vultures," Inés whispered, indicating the boys who had just passed.

He'd read about them. Genetically modified with super-tough stomach linings, exceptionally caustic stomach acid, and virulent intestines, all designed so they could eat virtually anything—including bacteria-laden carcasses. If food shortages ever hit Ceres again, this group was designed to survive. Rico mentally shook his head. How a culture could ban nanobots and then allow deep cerebral implants and vulture genes spliced into their children mystified him. It seemed pretty much blatant hypocrisy and, to him, appalling on a visceral level.

Along the main corridor ahead of them, stalls with tables and tanks and large smartwall demos hawked all manner of genetic enhancements. Rico could smell food cooking and, in spite of the dining imagery the vulture teens called to mind, his stomach rumbled.

A woman wearing a glowing red dress met his eye and stepped in between Inés and him. She had white hair tipped in green. He went to move around her, but the woman sidestepped, blocking his path. "How you like me, ya?" She leaned forward, "Take you fun places, ya? Ook, ook." She had nice, distracting curves, true enough. She swished her dress, which had multiple panels of sheer cloth, and then did a little twirl. In the low gravity, the dress swirled as if made of tendrils of smoke. Underneath she wore skin-tight legging pants. She ran her hands over her breasts and the material briefly turned transparent.

"I'm with somebody."

"She come, too. Special, special. Ain'no'law 'gainst that, ya? Yer lady, she no min'. No law'gainst somethin' somethin', not on Ceres. You no been here 'fore, right, flyboy?" She tapped his green spectrum armband.

"No, ma'am," Rico said.

"Fix you up, right quick, ya. Free go'round fer first timers. On da hoose. Goov'men' dey pay, ya. You coom now." She raised her eyebrows at him a few times. "Coom later." He smiled and grabbed a guide bar to pull himself around her, but she eased her way in front of him with quick grace. She started her patter again, but suddenly, Inés appeared over her shoulder and whispered, "Back off sistah, ya? I no share, no play nice. Denks now."

The woman made a face and shot off as quick as a frightened fish after more accessible prey. Inés took his hand and pulled his arm a little more forcefully than she really needed to. Rico carefully suppressed a smile. They moved along the right side and around an outer edge of the plaza until they came to a series of privacy booths lining the walls from floor to ceiling, with angled bounce pads to reach the higher levels. In a sense, it reminded Rico of a hotel, replete with balconies, but entirely self-serve and accessed from the outside. You just jumped up, landed on a platform, paid for your chosen room, and went in. A steady crowd of couples and cleaner robots streamed in and out of the booths.

Rico watched as she jump-hopped her way to a top floor room. He pushed off and followed after her. She inserted her ID and then pulled him inside the privacy booth when the door hissed open. The booth was cramped, with one small bed, a bright lime green in color, that folded down from the wall and included netting to help hold one down in the low-g for sleeping—or other activities.

She caught him grinning and poked him in the chest with a finger. "Don't get your hopes up, gaucho. We've got work to do."

Another door on the sidewall had a credit slot and she inserted her card. The adjoining room was vacant, so the door slid open. Then, she tapped on the smartwall icon and said, "Search query: Cecilia Azevedo, public records."

The mechanized voice of a Candra-unit spoke. "Cecilia Azevedo. Female. Age: 35. Occupation: pottery designer, programmer and certified 3D printer. No criminal record. No watchlists. Full Cerean citizenship."

"Private comm, please, eyes only. Inés Villaverde to Cecilia Azevedo."

"Confirmed. Please hold."

A long time passed, and Rico did not break into her reverie. Ghosts from her past clearly haunted her, being once again on extra-planetary soil, and he had no right to trespass there. She also clearly had a plan, and he trusted her, so he waited. Besides, he knew all about wrestling with the ghosts of one's past.

Finally, a woman's face appeared on screen, with the typically rounder face of a longtime Belter. Her dark hair, tied in a knot, and dark brown eyes, however, reminded him of Inés.

" Olá, irmã," Cecilia Azevedo said.

"Hello, sister," Inés replied. "Is this line secure?"

"Momento." Her arms moved in front of her as she ran something on her smartwall. "Yes. What's going on?"

#

Cecilia showed up twenty minutes later, with a friend in tow. "This is Arnab. He is a makeup, wig, and prosthetics artist." Arnab stood well over two meters tall—he definitely would have hit his head on the doorframe at his abuela's house, back in Puerto Rico. Arnab's slightly brown skin, combined with the common Indian given name, told Rico the man's lineage. Arnab bowed and set a large suitcase on the green bed.

"Cece has told me you need some disguises." He placed long, spindly fingers on his chest. "Fortunately for *du*, I am on vacation, because we have twelve different shows going on right now at The *Morshu* National Theater. We are *insanely* busy." He clapped his hands together in excitement, leaned toward them, and whispered, " Doing some detective work, yes? How marvelous! I feel as if I'm a spy!" Then, in a normal tone, he said, "We'll get you set up just so."

Cecilia said she'd be back shortly and left while Arnab started work on them. He moved quickly, applying skin and hair dyes, contact lenses, and lumienna tattoos. Arnab held up a mirror and said, "All of the mods are perfectly safe. No nans of course, and no toxics." Rico had shocking red hair on top that faded into orange and then settled into bright yellow down by his ears. His contact lens matched his hair, with tinges of fire and glints of gold. A serpentine iris—popular among the clubbing crowd—made him particularly trendy. His lummie tattoos shimmered with the hues of a dying campfire and stood out starkly from his now paler and rounder cheeks. Tricks of prosthetic wedges and skin shading made him appear tall and spindly. He could almost pass for a short Belter now. Arnab's skills impressed Rico.

Inés, made up to complement him, picked up the other end of the spectrum. Her skin was transformed to nightshade purple, fading to light blue at the fingertips and toes. Her hair transitioned from a hint of yellow at the tips immediately to green, with swirls of blue and purple that followed the curves of her hair. Shimmering glints of blue-white pulsated in her hair as well as on a long, phoenix tattoo that started on her neck. The wings spread wide across her shoulders, with the tail feathers disappearing tantalizingly between her breasts.

Rico did not recognize himself, much less Inés. There was no way Martel, Lara or Pedro would recognize them now.

Inés said, "Arnab, this is simply amazing. You are a master."

The tall Belter bowed. "You darlings stay put until Cecilia comes back. I know she's got something special in mind, because I hooked her up with a few friends of mine." He winked and then disappeared.

"We didn't pay him anything," Rico said.

Inés shrugged. "I'm sure he'll bill us." She perused her mien in the mirror and beamed. With a mischievous glance his way, she said, "Fire Serpent looks good on you. That whole bad-boy image." Her grin teased him. He smiled back at her. Contacts made her irises appear large and round, as if inspired by a hunting owl. They gave her an alluring, sultry look. Staring into those dark wells, Rico felt himself increasingly distracted.

He wrapped his arms around her and she turned into him. Their lips met and fiery passion washed through him. He kissed her long and deeply. His head spun but, as fantastic as this felt, he needed to keep his wits about him. He pulled back, blood pulsing through his veins, and shook his head.

"Well, now." He took in a deep breath and blew it out. Inés beamed at him and broke into a heartfelt chuckle.

To switch gears he said, "We're not going to get off this rock with him."

"Martel? No. We'll have to kill him."

"Just like that? No hesitation?" Rico frowned at the statement, ice water dashed on his good mood. He shook his head. "No way. If we do, we're no better than he is."

A flash of irritation crossed her face. "Rico, you know as well as I do that if we hesitate, people die. We have no choice. If you want justice for Taz and Zavier, you'll have to get it the Jupiter way."

"Cold and in the dark?"

Inés just raised her eyebrows and tilted her head at him. He recognized the semi-challenge.

Rico weighed her words and the situation in front of them. If they didn't kill Martel, the man would get away with countless murders and acts of espionage. Plus, Ceres would undoubtedly have the AMMATT drive. They would get it eventually anyway, but if they got their hands on it before everyone else? That could destabilize the entire system. Ceres had longstanding grudges with both Earth and Mars. Who knew what they would do with the technology? Hundreds of thousands could die. Maybe more. On that score, they were too late anyway. If Martel had asylum, then Ceres most probably already had the antimatter data. Holland being as shrewd as she is, she would have demanded proof of Martel's claims.

He pushed down thoughts of his friends Taz and Zavier, and tried to get some perspective on all of it. If they could stop Martel from passing along the AMMATT specs, then maybe his thinking would be different, but that was a done deal. Nothing could be done about it now. At last, he shook his head.

"No, Inés. I don't agree. Curtis is wrong, and so are you. There comes a time when we have to stop just surviving, stop living on the frontier, and start living like human beings."

He saw her face flush in anger, and he realized he was not exactly being diplomatic in his choice of wording.

"It *is* people living like human beings, Rico. Just being people. The good and the bad and the ugly. People can be wonderful, and they can be awful. Forgetting that can get you killed."

He wanted to argue with her, but what could he add that he hadn't already said? He knew all about the ugly side of human nature. That's why we have to fight against it, he thought. He wanted to remind her that he'd wanted to kill Trigger, that he understood the pulsing demand to kill the evil, to snuff it out before it could kill again. Instead, he held up a hand to stave off furthering arguing. "First things first. We need to find Martel, and we need to find Raheem."

"If he's still alive. If I were Martel, I would have dumped him before docking Ceres. He's too much of a liability. He knows too much."

Unfortunately, Rico had to agree. Raheem was probably another casualty to add to the long list of Martel's body count. He was about to say as much when the door chimed. They could see Cecilia through the one-way translucence. She had a deliberate air of nonchalance and held two large bags. Inés palmed the door pad and let her in.

Cecilia opened the bag and pulled out one red security uniform and one gray uniform. She held them up with a big smile. "Ta-da!"

"Where did you get these?" Inés asked in a hushed tone, even though the booth was completely soundproof.

"A friend of Arnab's is in costuming. Brilliant, are they not? Put them on." Cecilia handed the red one to Inés and the other to Rico. Apologetically, she said, "I thought you'd be able to move around better as an asher than as an officer."

"I take it an asher is a tech?"

"Sim," she said in Portuguese and then translated. "Yes. Ashers is their nickname. They collect all the data. Run all the scans."

"Won't they know we're not local law enforcement?"

Cecilia shook her head. "Security gets rotated around the planet regularly, to keep graft down, and to decrease the chance of another security … issue." Rico surmised that, in this case, the word "issue" was a Cerean euphemism for rebellion. She reached into the bag and pulled out a scanner identical to the ones the techs had used aboard the *Indigo Saber*. Then, she grabbed a third gray jumper out of the bag and began stripping down. She had the longer, stretched-out frame of a lifelong Belter and high, pert breasts unaffected by gravity. Her face shared the same Brazilian beauty as Inés.

Inés said, "Cece, what are you doing? You cannot do this."

Cecilia gave Inés the same hard stare that she had given Rico before. Must be a family trait.

"I can. And I will. I know this planet better than either of you, and I owe you. *We* owe you. For what happened to your—our—brother." Cecilia zipped up the suit and the gesture was as final as a gavel slamming down. Case closed.

The door chimed again. This time, through the frosted translucence of the door, Rico could make out a security officer, clearly carrying a LLAM.

"Not good," Rico said. They didn't have a single weapon on them, and they were stuck in a box with no weapons and only one exit that just led to another room.

"It's okay," Cecilia said and palmed the control. There on the platform stood Arnab, complete with uniform and what appeared to be a real station assault rifle.

"Hey, guys—" Rico started to protest, but Arnab held up a warning finger and flicked his gaze around upward. The universal signal for "someone may be listening." Ceres must have AI audio monitoring and listening for certain key words.

Arnab smiled at them. "Come along," Arnab he said. "We've got work to do."

Cecilia reached into the large bag on the floor, pulled out two more LLAMs and handed them to Rico and Inés. Rico inspected his. Fakes, but convincing ones.

He cringed inwardly. He hesitated to pull civilians into this mess, but it was their call, and there was little he could do now without drawing attention to themselves. Rico raised his hands in defeat and gave a single nod.

- NINETEEN -

Martel was not onboard the ship. However, Lara was.

She protested vehemently when they demanded access. She threatened to call Arnab's superiors—which would have been interesting to see—and swore profusely at Inés and Arnab since, in accordance with their charade, they were the officers in charge. She did not, however, recognize Rico, nor did she make any actual calls. Arnab threatened to arrest her if she made a move to call anyone. He played his role very well. Ceres personnel had not been able to find anything on the *Kukri*, but they had lacked something that Rico and Inés had with them: a DNA sample from Raheem.

The detectors found concentrations of DNA on the chair where he and Lara had been sitting, and then on a hatchway leading deeper into the ship. An outline of a hand showed up distinctly. Arnab kept Lara busy and Inés stayed in the control room as well, searching for any hidden computer files that the Cerean ashers may have missed. Rico and Cecilia went deeper into the ship.

Rico followed the occasional handprint smeared along a wall, and once, on the floor, where Raheem might have intentionally fallen to leave a clue in the hopes that someone would find it. Still, they found no sign of the man, from stem to stern. Rico had thought they'd find a hidden compartment in the cargo bay, but they found nothing. No Raheem. No blood. No nanobots. No hidden rooms. And, no sign of Martel or Pedro, either.

"Now what?" Cecilia whispered.

Rico flattened his mouth in a hard line. No way were they giving up now. "We keep searching."

They double-checked the entire cargo area but found nothing. Not even a handprint. At least, not one belonging to Raheem.

We must have missed something, but what? On the way back out, they saw it. The last room before the cargo room had a large print of the left hand. He'd seen that one and assumed that meant they would find more in the cargo hold. Now, panning the detector back and forth, Rico found a handprint on the *right* side of the doorway as well, along with small flecks of blood. Raheem must have put up a struggle when they told him to go into this room and grabbed both sides of the hatch frame. Beside the right hand print an 'x' had been hastily smeared with sweat.

The inside of the room appeared to be just a typical berth for a low-pay-grade worker, with one exception: the detector revealed a long streak where they must have dragged him across the floor. It led over to the bunk, and disappeared right underneath the stowage shelves. Rico slid a drawer open. Nothing. They tried moving the bed and shelves. No spin. Bolted or soldered right to the floor.

They'd found something, but they had no way to access it, short of laser cutters. Cecilia said she could get hold of one of those, but Rico wanted to hold off for now.

Rico commed Arnab and filled him in. He told the towering Cerean to lean on her, and he did so with great gusto. He confronted Lara about the hidden cargo hold. She, of course, refused to cooperate or to admit to any wrongdoing. She also demanded to see Martel—and a lawyer—as well as the planet Omsbud.

"Cecilia, do you have a wristcomm that will bypass the *Kukri's* communication network and patch us into Ceres channels?"

"Of course."

"May I?" he asked, extending his hand for her comm. She handed it over and he asked her a few questions. Then, he hit the appropriate icon and said, "Secure comm to Chief Curtis, Priority Code 999. Eyes only. Threat imminent." It was similar to what he'd heard Curtis' assistant say, but that priority code had had a suffix, which Cecilia had identified as a personal ID code. Rico didn't have Curtis' ID code, but hopefully the AI would compensate and the call would go through.

It did.

Immediately, an annoyed face appeared on the small screen. Her close-cropped hair almost bristled. "Who is this? Why aren't you following standard protocols?" She leaned in and peered at her own wristcomm. Seeing a man that she did not recognize with colored hair and a snake's eyes, she reined in her response. Clearly, Rico was not one of her own, but he was wearing an asher uniform. Rico could see the questions and possibilities churning through a rapid mind.

"Okay, young man, you're not on my transfer roster, but you have my attention. Who are you, and what do you want?"

Rico filled her in with military efficiency. He was

taking a gamble. If he'd read her right, they might get off the *Kukri* and back onto the station with minimal fuss. If he was wrong, they'd end up in a cell and having their DNA harvested to make bail.

Chief Curtis stared at him for a moment. Then she grunted, once, gave a clipped nod, and cut the comm.

The resulting swarm of security personnel eliminated any hope of a subtle exit. Dozens of ashers and redpipes, as he learned they were nicknamed, descended on the ship. *I guess I've lost another bet,* Rico thought. He expected to be arrested any moment. They did not get arrested, however. Instead an officer came over to them and said, "Schroeder and Villaverde?" They nodded. "I'm Orinsky. Stand over there." He pointed next to one of the command chairs. "Don't move. Please." He added as an afterthought. They did as they were told.

They watched from the bridge, on the smartwall as an asher ran a scanner and confirmed that a corridor hid under the fake berth.

As soon as the corridor showed up on scan, Rico heard the officer on the scene say, "Lockdown Protocol." Two of the techs drew weapons Rico had never seen before and pointed them at the hold. That was unusual, and he was itching to ask what they were, but held his tongue.

Orinsky turned his head to Kohler, who had a guard standing behind her. "I don't suppose you'd care to give us the security code?"

Kohler gave him a tight smile.

"Go ahead, Connors," Orinsky said.

The officer on the scene, presumably Connors, called in a crack-hack next. She got through the encrypted lock in short order, and the bed slid out of the way. A corridor led down and under the cargo hold.

Chief Curtis appeared on a Smartwall a moment later. "What do you have, Orinsky?"

"Right now, just a hidden corridor. Probably a smuggler's bay, Chief."

"Sync me in on the live feed, audio only. I'm still en route."

"Yes, ma'am."

The security personnel found all kinds of contraband, including pleasure-nanobots, assassin nanobots, and a cryo-chamber. They also found Raheem Kuzbari. He was floating naked in a tank of bluish liquid. Computer readouts showed his vital signs were near nil. His body metabolism had been dramatically reduced.

The officer on the scene spoke. "All clear. Medical move in." After that, Rico shifted his attention to Lara as Orinswky began grilling her.

"Why are you transporting nanobots, Miss Kohler?"

She held his gaze for a moment and then grudgingly said, "They're evidence. Kuzbari was the one with the illegal nanobots. We caught him. We're taking him to Mars for a bounty. The bots are evidence. Everything was secured.

The man glowered at her. "*Any* nanobots must be declared. You're in violation of several planetary laws, Miss Kohler. You were informed of this before docking. Do you have a warrant?"

"Yes."

Rico resisted the urge to snort.

"We can confirm this, you know."

"Absolutely. Go ahead." Lara didn't bat an eye.

They must have someone in their pocket back on Mars, Rico thought.

Orinsky continued, "You are confined to the ship until further notice, Miss Kohler. Charges will be pending. Your AI and your ship are on lockdown. No calls in or out. Do you understand?"

Lara nodded and bit her lip. For once, she seemed a little less sure of herself.

Raheem arrived on the bridge, dressed in lounging attire, and a lot less refined than usual. His wet hair needed a comb. He seemed weak but ambulatory. A towel hung over one shoulder.

Chief Curtis arrived the same time. "I'm sorry, chief," Orinsky said. "He insisted on coming to the bridge."

Curtis gave Orinsky a sour expression, promising a dressing-down later, but addressed Raheem instead. "You're being accused of dealing in outlawed nanotechnology. Do you have anything to say regarding these charges?"

Raheem took his time replying. He surveyed the room, and then casually went back to drying his hair some more.

"I assume you know this ship is not in my name?" he asked.

Curtis gave him a grim nod.

"And you do realize that I was the one in the cryo-tank, against my will?"

"What we know, Mr. Kuzbari, is that you were in a cryo-tank, hidden out of sight and detection. They could just as easily have been smuggling you for one reason or another."

Raheem, ever cool and collected, gave a thin smile.

"Miss Kohler here, along with Pedro and Teddy Martel, are opportunists and terrorists. They are the criminals here. Not I."

"Miss Kohler is claiming they captured you for a bounty and that they have official documents from Mars verifying that."

"And you've seen this supposed documents?"

Curtis turned to Lara. "Miss Kohler, if you don't mind?"

Lara's mouth quirked up in the slightest of smirks. "Certainly. Do you mind?" She gestured at the control panel.

"Orinsky, watch her every keystroke."

"Yes, sir."

A moment later, Lara sat back and, waved at the smartscreen with a flourish. Curtis flipped through the images, taking her time. She perused the electronic signatures and watermarks.

"These seem official enough, and they were dated six months ago."

Raheem appeared thoughtful, staring through the bridge floor, and said, "Ah."

"That's your answer? 'Ah'? You can't do better than that?" Curtis gave him her best skeptical scrutiny.

Raheem's demeanor perked up with a visible effort, and he said with a winning grin, "How about 'Ah,'—and, 'I'd like to apply for sanctuary?'"

"What?" Lara exclaimed. "That's outrageous."

"What?" Inés echoed.

"Actually," Curtis said, "this is perfectly within his rights, as you well know, Miss Kohler." She leveled a knowing gaze at the thin woman.

"Dr. Kozbari, are you sure? Interplanetary treaty requires me to inform you that you will be required to remain on planet for seven years doing any and all tasks as assigned. Further, your DNA will be catalogued in perpetuity, and any offspring from such genetic material will remain on Ceres until they reach their majority."

Rico stepped forward. "Raheem. Think about this. Did you hear her? You're talking *seven* years here—no exceptions."

"I'm aware, but what choice do I have, Rico? They've got papers." A slight upturn at the corner of Raheem's mouth gave the impression that he found the situation funny, or at least amusing. The realization threw Rico off for a moment.

Raheem went over to Lara and said, "Don't take it so hard, dear." He took her by both shoulders, and she flinched, just slightly, when he did so. "I've always wanted to relocate to Ceres. I hear it is a planet of great opportunity." They could have been cousins, with their dark skin and hair. He gave her a peck on both cheeks and added, "Thank you for the lift, darling." Lara stared at him, nonplussed, but clearly unwilling to say anything that might implicate herself. Her face turned stormy. She pursed her lips and crossed her arms. Raheem made his way casually over to a chair and collapsed into it with a little less grace than usual.

"Orinsky, has he been scanned for bots?"

"Yes, ma'am. Down in the hidden stasis room."

"We're done here. Assign two ashers here for guard duty. You take the rest and get him to medical and then put him in a secure guest room."

Lara jumped out of her chair, incensed. "This is ridiculous! This man is a felon and a fugitive. I demand to speak to Teddy—Ted—Martel and President Holland."

"Your requests have been noted, Miss Kohler, and are being considered. If you'd care to lodge a formal complaint regarding my performance, you may do so. Eventually. For the time being, sit down." She jabbed a finger at the chair Lara had recently vacated. With as much dignity as she could muster, Martel's mistress retook her seat.

Most of the security officers, ashers, and the medical staff escorted Raheem from the ship, and then Chief Curtis walked over to Rico and Inés. Cecilia and Arnab stood close by them.

In a low voice, she said, "I could have the two of you locked up just for the uniforms you're wearing."

"Yes, ma'am," Inés said.

The woman had a soft face, despite her severe tone and militant haircut. She surveyed the room and added, "However, since you discovered the smuggler's hold, and a large cache of nanobots, I'll let that go. This time."

"Thank you," Rico said.

Curtis met Rico's eyes and gave a sharp nod. "Now. You four—"

Lara Kohler lurched to her feet, the angle of her body wrong. She tottered and raised a hand to her head, wincing. Wide, panicked eyes darted from Orinsky to Curtis as she tried to speak. She got out,

"Unnh," and then her eyes rolled up into her head. She fell to the bridge floor. Her body started convulsing, her legs kicking at the plate decking. In the low gravity, each kick and convulsion raised her body off the floor slightly in an eerie mockery of trauma. Two officers and an asher reached her before Curtis and had to push Lara back down. One of the young men checked her breathing, and then spoke rapidly into his wrist comm, "Medical emergency, Bay 3-3-4, ship *Kukri*."

Curtis swore. "Computer! Bridge med kits?"

"Starboard side of the co-pilot's chair," an unconcerned and disembodied voice relayed.

An asher had her scanner out before the other was even off his comm. "No breathing. No heartbeat. No brain activity."

They quickly laid out sensors on Lara's brain and chest. The AI's voice came over the speaker. "Permission to deploy medical nanobots."

"Denied," Curtis snapped.

The factual voice droned on, "Miss Kohler will die without—"

"Denied I said!"

"Clear!" The asher said and activated the stims. Kohler's body arced upward in an unnatural manner. The tech checked her scanner. "No pulse, no brainwaves."

The first asher reset and zapped Lara three more times but with no change. She was gone.

"I'm sorry, chief. As far as I can tell, she had a massive stroke, but the med guys will have to examine her to know for sure."

"Massive stroke my ass." Curtis stabbed at a

smartwall. Her face was a livid red. "Orinsky, report," she snapped.

"Orinsky here."

"Bring Dr. Kuzbari on screen."

"Yes, Chief Curtis? How may I be of assistance?"

"Lara Kohler is dead."

Raheem kept a bland expression on his face. "My goodness. How unfortunate."

"A healthy woman in her prime, dead of an apparent stroke." Chief Curtis glared at Raheem for a three count. "If you had anything to do with this, I will have your ass. Officer Orinsky, have medical scan him again. Thoroughly."

She stabbed a finger at Rico and Inés. "You two. Come with me." She then pinned Cecilia and Arnab with the same lethal stab. "You two as well."

- TWENTY -

Curtis sent them with an escort to their rental room, where they changed out of their illegal uniforms.

While the guards were distracted by Cecilia and Inés, Rico grabbed Arnab's arm and whispered to him, "See if you can find Raheem Kuzbari. Find out if he's safe. What happened to him."

Arnab gave him a solemn nod.

The guards sent Cecilia and Arnab on their way with admonishments not to pull anything of this sort again. The prop weapons were confiscated back on the ship, and the real officers took the costume uniforms as well.

Before stepping off the balcony ledge, Cecilia glanced over her shoulder with a forlorn expression, as if she wondered what would happen to Rico and Inés, and if they would be safe.

Rico wondered that, too.

He had expected the security detail to take them to a holding cell or Curtis' office. Instead he and Inés were placed in a heavy-duty transport with no windows and four armed officers with red piping on their uniforms. Black onyx glass lined the walls, but if there were any smartwalls, they did not activate at Rico's touch. The transport drove on autopilot, and no external view came online. The vehicle same to a smooth stop, and they exited into a barren access tunnel. Nothing but cement and a few pipes.

The officers passed them off to men and women

wearing black brocade displacement vests, the design inspired by formal Modi jackets. Two men, one woman and an android. The android was a giant brass statue, almost like an old Hollywood acting trophy that Rico could not recall the name of at the moment. The android stood close to two-and-a-half meters, even taller than the Cereans.

They were then ushered through a series of hallways and past myriad offices until they finally reached a large office lined with wood and long milk-white stone panels inlaid with mosaic pictures of events that Rico could not identify other than in generalities. A station battle. A space battle. A man, waving to the viewer, a woman doing the same. The Cerean flag with a red border on the bottom, midnight blue background, dot in the middle —representing Ceres—and a blazing sun on the far left. Feeding a starving child. A cocoon and a meta-human basking in the sun's glow.

Their escorts stopped at the entrance to a large office. Rico and Inés waited to be presented. Three people sat in black leather chairs. Two Rico recognized immediately. The first was Chief Curtis, the second President "Rockhard" Holland. Her sparse, short form seemed out of place on Ceres, where the Belter physique ran long and appeared plump. She seemed a diminutive doll next to Curtis, but only in size. Her features were as hard as the rock from which the underground tunnels of this planet had been chiseled, and her eyes held both the coldness of the depths of space, and the hint of the fire of distant stars.

Oh crap, Rico thought. Why on earth are we being

brought to the President? Inés leaned close to his ear and whispered, "*Aquí Hay Gato Encerrado*," which literally translated as, "There's a trapped cat in here." What it really meant was that something was very wrong here.

Schroeder gave one slow nod and thought to himself, *We should be way below her pay grade. We must have poked a much bigger bear than we thought.* He waited to see if it would bite them.

"Do we know where Martel is now?" Holland asked her two subordinates.

"No," the third person said. He was local, judging by his appearance and his uniform. Same uniform as Curtis, but with more ribbons and piping sewn on. Clearly a superior officer of some sort. The Cerean officer shook his head and said, "He's off net."

Curtis cleared her throat and said, "That's rather unusual for a law-abiding individual."

"Yes, it is, Chief Curtis," President Holland said. "Superintendent Oberkell, I want his ship under protective guard, and I want his safety secured as soon as possible. Freeze his credentials. But remember, Martel is a class-A applicant—high priority and to be given every accommodation. Even if he is off-net."

Oberkell. Rico recalled the name but it took him a second to place it. Curtis had called in a report to him. The man was up her chain of command. He seemed innocuous enough, but Rico knew not to trust appearances. He had dark gray hair, subtly wavy, with gray eyes to match, and a soft, genial face. His presence projected a sense of command and comfort with himself, but if not for the uniform Rico might have thought him a businessman.

"He will be quite upset about Miss Kohler's sudden death," Oberkell said. He inclined his head toward Curtis.

The chief shrugged. "The only thing med can tell us is that she died of a massive stroke."

"Nanobots, Chief Curtis?"

"None in evidence, no."

Holland squinted at him. "What are you implying?"

"There were minute toxins in her stomach that normally would not be there. These may have been from nanobots that migrated after her death, so that they would be dissolved there."

"Can we prove that?"

Cynthia Curtis shook her head. "Med says no. The elevations could have come from something she ate or drank recently."

"Has the body been processed yet?" Holland asked.

Curtis pursed her lips, and shifted in her seat. She glanced over at Rico and Inés, who were still waiting over by the door during this exchange. "No. They're waiting for approval from our office."

President Holland turned her steely eyes their way and smiled thinly. Rico was not at all deceived by her hospitality. "Captains Villaverde and Schroeder. Please, come in." Once they had sat down, she said, "Would you care for some Cerean water? It's the most pristine in the Belt."

Before Inés could offend their hosts by refusing, Rico said, "Sure, that would be great."

Introductions were made. Victoria Holland,

President-for-Life. Rick Oberkell, Superintendent for Planetside Security. Chief Cynthia Curtis they already knew.

"I understand the urgency of your mission, but I'm afraid we cannot help you. Martel has formally requested asylum, and he has a longstanding relationship with Ceres."

Inés could not hold her tongue. "So Ceres maintains longstanding ties with terrorists connected to Adala? That's interesting."

For a moment, the Cerean president stared at Inés with flat eyes, and then she said, "Cerean policy is that those who request asylum will be granted it. Conditionally. They must agree to remain on planet for seven years. Further, they must agree to serve the interests of Ceres during those seven years in whatever capacity they are assigned. They may not leave the planet for those seven years for any reason, personal or professional."

Holland paused while a 'bot brought water and refreshed the president's tea.

"You've heard horror stories, I'm sure. Exaggerated stories about Ceres. That this is Frankenstein's lair. Freakish creations. Human-spider hybrids. Shark genes spliced with humankind's." She gave them a mocking smile over her teacup. "Some of them are true." Then lowered the cup and faced them directly. "But not most. Why would we create a spider-soldier when mechanicals can do everything easier and without the long-term implications? No, no spider-soldiers here. But a little DNA to boost the strength of a human? A little gene therapy from a certified genius to heighten the intelligence and creativity of our next generation? Absolutely. An improved immune system to ward off viruses and bacterial infections? Most definitely."

She stood and walked over to one of the mosaics. She traced a double helix, and continued. "We have the most extensive genetic archive in the solar system. Every plant, every animal. *Every single creature.* We can reestablish the human race from right here. We have every possible trait on our small planet. Every physical characteristic. Every race. You want them taller? Shorter? You want a timid human? A loyal bookkeeper? A rampaging warrior, without fear of death? *We* can create them. Lovers, scientists, murderers, poets, teachers. We have them all here in cold storage. We are the saviors of humanity. The guardians of our posterity. We bank them all here."

"Why in all space would you want murderers?" Inés asked.

Holland lifted her chin at Inés with undisguised disdain for a brief moment. "You are clearly not aware of the needs of the state or the realities of life at our level. Murder is a tool. A rather effective tool. Most leaders are too cowardly to admit that, but they all embrace it. A knife in the dark, arsenic in champagne. How many wars are averted, how many interests advanced by assassination?"

"What about World War I? That started with an assassination."

"An anomaly."

"Didn't the Bay of Pigs start after a botched assassination?"

Rico didn't recognize the reference. Inés loved political history, though. Rico knew some, but not as much as Inés. Holland recognized it or bluffed. Either way, she waved the question away. "Poor execution. Doesn't the old Earth Bible even say there is a time to kill? It doesn't matter. The point is that we never know what we might need in the future. We must save everything. To colonize a hostile world. To rebuild after a pandemic. You think we would survive a plague just because we are in space, hmm? You've not read enough fiction if that's the case. Too many ships. Too many rats. We'd go up like a wooden house on fire. Poof!" She exploded her fingers outward, and then unconsciously wiped some spittle off of her lip.

Rico thought, *This woman is absolutely insane. She may have some valid points, but she's spacewalking without a tether.* Then she spoke as if reading his mind.

"Ah, your expression betrays your thoughts, Captain Schroeder. "You think we are paranoid, but we are paranoid by necessity."

Holland leaned forward and tapped the screen on the table. Several windows opened up, including pictures of Lara Kohler's autopsy photos. The delicate curves of her cheeks were ashen now, but still beautiful. She looked like a sleeping evil princess waiting for her evil prince to come wake her up. She'd been dangerous, but Rico was still saddened to see her dead.

She'd made her choice, though, and paid for it.

He wondered if Raheem had killed her. He had a strong suspicion that he had.

"Paranoid by necessity, captains." She tapped the photos as if they were the culminating evidence in a trial. Perhaps they were, and Holland planned to sentence them right here. Again, as if reading his mind, she continued, "Superintendent Oberkell and Chief Curtis tell me that we do not have enough evidence to arrest anyone on this crime. We are not without laws and ethics here on Ceres. We could, however, hold you indefinitely, according to Cerean penal codes."

President Holland sat back and sipped her tea, waiting and gauging their reactions. Rico and Inés met her gaze with aplomb. Inés did not even scowl at the woman.

Something didn't sit right. Rico tried to take a mental step back to figure it out. He decided to drop a ball and see if it went spinward.

"Pardon me, President Holland. May I ask a question?"

She gave him a quick, assessing look and a nod.

"Do you get involved in every offworld case involving asylum? Do you, personally, meet with all the investigators?"

No one moved for more than ten seconds, though it felt much longer. Holland drank again from her cup, then said, "No, Captain Schroeder, I do not. However, as I said, Mr. Martel has a long-term relationship with Ceres. He is a friend of the State, and we care about his wellbeing."

"Hmm. I think it's more than that. From what I've learned of Martel, he's got three primary interests: nanobots, which, given the strict prohibitions in that technology here I cannot imagine the Cerean government would be interested in. Terrorism, which, again, doesn't seem the sort of activity that a government in good standing in the solar community should condone, even indirectly."

This time Rico paused to take a drink of water. Let them stew, he thought, and wonder whether or not he was being facetious. He set his plas back on the table.

"But Martel just stole a considerable amount of technology from several corporations and governments. The prototype is sitting in one of your docking bays, and, Madam President, you just requested that it be—how did you put it?—put under 'protective guard.' An interesting choice of words. No doubt the stolen research files are somewhere on board as well. It makes one curious as to the Cerean intent regarding the ship and it's technology."

"Young man—" Oberkell had sat up straight and his face was red with barely contained fury. President Holland held up a skeletal hand, stopping him. Rico sensed the two guards move behind him. He heard a whisper of cloth, a creak of metal. He knew he was playing a dangerous game, but if he wanted to catch Martel, he needed to go all in.

Rico sat, impassively, his face blank, waiting for her next move. Minutes seemed to tick by.

"I'm quite certain you are not implying that the Cerean government would be condoning espionage, Captain Schroeder. That would be rather impolitic of you, and even the suggestion could cause an interplanetary incident."

"Of course not, ma'am. However, I'm also sure you can see how granting someone like Martel asylum—especially while he's in possession of stolen AMMATT drive technology—could be of concern to a great many invested parties."

Holland rapped on the real wooden table with her fingers. The noise sounded dead and hollow in the room.

"Do you know *why* such an accusation would raise interplanetary tensions, Captain? Have you reflected on how the AMMATT drive will destabilize the entire solar system, Captain Schroeder? Whoever holds this technology will have a devastating amount of power in their hands. Whoever does not will be at a considerable disadvantage. Such an imbalance could lead to upheaval. War, perhaps. Collapsing governments. Famine. Entire colonies wiped out."

"Maybe. Seems a stretch." Rico shrugged. "These days, if there is a buck to be made, people sell whatever they can get their hands on. The same is true with the AMMATT Drive."

"Can you guarantee that, captain?"

Rico met her gaze and said without hesitating, "No, definitely not."

She gave him a grim smile. "I thought not."

"I can, however, guarantee that certain corporations and governments would be annoyed enough to lay sanctions on any party harboring a terrorist and spy who had picked their pockets."

He considered laying out some of the sanctions that could be laid down, but decided not to overplay his hand. Not to mention the fact that he was way outside his pay grade with the threats he was making to a planetary leader. Holland's pursed lips and pinched eyes told him of the cold fury burning inside of her. Besides, she was apparently brilliant as well as paranoid. She would have a very clear idea of the crap about to rain down on her head.

It did not take her long to make up her mind.

"Enjoy the remainder of your stay, Captain. Good luck with your hunting. Be careful. Accidents have been known to happen in our rougher population cells. Of course, accidents can happen anywhere, even back in Peru or Brazil. Isn't that right?"

Inés sat up straighter in her chair, and Rico lightly touched her arm. Rico had been threatened before. Sometimes it felt like a stab of cold in his guts, especially when he considered his grandmother, his old abuela, and Inés' siblings and nieces and nephews. But being threatened did not paralyze him or even fluster him. He thought grimly that maybe he'd been threatened enough that such verbal sparring caused only a minor adrenalin spike now, a momentary uptick of the needle.

Holland let out a congenial breath and smiled warmly, with all the friendliness of a viper. "Well," she continued, "I trust you will convey our cooperation to those concerned. The ship, unfortunately, must be impounded for illegal contraband. Smuggling nanobots is a most grievous crime on Ceres."

"Naturally," Rico said, keeping his sardonic tone in check.

To Curtis and Oberkell, she said, "Keep me in the loop, officers."

With that they were dismissed, and the security guard escorted them out. The brass giant remained behind to protect the Cerean head of state from whatever paranoid delusions haunted her twisted and crenulated little brain.

They waited while Oberkell and Curtis conferred for a moment a short distance away. Inés leaned over to him and kissed him on the cheek. "I think I just fell in love with you in there." Rico laughed, and she added, "You were awesome, Chico."

Oberkell walked by and gave them a perfunctory nod. His eyes were stony and his jaw set. He didn't seem quite as genial anymore, and Rico hoped they had not made an enemy that would trip them up. Chief Curtis had walked up at the same time, and she led them to a driverless ground car. She waved them in and surprised Rico by getting in as well. She said to the AI, "Candra, autocab, main water lines." The car took off and buildings zipped by.

- TWENTY-ONE -

Chief Curtis settled into the seat, and visibly relaxed as microprocessors began massaging her back. "Tell me about your pursuit of Martel so far."

Rico filled her in, and when he finished a silence fell. Curtis didn't say anything, but she clearly had something on her mind. Rico and Inés exchanged a glance, but waited her out. When she spoke next, the conversation went in an unexpected direction.

"Miss Villaverde, I know it was several years ago, but I'm sorry for what happened to your brother. That was a bad business."

Inés kept her composure, but her stricken countenance revealed old wounds newly reopened upon landing on Ceres. She nodded and said, "Thank you."

"*Você é bem-vindo.* You're welcome."

Inés eyes-widened, surprised. "You know Portuguese?"

"Yes. My mother was a surrogate, too. There's a lot of Portuguese blood on Ceres. Portuguese, Indian, German, a lot of Swedes—others as well, of course."

"I'm confused," Rico said. "All due respect—and meaning no offense—why would you care about what happened to her brother? Harvesting DNA is *modus operandi* here on Ceres. Isn't that what President Holland was alluding to with Kohler when we walked in? You guys are preparing to take samples from her as well. Holland's a hoarder. She can't get enough. Your population crisis is long past, but she's still obsessed with collecting DNA." Rico stopped short of explicitly calling her crazy, since he didn't want to end up in a cell of his own.

"No, no offense at all, Captain Schroeder," Curtis said dryly. "Genetic cataloging is our sacred cow, our state religion. For many Cereans, especially those in power, it is sacrosanct." She made no apologies. She just laid the truth out there to dry up in the sun.

"Moreover, patterns are hard to break. Policies, once in place, are hard to change. However, our research has helped a lot of people, and cured a great many diseases. Cerean advances have made space more habitable."

"And pushed the boundaries on what it means to be human," Inés threw out there, "without the permission of those making donations."

Rico noted that Curtis never answered his question about Inés' brother, but he didn't push the matter.

"Their permissions were implicit as soon as they made station dock," Chief Curtis said, a bit of annoyance creeping into her voice, "but we're not going to agree on the semantics here. Let me cut to the chase. *Your* chase, actually. If you want to find Martel, he'll be in one of two places." She ticked them off on her fingers. "The barrens, those are the inactive mines, above and below the surface on the outskirts of civilized Ceres. The more logical place, though, is the Borras Vila just before the mines."

"Borras Vila?"

"Sorry. It's what we call slums here on Ceres. Roughly translated, it means village of the bottom of the barrel. When the population was exploding on

Ceres and in the 'Belt overall, we needed water. A lot of it. Entire towns sprouted up around ice harvesting and the filtration plants. Now, with slower growth, the ice collecting has declined as well. A large number of apartments out at the Barboza Aquifer are empty or contain squatters, and it's become a ghetto. The Borras Vila, while primitive, has trading and supplies of a sort; the barrens do not. It Martel hid there, he'd need to bring his own supplies."

Rico, skeptical about her suddenly forthcoming manner, asked, "Why are you telling us all this?"

The woman ran her disconcertingly long, Belter fingers through her short hair and turned her face toward them. She formed a triangle with her hands, and tapped her fingers together.

"I'm not entirely sure. I believe in Ceres. I believe in her right to survive, but that doesn't mean that I agree with everything that goes on." She paused, making eye contact with both of them, as if willing them to understand some unspoken meaning. After a moment, she went on. "It's my job to uphold the law. That doesn't mean it's always pretty, Captain." She glanced away for a moment and then turned back to them. "Ghosts don't go away, you know. They accrue."

An awkward silence fell on the group. Whatever sins Curtis may or may not have committed she kept to herself. She shook off her somber mood and said, "Change may be difficult, but that does not mean there are not those who believe in change. I cannot help you beyond the information I've just supplied. You may have gotten a green light from Holland, but don't think she's happy about it, and she is not someone you want as an enemy. If you repeat any of this, I will, of course, deny it."

"What about Raheem?" Inés asked.

Curtis' face clouded over. "I don't trust that one." Her eyes drilled into them, her professional interrogator switch flipping back on. "Did he kill Kohler?"

Rico and Inés both indicated they didn't know.

Curtis pursed her lips and gave an exasperated exhalation through her nostrils. "He was in a hidden compartment, unconscious and presumably imprisoned. He could have been hiding in there, but that seems doubtful. Why would he bother? That weighs heavily in his favor. Lacking any evidence, he'll probably be released. I can't say when or for how long. I'll see what I can do.

"We'll head to the Barboza plant first, and then the barrens. Would you let Raheem know where we're headed, in case he can join us?"

"Are you sure you want to do that? Do you really think you can trust him?" Curtis asked.

Rico shrugged. "We can use any help we can get. Plus, I keep going back to that coded message he sent us."

"You know that could have been faked, or some sort of a setup."

"That wouldn't be out of character for Martel, that's for sure," Inés added.

"Granted, but it just seems too convoluted even for Martel. I could be wrong. Call it a hunch."

It was Curtis' turn to shrug. "Your funeral. Either way, just so we are clear: he's requested asylum, and that means he can't go off-planet."

"For seven years," Rico asked. "Is that really the case? Seven years, no reprieve, no exceptions?"

"Correct. He's ours now. Seven years. One hundred percent."

The cab stopped and Curtis opened the hatch and unfolded herself, climbing nimbly out in the low gravity. She shook Inés' and Rico's hands. "You understand, of course, we cannot allow visitors from off planet to run around with weaponry even for law-enforcement reasons. Planetary law. My apologies for that." She pointed, "Right across this plaza, there are a group of autocabs that will take you out on the routes that run along the water plants. Good luck. Oh, one more thing." She glanced around the plaza. "My understanding is that if you want to buy any souvenirs, you can purchase many hard to find items in the Borras Vila."

She gave them a brisk nod, and without waiting for a reply, turned and walked off.

* * *

They took a bullet-shuttle through the under-ground capitol city of Piazzi, where some of the buildings disappeared out of sight. Inés told them the locals called the floor-to-ceiling skyscrapers "stalags" after stalagmites. From her perspective, it seemed a dark joke on the word for the German prisoner-of-war camps. The pods traveled through clear tubes, and the buildings appeared to zip past them in a hypnotic blur. Rico had begun to nod off when Inés spoke, pulling him back from the edge of dozing off.

"You know," she said as they glided along,

"there's something else that's been bothering me about Raheem."

You too? he thought, but did not say it. "Yeah?"

"Why did Martel let Kuzbari live? They could have killed him at any time."

Rico grunted, but didn't say anything. It was a good question, one that kept nagging at him as well. He wondered if he'd made a mistake asking Curtis to tell Raheem their destination. Nothing he could do about it now.

He reclined the seat and closed his eyes again. One of the skills he'd picked up in the Corps was the ability to sleep anywhere, anytime. Before he knew it, a change in motion woke him up. Rico checked his wrist comm. Four hours had passed, and he had a message from an unidentified sender. He opened it read: "Ted at Dr. Numbia's. RK out. Acknowledge." He showed Inés.

A "Yes" icon blinked below the message. Rico clicked it and then watched as the letters disappeared in reverse order.

Inés eyebrows went up.

"Nice trick," he said.

"Ever heard of that doctor?"

Inés shook her head. "What do you think Raheem is up to?"

"Honestly," he said, "I haven't got a clue."

The shuttle had parked beside a dock with a chain-link fence to keep people out. Beyond the fence they could see a massive plant with pipes and tanks stretching for what must have been a kilometer or more. Dim lighting from some human-made source filtered down from the stone ceiling, and Rico thought he could see towering apartments in the distance. A sign identified it as Barboza Aquifer: Water Filtration Plant #6.

The air smelled of chemicals and sewage.

Inés and he exited the bullet-shuttle by pushing off and landing lightly on the platform. Moving in low-g was like being on a playground—almost all the fun of spacewalking without the constricting suit—or the threat of imminent death.

A clerk of some sort stood on the dock in navy blue coveralls, and greeted them. "Uh, Captain Schroeder and Captain Villaverde?"

"Yes," they said, wondering what they were walking into.

"Chief Curtis said you were investigators from off-planet and wanted to inspect the abandoned residence compound in Barboza?"

The guy looked to be all of fifteen years old and completely mystified as to why someone would want a tour of the last water filtration plant built on Ceres.

"That's correct," Rico said.

"Well, my name's Ket. Ket Johnson. She, um …" He trailed off for a moment and then regrouped. "She said you wanted to go to …" —He swallowed and clasped his hands — "to the Borras Vila?"

Rico nodded.

"Uhm. Are you sure? It's really not safe there."

Rico nodded again and gave him a reassuring smile. The kid gave a weak smile in return and then took them to a monorail with a single car suspended underneath. The young man paused before it and gave a grand wave as if introducing a celebrity. "Impressive, isn't it? Water is Ceres' biggest export.

We supply most of the 'Belt. Well, not Barboza, per se. We still treat a lot, periodically, though. The plants rotate processing volume to keep the equipment from freezing up."

He stopped and tapped his chin, thinking. "Oh, right. Sorry, I got sidetracked. Um, since we have so much water here, the engineers came up with this mode of travel. We call it the aqua rail. Water is shunted along main transport lines here at the plant, and the pod is pushed along like a bobber floating down a stream."

They boarded the pod, dangling like fruit from a tree, and Ket pushed a button, opening valves above them, and off they went. The pod actually floated along roughly comparable to an upside down sailboat, with the "sail" catching the water and sending them along. It wasn't as fast as the bullet-shuttle they rode over from Centri, but it did the job.

The number of tanks and the thousands of kilometers of pipes were staggering. Axion Station's and Branson Station's water filtration plants were only a fraction of the size, but then they were only treating their own waste. Ceres was actively mining the ice of the dwarf planet, treating it and exporting it. They had a fairly heavy industrial presence as well, and all that water had to be treated.

They rode above fat roundish tanks a couple of stories tall and between other, narrower ones twice as high. A forest of pipes of various colors—red, black, gray, blue—spread out beneath them. Large lettering that could be read from the aqua rail labeled everything with cryptic numbers and letters interpretable only by the inner circle of water filtration workers. Some had labels he could understand, "Greywater," "Bacterial Filter," "Sand Filtration," "Warning: High Pressure." Valves, levers, and gauges of various sizes were everywhere.

Ket chattered away enthusiastically while they rode. As with most water treatment plants, there were four main water systems that were kept isolated from each other: sewage water; industrial waste, which might contain mercury, lead or other toxic chemicals; greywater that did not contain sewage or industrial waste; and indigenous—sometimes called virgin—water, which came from ice on Ceres.

They passed ugly, utilitarian apartments along the way. Rico thought of towers created by stacking blocks sloppily atop one another. Rico's lips curled up as he watched a group of children jumping off balconies of one stalag and circling around using some form of propulsion. They appeared to be playing tag. Rico pointed them out to Inés, and they both smiled at the sight.

The pod approached the far wall of the massive underground cavern, and Rico felt the walls closing in. They stopped at a platform with more apartments, and Ket opened the door. It looked as if someone had taken five old-Earth-style skyscrapers and pushed them into a soft clay wall. The fronts of the buildings were almost flush with the cavern. No lights could be seen from any of the windows. No one went in or out of the bank of doors lining the front of the buildings. No one hung out talking or eating on the large plaza near the pod station. A disquieting tension thrummed in the emptiness. One thought came to Rico's mind as they stood before the abandoned residences: ghost town.

Ket cleared his throat. "Well, um." He coughed into his hand and cleared his throat again, darting glances up at the gloomy roofscraper. "I need to get back to operations and check some, uh, readouts. You can call me when you're ready to, uh, head back."

Their tour guide left so quickly they barely had time to thank him. The pod disappeared from view behind a cluster of tanks. Rico felt a little bit stranded.

The platform jutted out from the third floor, with two floors beneath them, which Rico saw when he peered over the edge. He spotted a girl's face staring up at them, open-mouthed, before an adult hand grabbed the child and pulled her back out of view.

Rico guessed the building before them stood over twenty stories tall. "This could take awhile."

"*Fala sério*," Inés said in a hushed tone.

"I always talk seriously," Rico replied, and Inés shot him a half-smile at their old joke. The two of them hop-walked in the stride of low gravity toward the middle entrance. Rico definitely felt as if they were being watched.

"I really wish we had some weapons here," Inés murmured in a singsong voice.

"Ayup."

Large panes of green-tinted glass hissed open as they approached. They walked through and into a lobby area. A desk lay ahead of them with a plexscreen on top. Off to the left a bank of float tubes sat currently unused. A light flickered on, off, on, off. Dust particles floated in the air.

To the right, broken chairs and tables lay scattered around the floor. A few pots as tall as Inés held dead plants. One overgrown tree still thrived, probably because of some automated waterline. On the opposite end of the room, beyond the far doors, they could see additional trees in a courtyard. These, too, were full of green leaves, and some even bore fruit.

With a nod, Rico headed outside. Beyond the lobby, there was indeed a courtyard, oval in shape and lined with abandoned offices and stores. A large oak tree filled the center square and reached up half as high as the building Rico and Inés had just exited.

As their eyes drifted upwards, he and Inés both started in surprise as they saw several balcony platforms, all without handrails, and several women and men. The people either stood or sat with their legs dangling over the edge, but all of them held some sort of weapon. Dozens of disruptors, LLAMs and lasers pointed down at them.

"Welcome to *Fim da Linha*," a voice said from above them.

Rico raised his hand in greeting, and translated the Portuguese phrase in his head, "End of the Line." *Well, let's hope not.*

"Hello," he said, holding his arms up and away from his body. Inés mirrored him.

"State your business," said a man with the grayish skin and elongated body of a Belter. No weapon was visible in his hand, but his eyes held plenty of malice of their own. He had the wrinkles of someone who had not had any prolong treatments in a long time.

"We're … here to deliver a package," Rico said slowly.

"What kind of package?"

Rico glanced around and saw scores of other eyes

watching them from windows and balconies.

"Medical, I guess. Dunno. Guy didn't tell us."

The spokesperson grunted. "Let me see it."

Rico met his gaze and said, "No can do. I lose my rep, no more deliveries."

The old man glared at him, a distant sun beating on a barren and lifeless surface.

Finally, he said, "Who's the package for?"

"Dr. Numbia."

"Never heard'a him." Some of those in the gathered crowd were smiling—vultures hovering, waiting to feed on the dead. Others had grim or outright hostile expressions. They definitely did not make Rico feel welcome.

"We can pay for an escort. Untraceable credits."

They haggled for a while and agreed on a price. Rico slid a generic credit card through a portable scanner and transferred the amount from his account to the old man's. The old man pointed to a third-floor apartment, and a young kid did a somersault off the balcony and bounced over to them. She stood rock still and waited by the old man.

"I see you have a nice variety of weapons here," Rico said. "I'm a bit of a collector myself." He held the old man's gaze. "I'd pay a good price for two LLAMs."

The old man shrugged and said loudly, "Anyone interested in selling these two floaters?"

"How much?" someone called down. They haggled a bit, and agreed on a price that was probably about three months salary on Ceres. Rico paid it willingly.

"Take them to Doc Numbia," the old man said to

the girl.

"Yes, *avô*." When the girl used the word, *avô*—grandfather—Rico noticed the family resemblance in the cold, steely eyes.

No other goodbyes, no false pleasantries. Rico nodded and followed after Inés and the girl, who had already taken off. The girl—skinny, dark of skin and hair, and with large blue eyes—had a grace neither Rico nor Inés could match. She took two or three quarter-steps and then leapt into the air, gliding twice as far as they could, with one knee thrust forward and the other leg pointed backward. She reminded Rico of some real-life incarnation of Peter Pan. They started after her, and one of the residents of *Fim da Linha* grabbed Rico's arm. Heavy odor wafted off the man, and a scraggly beard hung in front of his face. "Hey, off-rockers. Want some Nahn-Nahn juice? Hook you up."

Nahn-nahn juice. Nanobots. Interesting. Nano-technology had been driven underground here, but not eradicated. Rico declined the offer, and followed after Inés and the kid. The ceilings were higher than Rico was used to. They needed to be—with such low gravity, you'd crack your head on the beams overhead if you bounced too high, and end up in the infirmary.

The girl led them an industrial-styled door labeled only G-568. She pointed at the entrance, still without talking, and then sprang back the way she had come. "Wait," Inés called after her, but she only gave them a glance and a half wave, and then she was gone.

Rico knocked on the heavy-duty door. No one answered, and after a minute or two, he tried the knob and the door opened into a waiting room. Chairs lined the far side of the room, paintings hung on two walls, and a miniature cannon occasionally fired globes of water from one side of the room to a fish tank on the other, the wobbly balls of water slowly floating down to the surface in the low gravity.

A gray rug had grease or dirt stains. A sturdy red plas coffee table sat in front of the chairs. No assistant, human or robotic, waited behind the desk. Next to the desk, another door led into the inner sanctum, but a security pad requiring a pin code, fingerprint and retinal verification barred access.

"Now what?" Inés asked.

"Now, we wait." He sat in one of the chairs.

She made an unladylike snort of disgust. Rico suppressed a smile. Inés hated to wait. She plopped down next to him in a semi-sulk, as much as one can in low-g, and crossed her arms.

Shortly after they had arrived, a large man opened the inner entryway. He was the most unusual man Rico had ever met. He appeared to be the result of a mad scientist experiment. Feline whiskers projected out from the crown of the man's head, as well as his forehead, cheeks and arms. Rico reevaluated his first impression. No, not a cat. There were so many whiskers protruding from the man's flesh, and his form so bulky, that it brought to mind a gorilla crossed with an exotic fish. His shoes were unusually large and misshapen as well, also suggesting some deformity.

The man wore a white, short-sleeved lab coat, mag-sealed, and stretched taught by biceps as big as small moons. He smiled and held out his hand.

"Good afternoon. I'm Dr. Numbia. I understand you have a package for me."

Rico wondered how he'd gotten that piece of news already. "Well, actually, we're interested in your … services." Rico gave the man a friendly smile, but careful not to overplay it. No need to make the guy more suspicious than he would be already. Especially since Rico and Inés both had LLAMs within easy reach. Whatever this guy's real line of work, no doubt it was not on the legal side of the law. Not way out here—and not if Martel was a customer.

"I see. How did you hear about my research?"

"A guy over at the Hole. You know, on Eunomia? He didn't give us his name."

"Hmm. What are you interested in? Augmentations? Downloads and backups?" He raised a hand, "You need to know up front, I don't do field work. If you need a donor, then apprehending and transporting are on you. However, mindwipes and storage are included in the fee."

Inés asked, "Do you have a list of fees?

The wide man gave a thin smile and tapped his head. "Nothing in writing, no. The nature of my work is … delicate." He sat down in one of the chairs, close to the door he had just entered. Rico and Inés sat on the opposite side, near the outer door where their silent guide had dropped them off.

Rico didn't have the whole picture yet, but what he put together did not sound good. Mindwipes were highly illegal except for the rehabilitation of prisoners. He decided to try a different tact to see if Numbia would bite.

"We heard you had some issues."

The man curled his lip, showing his teeth on one side of his mouth in a snarl. "I don't think I care for your tone. This is a whole new frontier. There are risks." He waved away the failures with a swipe of a massive hand. "We're talking about immortality. Youth on demand. A new life, a new body— whenever you want. The failures, well, those were unfortunate, but that was early on." He touched the top of the coffee table, palm flat, and a screen blinked on. The whiskers on the back of his knuckles waved in a disconcerting yet mesmerizing manner.

A graphic of the brain appeared on the tabletop. He spun the image around so it faced them. "My technique uses a biocyber drive, which will hold every thought and emotion you've ever had—even the ones you've forgotten. With enhanced neural connections, all your memories will be more accessible than ever before. You will be smarter, make connections faster. *Life* will be more vibrant, all without the limitations and risks of nano-technology. *I* know. I'm living proof." The whiskers on the man's head and bare arms quivered with what Rico assumed was excitement, but you never could tell for sure.

Rico's thoughts raced, sorting through this new information. Wetware experiments. Not just experiments but, apparently, successful redesign of the brain itself. Very dangerous stuff.

Inés scoffed at the screen and then glowered at Numbia. "Come on. Brain downloading? They've been trying to transfer the psyche for over a hundred years now. It's a myth. Right out there with the Fountain of Youth and transmuting lead into gold." She turned to Rico and said, "C'mon, hon. This guy is a snake oil salesman." She whipped back to Numbia. "The closest anyone ever got were freaks that could spit back memories, but that was all. The essence of the person? The spark? Gone. They were zombies. How is your process any different?"

"The details are both technical and proprietary," Dr. Numbia said stiffly. He pointed to the screen where synapses or some such thing sparked and glowed in the brain graphic. "Suffice it to say that these enhanced connectors are foundational to both the storage of engrams—memories and personality— and the successful uploading of that information into a brain. Without them, you are correct. Uploading and successful downloading has … unpleasant results."

Rico raised a placating hand. "You'll have to forgive my wife. She's very protective of my well being." He patted her hand. "I have Az-three. Early stage. The doctors tell me they can greatly slow the degradation with medication and nanobots, but that the end result will eventually be the same."

Rico pursed his lips in a frown at his fictitious demise. After a beat, he continued. "So are you saying that you can download every single memory, the emotions, the sensory experiences—everything— into some sort of backup device? Then you, what? Fix my brain with those improved synapses or whatever and reload 'me' back into my refurbished brain?"

"Essentially, yes. That's one option."

"One option?" Inés asked. "What are the other options?"

Rico winced mentally. She had asked just a little too eagerly.

Dr. Numbia sat back and crossed his arms. Uh-oh,

Rico thought.   Something in her tone or their questions had tipped him off. "Who did you say referred you?"

Rico shrugged. "Tall guy. Belter. Brown hair."

"I see." Then, without warning, the man said, "Candra, black out!" The room went pitch black.

- TWENTY-TWO -

Numbia must have prepped some programming for just this scenario. His AI responded instantly. Even the table display and the fish tank light winked out. Rico made a grab for him, but Numbia kicked the table into him, cracking into Rico's shins and tripping him up. *Two exits from the room. Which one?* Rico made a guess: back inside. He stepped around the table by feel, moving blind, and bumped against a plas chair. He pushed it aside and moved on.

A green glow suddenly suffused the room from the wall beside the inner door, and Rico saw that it had lit as Numbia palmed the door lock. Inés had gotten ahead of Rico. She grabbed the man's elbow but, with surprising speed and viciousness, the doctor lashed out. He popped his arm back, elbowing Inés in the face, and followed it with another to the gut. Rico heard her cry out from the first blow and then gasp as the air shot out of her lungs.

Rico lifted his gun and racked it, the characteristic whining-hum sizzling in the air as it surged into ready mode.

In the low gravity, Numbia easily shoved Inés in an upward arc right toward Rico, blocking any decent shot. Rico let his gun go to catch her, the weapon dangling from the strap around his neck, but he was too slow. Inés flew into him and they both tumbled backward against the far wall. Rico struggled to his knees just as Numbia disappeared into the hallway. The door started to close. Rico grabbed a chair and dove for the opening, shoving the chair into the closing gap. There was a loud crack—no safety stops here—but the plas held.

Rico threw a glance back to Inés who was propped against the wall, blood pouring from her nose. Still trying to catch her breath, she waved him on.

LLAM up and ready, Rico stepped into the hall checking for threats on both sides. Empty. He heard the whisper of a slide-door come from his left and ran that way.

He passed a few doors labeled as exam rooms on the right. On the left, there were only two doors, both at the end of the hall. One was just another exam room, but the other bore the label, "Bio-Drives." Rico palmed the door and it whisked open. He tensed at the noise, which in the empty hallway sounded as if space thrusters were firing.

Inside, he saw a wall of stainless steel doors, three rows of them, each less than a meter wide and a meter tall. He could see thirty just from the entryway. He stepped in, shifting his LLAM, and opened the one closest. Tubes and wires went into and out of a clear plas box. A strip of lights on the left blinked green, with one blinking yellow. Six rectangles floated in bluish liquid, making it difficult to determine colors. Green or blue or gray. Rico leaned in and saw a crenulated surface. They reminded him of something, but what? His first thought was a brick of noodles that needed reconstituting. Then it clicked—brain tissue. The dips and valleys of the smooth surface reminded him of a human brain. *Jesus help me. This must be where Numbia is downloading or backing up people's brains.* A disturbing question came to mind: *Is he growing brain tissue or "repurposing" it?* If he was reusing brain tissue, the next question was whether or not the donors were alive or dead when they'd had their brains harvested and stuck in a tank.

Rico quickly left the area and saw that Inés had passed him while he discovered the brain servers or whatever they were. She spun toward him, LLAM ready, and he held his hands up. They continued as quietly as they could down the hall to where it turned to the right. Rounding the corner, Rico saw three doors—double-gliders on the right, another farther down on the opposite side, and at the far end a door with a frosted window, maybe an office.

No sign of Numbia.

He headed for the double-gliders, Inés guarding his back. As he approached, the gliders whisked open automatically. So much for subtlety.

Just as he stepped inside, they heard the sizzling crack of a disruptor from behind the door across the hall. "Rico!" Inés moved quickly, crossing the hall in three strides and shoved open the door. She stepped to the side, keeping out of the line of fire.

Rico went through low and rolled to the side, and for a second his brain couldn't process what he saw. A fly-cycle lay on the stone floor of an access corridor, the front tire smoldering and most of the rest disintegrated. *Disruptor.* An open garage door gaped to his right. On his left, Numbia was grappling with someone—a tall, non-Belter. For a moment, Rico didn't recognize who it was. Then he saw the man's distinctive green suit. *Raheem.*

Inés stepped into the threshold and leveled her

LLAM on the pair. She and Rico had already loaded ShockGels. If she fired, though, the charge would hit both of them.

Rico considered firing anyway. Raheem was not high on his favored list at the moment.

Numbia was struggling to grab the disruptor in Raheem's right hand. The pistol went off and a large chunk of the ceiling disappeared. The overhead lights went out, leaving only luminescent bricks dimly lighting both sides of the access corridor. With his left hand Raheem punched Numbia in the gut. The gorilla across from him grunted and just smiled. The Earther blocked three of Numbia's rapid blows, then Numbia kneed him in the groin. Rico cringed. Numbia raised a blocky fist for a killing neck blow. All the muscles in Rico's body tensed, but Raheem whirled aside, and the punch glanced off. The wedge-shaped man kicked Raheem's arm hard. The disruptor tumbled in slow motion to the stone floor.

Numbia stepped back with a snarl and pulled a laser pistol from his lab coat. Inés and Rico didn't give him the chance to fire. They both pulled the triggers on their LLAMs. Numbia jerked as electrical current ran through his body.

Just then, someone fired a laser pistol from inside the garage. The first shot went wide by a hair. The second clipped Rico's left arm. It felt as if he'd touched a hot stove. He gritted his teeth and dove toward Numbia's groggy body as Raheem flattened himself on the floor behind the burning fly-cycle and retrieved his disruptor. Clutching Numbia's clothes, Rico pulled himself down and around, fighting the low gravity. Inés scrambled in next to him. *Not much cover, but it will have to do.* Two laser shots scorched into Numbia's leg, and he screamed in pain.

Rico switched ammo. Time for body-seekers.

Body seekers were a last resort. The bullets could fly around corners and target any organic creature between 35 and 40 degrees Celsius. Hopefully there were not any stray cats—or hostages—around.

Inés popped up and fired off three rounds. Rico followed with two of his own, hoping their assailant had taken cover. He didn't wait to see if he hit the target. He ducked back down as a series of wild laser blasts came from the garage. Numbia screamed as another one hit him. Raheem rose to his elbows and fired his disruptor. The air cracked as if it was breaking.

They waited. Only Numbia's moaning broke the silence.

Raheem whispered, "Cover me," and scrambled around the fly-cycle toward the open garage door. Rico nodded. Inés gave the Middle Easterner's back a dirty look.

No one fired at him from the shadows. "Clear."

Rico joined him in the garage bay. Pedro, Martel's henchman, lay on the floor. Lucky for him, one of Inés' ShockGels hit him instead of the body seekers or Raheem's disruptor.

#

"With Pedro here, it's a good bet Martel is still around," Rico said.

"If he didn't take off already," Raheem said. He rubbed at his neck where Numbia had hit him.

"Thank you, by the way."

Inés found some cables in the garage. Raheem filled in Rico and Inés while they trussed up their captives. "After our good Chief Curtis let me out, I bought a fly-cycle—at twice the market rate, the charlatans—and came out here. Old Man Arroyo's granddaughter showed me the garage entrance. I parked out in the main tunnel. As I was walking up, some guy came out of the garage on that fly-cycle." He pointed at the burning heap. "I told him to stop and, when he didn't, I shot his tire. He took exception to that." In an admiring tone, he added, "Despite his size, he's quite agile. He jumped off his bike and onto me. The rest you saw."

"Does he always talk that way?" Inés shot at them.

Rico shifted his eyes from the knot he was finishing to Raheem, and then grinned at Inés. "Pretty much. I figure he went to Oxford or some other Ivy League school."

"Am I sensing some residual hostility?" Raheem sounded mildly amused.

Inés stepped in close to him and jabbed a finger at his chest. "That's right. I want to know whose side you're really on, and what kind of game you're playing. Why didn't Martel space you out there? I would have."

"And I'd like to know why the hell you killed Lara Kohler," Rico added.

"You two want to have this conversation now?"

Inés crossed her arms and glared at him. "I'd rather have this conversation here with you in front of me than have you behind me with a disruptor."

"Touché."

"Raheem's got a point, though, Innie. We need to keep moving." At the same time, Rico was determined that there would be a reckoning. Lara Kohler had been a criminal, true. But she had also saved Rico's life—and possibly the life of everyone on Chou Station by tipping them off. Rico had owed her, and he'd never be able to pay her back. It left him with a renewed sense of loss. Raheem and Inés both argued for Jupiter Justice the hard way, but Lara Kohler hadn't deserved to go out like that. He'd sensed more to her than a hardened criminal. And, despite Trigger's betrayal, Rico still trusted his instincts. He had too.

Inés started to protest and Raheem held up a hand. "Fine. I shall be brief." He inclined his head toward the door Rico and Inés had come out of. "Have you figured out what they do here?" Inés waggled her hand *mezza mezza* to indicate "sort of."

Rico said, "They back up people's entire being into biological data-storage devices. I saw brain-like wet-drives in one of the rooms."

"Yes. That is one procedure they do here. Another is that they transfer those personalities into a completely new body. But the clients must provide the victims. The hapless individual's brain is then wiped out and the 'new' personality uploaded."

"That's what Numbia was telling us, but that still doesn't explain why Martel didn't have you sucked out an airlock," Inés said, her tone more inquiring now than hostile.

"Doesn't it? Oh, I quite think it does. Martel was planning on moving in. He was going to have my mind erased, and then taking up residence in my body. Martel would conveniently turn up dead—no doubt in a conspicuous manner for easy discovery, and probably framing *you* in the process. Then Martel would continue his evil ways as the illustrious Dr. Raheem Kuzbari." He bowed with a flourish of his hand.

Rico and Inés stared at him, incredulous. Raheem arched an eyebrow and shrugged. With a weary sigh, he said, "Look, he and Lara took great pleasure in telling me as much on the ship. They are both cold-spaced killers." He looked pointedly at Rico. "Yes, she was beautiful, charming...and also very deadly." His gaze shifted between the two of them. "You got my message, yes? Otherwise, you would not be here. Why would I send such a message if I were working with Martel?"

"Maybe to lure Rico here. A trap, so he could be Martel's host."

Raheem laughed. "No offense to Rico, but we've hardly been enough of a nuisance to Martel to warrant that sort of grand revenge. No, I was simply an available body at an opportune time."

"So how do we know that you're not Martel right now?"

Raheem scoffed at Inés. "I expected more from you. If I were Martel, how would I know about the hidden message? The one sent in the non-visible light spectrum, and the one I tapped out on Kohler's leg?"

Inés glowered up at the tall man. "You could have caught Raheem in the act, and figured out what he did. From there, you reviewed the vid you made, you arrogant chupacabra, and discovered the Morse code message as well."

"This is ridiculous. Why would I be attempting to capture Martel now?"

Inés laughed. "You could have done the transfer and left your old self as a sacrificial pawn. *You* just said so yourself—the old Martel has to be discovered."

"Yes, but dead. At the moment, he happens to be very much alive. We're wasting time. Either trust me or not, come with me or not, but I'm going after Martel."

"All right," Rico said. "Enough talk. We need to move if we hope to catch him." Inés started to argue, but he held up a hand. "Even if you're right, we still need to catch the guy. Everyone back inside."

Rico went through the garage to the small access door that Pedro must have used. Raheem and Inés followed. It opened into a meeting area, this one much nicer than the lobby they first encountered. An office glider stood ajar. A quick peek told them no one was inside.

Only one other exit led out of the meeting area. Rico made eye contact with Raheem and Inés, his palm poised over the glide control. When they both nodded, he pressed it and the door whisked open. There were two gliders across the hall, spaced wide enough to probably indicate separate rooms.

They heard someone curse far down the hallway to the left. Rico took in a breath and stuck his head out. He saw Martel and another man before he ducked back. He really didn't want his molecules disintegrated today, or any other day, actually.

As he debated what to do next, an object drifted languidly in the low gravity across their field of vision. Light glinted grudgingly off of flat metal.

"Grenade!" Rico yelled by instinct and hit the close icon. The glider whisked home with speedy efficiency.

They heard a muffled bang, but felt no concussion through the thick door.

"Doppel-banger?" Raheem suggested.

"Most likely," Rico responded.

"Let's not go through that again."

"Agreed."

"Again?" Inés said.

"Later," Rico responded.

Raheem said, "How long before the gas dissipates?"

"Depending on the size of the corridor and the air exchange, maybe five minutes."

"Great," Inés said, rolling her eyes.

While they waited, Inés hacked into the computer system, activated the air filtration system, and found the security cameras. She pulled up the corridor outside on the smart panel. Martel and another guy were hurriedly wheeling a large cart down the corridor toward another set of double gliders.

Inés mumbled to herself as she typed away at the keys on the desk. "Come on, come on." Rico recognized a few Portuguese swear words.

"Gotcha!" She sat back with a smile. Martel and his companion got to the double-doors and the tall, rail-thin man palmed the lock. Nothing happened. He tried again. Nothing.

Rico, Raheem, and Inés chuckled as they watched

the two men argue and try getting through the panel.

"Wait," Raheem said suddenly, his face grim. He tapped one of the miniature views, and it opened up, taking over the smart panel on the desk. It showed a warehouse-type area with large boxes and crates— and several vehicles.

Raheem ran for the exit that led back to the garage. "Keep after them. Don't let them double back."

"Where are you—" Rico started to yell, but the door snicked shut, and Raheem was gone.

"Uh oh," Inés said.

Rico turned back to the screen. Martel was pointing a pistol at the tall guy. Teddy Martel, the mystery man of many names, gestured with the gun.

Rico thought Martel might shoot the guy, but instead the accomplice moved to the side. Martel fired at the door. A disruptor beam punched a three-meter hole through the jammed egress. After a pause for the weapon to recharge, he fired again, and then they had plenty of room. Unfortunately for the culprits, a disruptor beam is a sloppy weapon, and now the floor was steaming slag. The cart went down a bumpy slope, caught on a ridge, and tipped over into the warehouse. Steel containers hit the floor and rolled away from the cart.

"Okay, let's go," Rico said.

He opened the door for a second time. The air smelled pungent, and their eyes stung, but they could move through the hallway easily enough.

They passed through one set of double-gliders Rico had not noticed on the monitors, and came to the one Martel had disintegrated. They crept through the melted door. Two abandoned steel canisters had rolled to a stop near a pallet hauler.

Rico and Inés squatted down behind some large crates and listened.

Nothing. They peeked over the top. No sign of Martel and the tall guy. Then a motor thrummed and the massive paneled-wall at the front of the warehouse slowly lifted.

Both of them swore as the truck started moving, a quiet electric whine.

They stood and fired full out, but they only had anchor bullets. LLAMs were not built for piercing metal.

They fired anyway.

The truck slid silently into the main tunnel, the one they came down with the girl who was apparently the old man's granddaughter.

Then, unexpectedly, the passenger side of the cab of the truck disappeared with a crackle, the front tire, the door, and the passenger seat just gone. The front right side sagged forward like a shot elephant, listing so they could see the entire passenger side. Inés and Rico ran toward the truck. Raheem stepped into view, pistol out. He held it on the cab, waiting for the driver to make a move.

He glanced over their way, turned back to the cab, and said something they could not hear. Then, before Rico and Inés reached him, Raheem tensed, crouched down, and fired his disruptor into the truck's cab. When Rico and Inés got there, all that remained was the smoldering remains of a steering column, and the legs of what was once a man.

Inés covered her mouth and closed her eyes. Rico

felt his gorge rise at the smoking limbs.

Nausea and rage washed through Rico. Adrenalin and fatigue assaulted his body. After all they'd been through, he'd wanted to nail this guy. To get Martel, yes, but not this. He'd wanted him to pay. He'd wanted the bastard to stand trial. He felt angry and cheated.

And, if not, truth be told, some small, dark part of him had at least wanted to pull the trigger. Maybe. He wasn't sure. He'd come close to killing Trigg McAboy all those years ago but stopped himself. Would he have this time? He just didn't know. Now he'd never know.

All his frustration and adrenalin and turmoil turned in on itself, mingled with his guilt and anger over Lara Kohler's murder, and then exploded outward, a star about to go nova. He stepped in close to Raheem, invading the man's personal space. He barely kept from grabbing the man.

"Why the space did you kill him? You could have captured him."

"He went for his disruptor. I had no choice," Raheem said and locked onto Rico's gaze. Truth...or lie? Rico felt the challenge in those dark brown eyes.

"Well, that's pretty darn convenient, Kuzbari."

Raheem stood his ground. "I wouldn't exactly call *any* of this convenient, Rico."

The two men stared eye to eye for a moment longer. Rico wanted to slug him, have it out with him. The tension vibrated for a moment longer.

"Justice," Inés whispered. "Jupiter justice."

Raheem inclined his head and slowly agreed, watching Rico's eyes carefully. "If you will."

Rico turned away before he did something he'd regret. He walked a short ways down the corridor in a cold, roiling fury. He glared at the wall before him, not seeing it.

He couldn't say he was necessarily sad about Martel's death, or even the other guy's, for that matter. But he didn't kill without a clear and imminent threat.

It just wasn't his way.

After a few minutes, Rico walked back and said, " Let's call this in. I want to get the hell out of Dodge."

- TWENTY-THREE -

Chief Curtis arrived forty minutes later with a full ensemble of forensics, tech, and hazmat guys. Raheem had tipped off Old Man Arroyo that the End of the Liners should make themselves scarce for a while. They had done just that.

It turned out that the silver canisters held bio-cyber drives. Two, stowed in the truck, apparently contained the backups for both Martel and Dr. Numbia. The three that had been abandoned were eventually identified as Lara's, Pedro's, and one Calvin Harris.

The guy they had captured was not, in fact, Dr. Numbia. He was Numbia's personal assistant and bodyguard. When potential clients came, he would impersonate Dr. Numbia to screen them. Dr. Numbia had died in the cab of the truck with Martel.

Rico's laser wound—from Dr. Whiskers, as Inés referred to the Numbia imposter—had been tended to. It smarted, but he'd had worse, and he'd live.

Pedro and Calvin had, inevitably, applied for sanctuary. It had, of course, been granted. Rico and Inés were equally disgusted, but there was nothing they could do about the situation. Raheem took it in sardonic stride. "The universe is a harsh and unfair place, especially out here. The new frontier is an ugly place at times. Find satisfaction in the minor victories you achieve. Hold on tight to whatever joy you can find."

By the time Rico and Inés had left Ceres, the

government had decided to incinerate all the canisters, including the more than one hundred bio-drives still in the lab.

Twenty-three actual people, all in a state of cryogenic hibernation, were revived. Computer records revealed that every one of them had been mindwiped. Their original personalities had not been saved. Why would they be? The original inhabitants of the bodies were not, after all, paying customers. They were simply kidnap victims—young, beautiful, healthy people in the prime of their lives who had been in the wrong place at the wrong time.

Since the clientele who had planned to use Dr. Numbia's services all had to supply their own future bodies, most of them would be convicted of kidnapping, and first-degree murder of a psyche. What to do with the stolen bodies was a trickier question. They had memories implanted in them, from the clientele who had eventually planned to occupy the stolen bodies. Months later, Rico learned that the Cerean courts decided to mindwipe the individuals a second time, erasing the co-conspirators' memories, and giving the abducted hosts new personalities. It wouldn't bring them back, but the thieves would not be able to benefit from their crimes. A fresh start, albeit not an ideal one. It was the best they could do. The more cynical comms insinuated that the decisions also increased the population of Ceres by default, but Rico didn't quite believe that line of thought.

The system being flawed, and susceptible to the abuses of money and power, some of the Numbia's clients would get away with murder. Inés had pointed out that that was a pretty good argument in favor of Jupiter Justice.

"Remind me to never get on your bad side," Rico had replied at the time.

It had taken a few weeks to straighten out all the arrests, the witness statements, and the interplanetary paperwork. While they waited, they visited with Cecilia and she took Inés around to see several other half-siblings. They were even able to track down some biological children of Ines' brother. Finding out she had actual nieces and nephews on Ceres lessened some of the sting of her brother's death.

Arnab got them tickets to a play where he was in charge of makeup. The tall man took them backstage, introduced them to the star of the show, and then managed to get them into the best restaurant on Ceres.

After Rico had cooled off, he and Inés went and visited Raheem. Dr. Raheem Kuzbari settled into his new seven-year tenure on Ceres with his usual aplomb. "Not to worry," he said with a wave of his hand. "Seven years is but a blink. Besides, I will be keeping busy out here. Chief Curtis is giving me a job in law enforcement. She said she wants to keep an eye on me."

"Uh huh," Rico said. "Who's going to be watching whom?"

Raheem had merely spread his arms wide and smiled. Inés had laughed.

At one point, Rico pushed Raheem a bit. "Shame about Lara Kohler," he said. I think there may have been some potential there." He held Raheem's gaze.

"Potential?" Raheem snorted a laugh. "Potential for what? A quick romp? A knife in the back? She did rather fancy you, though. Maybe you would have gotten both."

Rico grunted. Gaze unwavering, he continued. "Heard through the grapevine that you broke your tooth. How's that coming along?"

"Oh, fine. Must have broken it during that scuffle with that gorilla, Calvin Harris."

"By the way, this has been bugging me, if you'll pardon the pun. Why didn't Martel find all those tracker bugs on the ship?"

"Ah," Raheem said, a slight smile on his face. He held up a finger. "I'll tell you how *they* work if you tell me how you can communicate so quickly with Axion and earth."

"Hmm."

"All right. How about this. If I guess how your new comm works, you just confirm it?"

Rico just lifted an eyebrow. He could be noncommittal as well.

"I'd guess that you're using tech similar to your matter-antimatter annihilation chamber. For your AMMAT engine, you're teleporting the molecules in. Easy to figure out from your screens and your comms." He waved that aside as trivial. With an eager grin, he leaned forward. "My guess is that your comm uses teleportation as well."

"Well, I cannot confirm or deny that, officially, of course. You know, teleporting particles first happened more than two hundred years ago. Turning that into a predictable communication has taken a bit longer than optimists predicted—but it is only a matter of time." Rico couldn't help but grin. "Bound to happen sooner or later."

"My guess would be sooner," Raheem said dryly.

"And your nanobots?"

"Simple. They're light deactivated. As soon as light hits them, they shut down."

When they finally left Ceres several weeks later, Raheem met them at the docks. He shook Rico's hand and kissed Inés on both cheeks. "Be well, my friends," he said.

"You, too, Raheem."

With the antimatter drive fully functional, the ride back to Axion wasn't long, but Inés and Rico still managed to take their time and enjoy the ride.

* * *

About a month after they left Ceres, Rico received a communiqué from Raheem.

> TO: Captain Federico Schroeder
> FROM: Raheem Kuzbari, PhD, Ceres
>
> Rico ~
>
> Congratulations on your team winning the AMMATT Prize. Alas, the universe is not always just! But I am just joking with you. Which reminds me. I quite agree with something you said: there are some injustices one should never get used to.
>
> As such, I have sent you a small gift. I think you and Inés will enjoy it. It's

from the hydroponics bay at Dubai Intergalactic. I'm fairly certain that the stuff you gave me should be classified as a biohazard.

It was an honor to work with you. See you in seven years—if not sooner. One never knows.

Regards,
Raheem

Inside the package was a two-pound bag of coffee beans. Rico laughed. He and Inés had plans tomorrow night for the long overdue fancy dinner he owed her on the main wheel of Prime Station. Maybe they'd have fresh coffee in the morning.

About the Author

Donald J. Hunt grew up near Rochester, New York, where his love of writing was kindled, no pun intended, through impromptu writing contests in Mrs. Shannon's fifth grade class. Those early explorations into the imagination sparked a nagging passion to weave tales. That insistence ebbed and flowed but never left.

Don has taught at the middle school, high school and university levels. He has compiled a lot of ideas, partial scraps of stories, and reams of notes. *Jupiter Justice* is his first complete novel.

His life journey eventually took him to the suburbs of Chicago, Illinois. He lives there now with his wife and two children. He is striving to indoctrinate the children into the ways of the Force and all things Geek. The dog, Indiana Jones, and the cat, Buffy the Vampire Slayer, wholeheartedly support his endeavors.

* * *

Read It, Share It!

In the age of social media, the best publicity a book receives is from *you*, the reader. If you enjoyed this book, share it on your favorite social media venues—and write a review on Amazon.

I would love to hear from you—

You can:

Follow me on Facebook at
www.facebook.com/hunt2020

Send me an email: **theworldsofdonhunt@gmail.com**

And/or get updates on my projects at:

www.donaldjhunt.com

Made in the USA
Middletown, DE
18 October 2015